Change
for
Lakewood Med

Book 4 of the Lakewood Series

TJ Amberson

CHANGE FOR LAKEWOOD MED
Book 4 of the Lakewood Series
by TJ Amberson

Text ©2022 TJ Amberson
Cover design ©2022 Maria Spada and TJ Amberson
All rights reserved

ENGLISH TRAILS PUBLISHING, LLC
Paperback ISBN 978-1-7366513-1-5

For Cookie,
the best writing buddy a girl could ever hope for

Books by TJ Amberson

Love at Lakewood Med
Back to Lakewood Med
New in Lakewood Med
Change for Lakewood Med

Fusion
Between
The Kingdom of Nereth
The Council of Nereth
The Keeper of Nereth

One

This can't be right.

Eyebrows rising, I quickly re-read the triage note for my next patient, wondering if I misunderstood what it said.

Nope. I didn't misunderstand. My patient really is here in the emergency department because of hot dogs.

I push back my chair from the desk that has been my base camp during my shift, and I get to my feet and scan the complete insanity that is Lakewood Medical Center's emergency department. I soon zero in on the long lineup of patient-occupied stretchers that are crammed up against one wall of the ED's main hallway. Like everywhere else in this outdated, undersized emergency department, the hallway treatment area is as chaotically busy as ever. Nonetheless, it's not hard to spot my patient amidst the havoc: Mr. Charlie Benyon, the thirty-year-old gentleman in tropical-print clothing who's currently seated on one of the hallway stretchers and observing the madness of the ED with an entertained smile on his flushed face.

Between the patient's stable vital signs, which were recently obtained in triage, and the extremely comfortable way the patient appears to be feeling at the moment, it's evident Mr. Benyon isn't in any acute distress. So before heading over to meet him, I take the opportunity to grab my water bottle from my bag and gulp down some much-needed hydration. All the while, I continue observing my patient from afar. It never ceases to amaze me how much information can be gleaned about patients in the first few moments of putting eyes on them— even when doing so from across a wild, crazy ED. And there's no place where being able to do a rapid-yet-thorough analysis of someone is more critical than in an emergency department; around here, a second or two to assess a situation is often all a doctor has before needing to decide how to intervene.

I drop my water bottle back into my bag, realizing this was my first chance to hydrate in hours, and I continue observing my patient. I have to say, I'm kind of impressed with the guy. It's not easy for someone to stand out from the flocks of people who swarm this ED all day and night, but Mr. Benyon has managed to catch my eye. That's especially notable since, as a second-year emergency medicine resident here at Lakewood, there's little a patient can do to truly faze me anymore. It's really no big deal if a patient insists on wearing a superhero cape, or if the patient chooses not to wear anything at all. I don't mind when a patient scream-reads a manifesto about how gummy candies are plotting to take over Planet Earth. And I hardly miss a beat if a patient prefers to sit cross-legged on the floor and perform an exorcism ritual on behalf of the department, like that woman who's farther down the hall is doing at this very moment.

Actually, come to think of it, having an on-call exorcist as a consultant for the ED wouldn't be such a bad idea . . .

Anyway, despite the unpredictable and zany nature of this place and many of its patrons, it's still hard for me to overlook Mr. Charlie Benyon, thanks to his blindingly bright tropical-patterned shirt, which is unbuttoned almost down to his navel, revealing his exceptionally hairy chest and robust beer gut. Also as part of his ensemble, Mr. Benyon has fluorescent-colored, fake leis draped around his neck, and he's wearing yellower-than-the-sun cargo shorts that are bordering on indecent in their degree of tightness. I suppose what makes Mr. Benyon's tropical ensemble even more conspicuous is the fact that it's late September, and it was forecasted to be fifty-two degrees and rainy today. (I wouldn't know for sure about the weather, though, since I've been inside the windowless ED since eight this morning.)

I flick my hazel eyes up to the clock on the wall. It's almost five pm, which means my shift will be ending soon. That doesn't mean I'll be done with work, though. I won't be expected to pick up any more new patients, but I'll have all my notes to finish, which will take me another several hours.

With a sigh, I go through my well-practiced ritual of squeezing and relaxing my toes inside my clog-style shoes, trying to get my weary feet to stop aching. As a resident physician here in the emergency department, chances to sit down are rare, and the chance to sit down for any meaningful period of time is almost a non-occurrence. I've certainly gained an appreciation for the advice an upper-level resident gave me on my first day here at Lakewood almost a year-and-a-half ago: "Don't stand if you can sit. Don't sit if you can lie down." Better advice, perhaps, has never been given.

With my feet feeling better, I reach into one of the large pockets of my long, white doctor's coat, which is hanging over the back of my chair, and retrieve my stethoscope. After draping my stethoscope around my neck, I straighten the top of my hospital-blue scrubs and cinch my long blonde hair more tightly in its ponytail. I glance again at my white coat, but I opt to leave it on the chair rather than put it on.

To be honest, I've never been a fan of wearing a white coat in the ED. I suppose it might look kind of cool, but a long, flowy extra layer of white clothing is about the least practical thing someone could wear around this joint. In here, I'm usually overheated from rushing from one high-acuity patient to the next, there's a high likelihood I'll get splattered with blood at some point, and I'm frequently doing procedures that require me to remove my white coat anyway. I might as well wear a ballet tutu in here, for all the help a white coat provides.

However, despite a white coat's lack of practicality (other than the additional pocket space it provides, I suppose), I do wear my coat during most of my shifts. For good or for bad, I've learned that a white coat helps establish my role with those patients who otherwise can't believe I'm actually a doctor, resident or otherwise. I've lost track of the number of times when, even after I introduced myself to a patient, showed the patient my ID badge, listened to the patient's story, performed a physical exam, and provided the patient with a detailed explanation of my differential diagnosis and recommended plan for care, the patient politely smiled at me and asked: "But when will I be seen by a physician?"

Go figure.

Leaving my workstation, I maneuver across the center of the department, which is where the providers' workstations are located, and I head for the patient treatment areas. As I go, my ears are inundated by the ED's endless symphony of noise: announcements blasting out from the PA system, pagers going off, phones ringing, shouted conversations, the rumble of the x-ray machine as it's pushed into patients' rooms, medication pumps beeping, EMS personnel barking reports, babies crying, and patients screaming. At the same time, my nostrils are flooded with the potent aromas of cleaning solutions, a GI bleed, alcohol, marijuana, and sweat. And topping off the pandemonium is the endless hurricane of activity as doctors, nurses, ED techs, social workers, secretaries, radiology technicians, security guards, and EMS personnel rush to care for patients and perform their duties.

I can't help breaking into a smile as I take it all in. I love this place.

I merge into one of the ED's crowded corridors and start threading a path past the patients and staff members who fill it. I go by Dr. Henry Ingram, who's my attending for this shift. Henry's green eyes meet mine through the fray, and he slows his pace. I show him a thumbs-up in return, answering Henry's unspoken question by silently communicating that I don't have anything to discuss with him at the moment. Henry nods once and continues past me. I smile again. Henry graduated from Lakewood's emergency medicine residency program this past June and got hired to stay on as an attending, and he's fast becoming one of the favorite attendings in the department. Henry himself, though, remains quite the enigma. No one seems to know much about his personal life. He maintains a very mellow outward appearance; he even keeps his dark blond hair just long enough to be pulled back into a short ponytail at the nape of his neck like he's a laid-back "surfer dude" or something. The truth, though, is that Henry is one of those intensely quiet types who's scary-observant and profoundly brilliant. Henry doesn't feel the need to say much, but when he does, his words pack a punch.

I continue carving a route through the jam-packed corridor. As I go, I high-five Xavier Tan, one of the third-year residents, I smile at two of the great ED nurses, Tom and Kathy, and I exchange a nod with Austin Cahill, who rotated through here last year as a med student, and who now looks every bit the part of a first-year internal medicine resident, dressed in his button-up shirt, trousers, and long white coat. As I get farther down the corridor, I have to choke back a laugh when I catch a glimpse of Finn, one of the techs, through an exam room's partially open curtain. Brow furrowed, Finn is attempting to explain to a patient that the fiberglass splint he's about to put on the patient's broken ankle isn't edible.

I suddenly hear the huge glass door of the EMS entrance up ahead sliding open, and I dart out of the way, barely managing to avoid getting run over by the two paramedics who charge inside while pushing a stretcher that has an ashen-looking patient seated upon it. Based on the way the patient is working to breathe, his edematous legs, and the positive pressure ventilation device that the paramedic crew has strapped to the patient's face, I suspect the patient is experiencing an exacerbation of congestive heart failure, otherwise known as CHF.

Dr. Wilma Fox, another one of the ED's attendings, dashes over to meet the crew, and she stays at the patient's side as the paramedics finish wheeling the patient into one of the resuscitation bays. Following closely on Dr. Fox's heels are Maurine Endot, another third-year resident, and Tyler Warren, one of the ED's first-year residents. Two other nurses, Carrie and Pete, jog into the resuscitation bay, followed by another tech and one of the respiratory therapists, Brenna.

As the CHF patient gets surrounded by ED personnel, I resume heading down the corridor to reach my patient, but I soon have to stop again. The corridor is now at a temporary standstill because a radiology tech needs room to push a patient on a stretcher toward the radiology suite. In the transient lull, I shift my eyes back to the resuscitation bay to observe what's happening with the CHF patient.

As I watch the paramedics transfer care of the patient over to the ED team, I'm hit with a punch of excitement. During the second year of residency, each emergency medicine resident gets to spend one month away from the ED to do an EMS rotation. My scheduled EMS month isn't until April, but I'm already counting down the days. Without question, the EMS month is the off-service rotation I'm most looking forward to. Ever since I was young, after witnessing EMS providers help my younger brother on several occasions, I've been extremely interested in EMS work, especially how it overlaps with patient care in the ED. I'm even considering applying for an EMS fellowship after residency is over. I think I would love to be the EMS medical director for whatever emergency department I work in as an attending physician one day. I—

I snap to attention when I realize that one of the paramedics in the resuscitation bay is looking right at me. As soon as I lock eyes with him, the same skill set that I use to rapidly assess patients kicks in, and I find myself doing a split-second analysis of the paramedic in return.

Okay, wow.

I don't mean to be unprofessional, but there's no denying that this paramedic is hot. Super hot. He's a little over six feet tall, and if the way his gigantic biceps bulge out past the short sleeves of his uniform's white shirt is any indication, this paramedic is profusely muscular in that EMS-provider-who-poses-in-calendars-while-holding-a-puppy kind of way. Actually, this guy is so hot that the calendar people would probably ask him to pose with a puppy *and* a kitten. And maybe a fawn. The paramedic has high cheekbones, a light-brown skin tone, and piercing dark eyes. He has straight, dark hair that's cut short, military-style. And, I suddenly also realize, he's smiling at me with a charismatic grin.

Before I can react, commotion in the corridor causes me to pull my eyes away from the resuscitation bay. The temporary standstill has cleared out, and everyone is on the move once more. I promptly resume heading down the corridor without giving the resuscitation bay—or the hot paramedic—another glance.

Because it doesn't matter if that paramedic is super hot. It also doesn't matter that I'll probably see him again when his crew brings in another patient while I'm working. None of it matters because I swore off romance years ago. I learned the hard way that loving someone can lead to devastating heartache, and I vowed not to let my heart get crushed, torn into shreds, and drained of all its hope ever again.

I round the corner that leads to the stretcher-lined treatment hallway, and I again locate Mr. Charlie Benyon through the chaos. He's still seated on the edge of the stretcher, his legs dangling over the side, and he's now snapping in time to a song that's being sung by one of the other patients who's waiting to be seen. This evening's impromptu hallway entertainer is a woman who's belting out "Safety Dance" with drunkenly slurred speech. An equally intoxicated man is beat-boxing to accompany her, and another man is not-so-safely dancing in the corner. Even the woman who's sitting on the floor has paused her exorcism ritual to clap along to the song.

In other words, it's just another day here in the Lakewood Medical Center Emergency Department.

Mr. Benyon does a double take when he notices me approaching. He stops snapping and shows me a massive, toothy smile. "Hiya!"

I reach his stretcher and display a professional smile in return. "Good afternoon, Mr. Benyon. I'm Doctor Elly Vincent. I'm a resident physician here in the emergency department, and I'll be helping you today. I reviewed your triage note, but I want to ask a few more questions to make sure I understand what brought you in."

"Sure thing, Doc!" Mr. Benyon proclaims jovially. "Ask me whatever you want!"

Out of the corner of my eye, I can see that the patient who was dancing in the corner has now grabbed a mop from the supply closet. Without hesitation, he suspends the mop between two rickety hallway chairs and begins attempting to limbo underneath it while the other patients cheer him on. I shrug to myself. Yes, it's just a typical day here at Lakewood.

I shift my full concentration back to Mr. Benyon. "Sir, my understanding is that you were at your friend's bachelor party this afternoon, and after you ate several hot dogs, you began feeling sick. Someone called nine-one-one, and a friend rode here with you in the ambulance." I pause to glance around, but I don't see anyone who appears to be here with Mr. Benyon at the moment. "Is that correct?"

Mr. Benyon wipes perspiration from his forehead. "That's absolutely right, Doc! Not only did I eat twenty-one hot dogs in under fifteen minutes, I ate the buns, too! I was—"

"Dude, it was so epic, Charlie!" someone bellows above the chaos. "I recorded the whole thing on your phone, too!"

I turn my head, following the sound of the bazooka-like voice to its source. A man with a sloppy grin is strolling toward Mr. Benyon's stretcher. He appears about Mr. Benyon's age, he has slicked-back red hair, and there's a tattoo of a snake on the side of his neck. Like Mr. Benyon, this man is conspicuously decked out in a tropical-patterned shirt and colorful shorts. In one hand, the man is gripping a package of generic-brand cookies, which he undoubtedly got from the waiting room's ancient vending machine. In his other hand, the man is holding a phone. With his unsteady gait, bloodshot eyes, and glazed over expression, the man bears a striking resemblance to the many intoxicated patients who fill the hallway.

Seemingly oblivious to my existence, the man finishes staggering up to Mr. Benyon's stretcher, forcing me to step aside. A rush of alcohol floods my nostrils, making my nose hairs sting. With a burp, the man hands the phone to Mr. Benyon, and then he slaps the patient on the back.

"You were so awesome, Charlie!" the man shouts, even though he's standing only a foot or two away from his friend. "Had you kept going, you would have broken the world record for sure!"

I slide my eyes over to my patient once more.

Mr. Benyon sits up proudly and meets my quizzical gaze. "I was trying to break the world's hot-dog eating record," he explains to me in a hiccup. "Wanna see the video of me in action?"

"I do appreciate you offering," I reply politely, "however, I don't think it's necessary at this time for me to—"

Mr. Benyon shoves his phone in my face, holding it so close to my nose that I have to cross my eyes to view the screen. Once my vision comes back into focus, I find myself staring at a shakily recorded video of Mr. Benyon seated at an outdoor table on someone's covered patio. A bunch of guys are gathered around Mr. Benyon; most of them are holding alcoholic beverages, and all of them are decked out in tropical clothing. There's another guy working a grill, and he laughingly places a tray of hot dogs on the table in front of Mr. Benyon. Everyone shouts a five-second countdown, and then Mr. Benyon starts shoving hot dogs into his mouth with his bare hands, inhaling them as fast as he can. My eyes widen as I watch. I have no idea how Mr. Benyon didn't wind up requiring the Heimlich maneuver.

Mr. Benyon pulls the phone from my face. "That was some impressive stuff, don't you think?" He sounds awe-struck with himself.

"Impressive," I echo. "So how are you feeling now, Mr. Benyon? Are you experiencing any symptoms?"

Mr. Benyon pushes his sweat-logged, brown hair from his face. "Nope. I feel great. A little while ago, though, I definitely *wasn't* feeling great." He laughs and then peers up at his friend. "Hey, can I have some of those cookies?"

"I would prefer that you hold off eating or drinking anything until I've finished your workup, Mr. Benyon," I interject with calm, polite firmness. I remove my stethoscope from around my neck. "Would you mind if I examine you while I ask a couple more questions?"

"Not at all!" Mr. Benyon belches. He yanks off his shirt and throws it to the floor, and then he slaps his abdomen, making it ripple. "Examine away! I'm as healthy as a horse!"

I step forward, trying to reestablish my position beside the stretcher so I can reach the patient. However, Mr. Benyon's drunken friend doesn't take the cue to move out of my way.

"Excuse me, sir, I do need to stand there," I inform the man. I motion to the empty chair that's wedged beside the foot of the stretcher. "May I ask you to sit down instead?"

The man puts his beady eyes on mine, acknowledging my existence for the first time. Swaying slightly, he proceeds to look me up and down in a not-so-subtle way. The man's smile widens, revealing a mouth full of braces. He wags his eyebrows at me and says:

"Well, hello, Beautiful."

I keep my expression empty, determined not to let this man think he's getting a reaction out of me. However, I'm groaning on the inside. This is the last thing I want to be dealing with at the end of a long, difficult, busy shift. Patients, family members, or friends who act inappropriately are disrupting at best and dangerous at worst. I glance past the man to identify where the nearest security guard is located, just in case, and then I fix my eyes back on the man and say:

"Sir, I need to examine Mr. Benyon. Please have a seat."

The man smirks. "Oh, you're a feisty one, aren't you?" He finally relents and saunters over to the foot of the stretcher. He plops himself down on the chair. "I like sexy girls who are feisty."

I huff out a silent breath of annoyance and exasperation, turn away from the man, and begin examining Mr. Benyon. I try to position myself in a way that provides my patient with what shred of privacy there is to be hand in the middle of the hallway. Thankfully, at least, most of the other patients are watching the mop-limbo competition that's going on in the corner, so they're not paying Mr. Benyon any attention.

"May I ask what made you decide to try to break the world record for eating hot dogs?" I lower the back of the stretcher and help Mr. Benyon lie flat on his back before I start palpating his abdomen.

"I dunno." Mr. Benyon hiccups a couple more times. "One minute, I was enjoying drinks with my buddies, and the next thing I knew, I was being dared to eat all the hot dogs on the grill. I don't remember much after that."

I finish my examination and help the patient sit back up. "Well, according to the triage note, about the time you swallowed your twenty-first hot dog, you informed your friends that you were feeling sick. You wandered into the neighbor's yard and began vomiting in her autumn-squash garden. Understandably, the neighbor called nine-one-one."

"Really?" Mr. Benyon squints, like he's thinking hard. "I don't remember a garden, but I do remember feeling sick. Like I said, though, I'm not feeling . . ."

Mr. Benyon trails off, and his face takes on an ominously pasty hue. I have just enough time to jump back before Mr. Benyon leans forward, lets out a sound like a dinosaur, and throws up on the floor.

Everyone in the hallway stops what they're doing and looks my way.

"That was awesome!" Mr. Benyon's friend unsteadily leaps back to his feet, knocking over his chair in the process. He grabs Mr. Benyon's phone from off the stretcher and starts recording.

I blow a loose strand of hair from my face and look toward the workstation area, making eye contact with Miriam, one of the ED's secretaries. Miriam is a year or two older than me, and she has short brown hair with heavy bangs. Miriam's eyes drop to the mess at my feet, and her expression makes it clear she is not amused. Her expression doesn't budge as she proceeds to use the PA system to make a monotone request for someone from environmental services to come to the treatment area of the hallway.

I shift toward my patient once more. "Mr. Benyon, why don't you lie down on your side?" With far too much experience ignoring a pile of sour-smelling vomit on the ground, I lower the back of the patient's stretcher once again. "I'll go enter some orders. Your nurse will put in an IV, draw labs, and administer fluid and anti-nausea medication to help you feel better. We'll keep you here for a while, so we can monitor you while your body processes the alcohol and hot dogs that are in your system."

Mr. Benyon is smiling again. He gives me a thumbs-up. "Whatever you say, Doc!"

"Hey, Doctor Vincent," I hear someone else call out to me. "How can I help?"

Looking up, I'm met by the welcome sight of another of our great ED nurses, Hadi, sauntering my way. Hadi is twenty-six, so he's a year younger than me, but I would argue that he has the skills, smarts, and intuition to rival any of the veteran nurses around this place. Hadi also has a great sense of humor, which is not only an essential survival skill in this department, it always makes working with him a good time.

I step away from the stretcher to meet Hadi in the middle of the hallway. "Glad you're here. I was just about to go put in some orders."

Hadi's eyes move to the mess on the floor. He grins. "As soon as Laura assigned me to this gentleman and I heard what was going on, I knew you would be the doc caring for him." He looks at me again, this time with amusement in his gaze. "Only you and your notorious black cloud would somehow manage to bring in a guy who got sick while trying to break the world record for eating hot dogs."

I snort a laugh. "I would like to disagree with you, but I'm afraid I do tend to have a black cloud in the ED. I always have."

"Oh, trust me, I know. We *all* know." Hadi laughs again. "There's the typical Lakewood emergency department's level of busy, and then there's the completely-unexpected-and-weird-and-even-more-patients-than-usual-because-Doctor-Vincent-is-working level of busy." He shakes his head. "It's a good thing we all like you so much, otherwise we would have had you tossed out of this place long ago."

"I appreciate you letting me stick around." I laugh again. "Maybe I'll start warning everyone before I work next."

"Good idea. That will give folks time to don their riot gear, at least." Hadi starts backing up. "I'll go get everything Mr. Benyon needs and be back."

"Thanks. I'll go put in the orders."

Hadi salutes to me before he heads off. As I watch him go, I also see an employee from environmental services taking away the mop from the guy who was hosting the limbo competition in the corner, causing the other hallway patients groan with disappointment.

Chuckling to myself, I look again at Mr. Benyon. His color is back to normal, and he's resting on his side while re-watching the video of himself gobbling down the hot dogs. He rewinds the video to play it yet again, and I swear that I hear him whisper to himself:

"I know I could have broken the world record. I *know* I could have done it."

Convinced Mr. Benyon is doing all right, I turn around to go to my workstation, but I'm forced to an immediate stop when I nearly run into a man who's hovering right behind me.

"Excuse me," I say, startled. "I'm sorry, I . . ."

I trail off when I realize the man who's standing uncomfortably close to me is Mr. Benyon's intoxicated friend. Instantly, I'm wary about what will happen next. Sure enough, like I feared, the drunk man doesn't step aside to let me pass. Instead, he gives me another flirtatious wag of his eyebrows.

"Leaving so soon, Doctor Sexy-Feisty?" The man looks me over again in a way that churns my stomach.

"Yes, I'm leaving," I tell him blandly. "So if you will please excuse me . . ."

I step to my right to get around him, but the man mirrors my movement, inserting himself into my path once more.

"Aw, don't be like that. Don't leave, Doctor Sexy-Feisty."

Still obstructing my escape route, the man adopts a casual leaning pose against the wall, and he sticks out his chest, apparently trying to show me how buff he is. However, he's most definitely not buff, and so the end result is that the man looks like a rooster-peacock-human hybrid that's attempting to puff its feathers. Given how rapidly the man's face is reddening as he holds his position, I think he's actually in some degree of pain from straining so hard.

"Sir," I bark, "I need you to—"

"*Sir*, huh? Oh, I like that." The man pushes off from the wall and steps forward so he's only inches from me. "You can call me *sir* any time you want, Doctor Sexy-Feisty."

I stagger backward but collide into a cart of clean linens. I quickly gather my footing and make another attempt to get around the man. "Sir, let me pass. I—"

The man grabs me by the elbow. "Ah, so you wanna play hard-to-get? I can handle a girl who—"

Someone comes up from behind me, yanks the man's hand from my arm, and puts himself between the man and me. I whip up my head. My heart punches the inside of my chest when I see that my rescuer has extremely recognizable thick, wavy, jet-black hair. I catch a hint of his familiar, musky cologne, and my breathing hitches.

It's Grant Reed.

Grant is another second-year emergency medicine resident here at Lakewood. He's one of my best friends.

Grant also just happens to be the man who caused my heart to break years ago. He's the reason I vowed never to take another chance on love.

Two

Even though I'm standing behind Grant, I can tell that every muscle of his tall, chiseled frame is tensed. His whole torso is rising and falling with deep, measured respirations. His hands are twitching at his sides.

"Sir," Grant says to the man in a low voice. His tone is thick with restraint, but there's an unmistakable edge of warning to it. "I'm going to ask you to leave the treatment area of the emergency department and go to the waiting room. Now. Right now."

The intoxicated man is still smirking as he finally removes his creepy stare from me to look up at Grant's looming figure. Immediately, the man's cocky expression vanishes. His face pales, and he stumbles back from Grant, holding up his hands in a halting gesture.

"F-fine. Sure th-thing," the man stammers, his eyes wide. "I didn't mean to cause any trouble. I'll go. I'll go."

The drunk man slides far to his left, giving himself a wide berth to get around Grant, and then he ducks his head and scurries past both of us, headed for the heavy double doors that lead to the waiting room.

Grant turns, keeping a steely gaze on the man as he tracks him while he departs the ED. Only after the man is gone does Grant exhale and shift his stance to lock his stunningly bright blue eyes on mine. There's a crease between his brows, and his jaw is clenched as he asks:

"Are you all right, El?"

I nod. "Yes, I'm all right. Thanks."

This is not entirely true, however. I'm still mentally flailing to collect myself. I'm trying to shake off the intoxicated man's unwelcome, shudder-inducing advances. Plus, I've been completely caught off-guard by Grant's arrival this evening, and his current breath-stealing closeness has my heart drumming and my body tingling.

Grant always makes me feel this way. He always has.

I fell in love with Grant the first day I met him, back when we were teenagers. Grant was not only the most handsome boy I had ever seen, his intelligence, kindness, subtle humor, unflinching sense of duty, and loyalty swiftly and completely stole my heart. To this day, no man has ever come close to taking Grant's place. Yet Grant has no idea how I feel. All these years, I've kept my love for Grant a secret because I know it's for the best, for both of us.

Grant is still watching me closely. I blush under his searching gaze. I wouldn't be this rattled by Grant's presence if I had known I would be seeing him today. I wasn't prepared to run into him, however, and I definitely wasn't expecting him to swoop in and play hero. So I'm about as out-of-sorts around Grant right now as I was in high school.

The reason I wasn't expecting to see Grant in the ED this evening is because I know he just got off a run of overnight shifts, and he's next scheduled to work when he starts his EMS rotation in a few days—on October second, to be exact. Don't get me wrong: I don't obsessively check Grant's schedule. I don't need to think about him more than I already do. However, I periodically screen for Grant's name on the ED schedule, which is posted in the online portal that all the emergency medicine residents and rotating med students have access to. Like I said, knowing that I'll be seeing Grant helps me steel myself for the encounter a little bit.

I finally begin emerging from my Grant-induced stupor, and my mind flips into its more analytical mode of observation. I note Grant isn't in scrubs this evening, which confirms he's not here to cover a shift. Instead—and I'm not sure whether to be delighted or perturbed about this—Grant's blue sweater, dark jeans, and sturdy boot-shoes are making him look particularly handsome tonight. There's something about his casual-yet-put-together ensemble, and the way his clothes happen to perfectly accentuate his muscular frame, combined with the slight tousle of his hair and the hint of facial scruff along his jaw, that makes me weak in the knees.

I adopt a casual smile, as though I'm not speaking to the man I've been in love with for nearly half of my life. "I appreciate you getting that drunk guy out of here, by the way. While I'm sure he's a real hit with the ladies at parties, he has been a nuisance, to say the least."

Grant's eyes shift to the doors again. His expression darkens for a moment before he focuses back on me. "Yeah, I kind of got that impression."

There's another pause, and then Grant clears his throat and retreats a step, putting more space between us. I exhale, part of me missing his nearness, the other part of me feeling like I'm finally able to catch my breath. As he watches me, Grant's face takes on an impossible-to-read look. It's a look I know extremely well. It's the classic Grant Reed look. The look of Mr. Calm, Cool, and Collected. Mr. Never Rattled. Mr. Professional. Mr. Polite. Mr. Perfect Gentleman.

A little bolt of electricity zips down my spine. I swallow hard.

I need to get away from him.

"Well, I should go put in orders for my patient." I give Grant another smile. "Thanks again for your help."

I wave to Grant and start walking in the direction of the workstations. My heart lurches when Grant turns around and calmly falls into step beside me.

"Actually, I'll head over there with you," Grant says in his steady way. "I'm supposed to meet Doctor Priest at the charge nurse's station in a couple of minutes."

I shoot Grant a fast side-glance, taking in the view of his profile while he calmly continues looking straight ahead. I sigh to myself. As always, it's apparent that Grant is indifferent toward me as anything other than a friend. Why can't I feel the same way about him? Why do I have to be *in love* with him?

As Grant and I draw closer to the center of the ED, I notice Miriam, Carrie, and several other members of the ED staff glancing our way. Correction: they're glancing *Grant's* way, and they're watching him with unmistakably starry-eyed expressions. Heck, even an elderly woman on a nearby stretcher is giving Grant a flirtatious once-over.

Not that I'm surprised. Grant has always been the gorgeous, athletic, smart, kind guy whom everyone crushes on. Grant was the homecoming prince in ninth, tenth, and eleventh grades, and he was the homecoming king our senior year. He was the captain of the high school basketball team, and if it weren't for his decision to hammer out the rigorous pre-med curriculum in four years, he could have played point guard on our college basketball team, too. In other words, Grant has always been the perfect guy. The funny thing is, though, Grant never seems to recognize how everyone admires him. He's really that humble. Like I said, he's basically the perfect guy.

And every single day I have to pretend like I don't notice how perfect he is.

Grant and I reach my desk. I sit down and start putting in orders for my patient, and I ask him:

"So what brings you in to chat with Doctor Priest this evening, anyway?"

"I'm not sure, actually. In his email, Priest just asked me to meet him here. He didn't indicate what we would be talking about." Standing beside my desk, Grant is letting his eyes dart around the department while he uses one hand to ruffle his hair. I swear one of the secretaries let out a little titter of delight as he does so.

I arch an eyebrow. "You don't know what Priest wants to meet about? That's weird. I wonder why—"

"Elly?" someone calls out.

I turn in my chair and break into a grin. Rachel Nelson, one of our other first-year emergency medicine residents, is hustling toward me. On Match Day last March, I was thrilled to hear that Rachel had matched with our residency program. I first met her over a year ago, when she rotated through here as a med student. She initially came across as both a little bit shy and a whole lot particular, but it didn't take long for me to decide that Rachel is one of the most hard-working, dedicated, and determined care providers out there. Not to mention, Rachel definitely wins the award for the most pristinely starched white coat in the entire department. In the entire hospital, probably.

"Hi, Rachel, how are you doing?" I greet her. I decide to stay seated, since Rachel is so petite that it's easier for me to look her in the eye this way.

"I'm doing well, thanks." Rachel reaches my desk. She gives Grant and me a friendly-yet-professional nod before continuing to speak to me. "I'm about to start my shift, and so I wanted to inquire if you would like to sign out your last patient to me."

"That would be great," I tell her appreciatively. "The gentleman is Mr. Benyon, a thirty-year-old male who was—"

"Brought in by EMS because he was feeling sick," Rachel finishes my sentence, speaking in her no-nonsense way. "From the triage notes, I understand he was at a bachelor's party and became ill after consuming twenty-one hot dogs in less than fifteen minutes."

I can't help laughing good-naturedly. I should have known Rachel would already be on top of things.

"Exactly," I reply, still laughing.

Rachel's demeanor relaxes, and she cracks a smile of her own. "I also saw in the notes something about the patient trying to break the world record for eating hot dogs?" Her large brown eyes shine with curiosity. "Is that for real?"

"Indeed, it is." I snicker. "Mr. Benyon has it all on video, in fact, and I'm sure he would be happy to show it to you, if you're interested . . . actually, he'll probably show you the video even if you're *not* interested."

Rachel giggles. "Thanks for the warning."

"My pleasure." I'm still chuckling as I motion to my computer. "Anyway, I just put in orders for—"

I interrupt myself with a gasp that's probably loud enough to be heard across the whole department. I can't help it, though. Rachel is wearing a ring. A big, beautiful diamond ring on *the fourth finger of her left hand*.

With an excited squeal, I hop to my feet. "Oh. My. Gosh. Rachel, are you engaged?"

I hear other gasps from the ED staff members who are within earshot, and they all stop what they're doing and spin toward Rachel and me, unashamedly trying to get a view of Rachel's left hand.

Rachel ducks her head, blushing shyly, but I can see the smile of joy that's spreading across her lips.

"Austin proposed a few days ago," Rachel tells me softly. She lets out a sweet sigh. "I've never been happier in my entire life, Elly. I don't even have words to explain how happy I am."

"I'm so thrilled for you!" I yank Rachel into a hug. My inner romantic is exploding with glee right now. I may have chosen to forgo love for myself, but I'm ecstatic when romance goes well for others. I finally release Rachel from my zealous hug. "I'm over-the-moon for you and Austin! Congratulations!"

"Yeah, congratulations." Grant smiles at Rachel warmly. "That's awesome."

"Thank you." Rachel is still beaming—glowing, really—with what could only be described as a look of total bliss. "We haven't picked a wedding date yet, but we'll probably get married next summer, between our first and second years of residency."

"That sounds perfect." I drop back down on my chair, using my hands to fan air past my face. "I assume your sister, Julie, is going to be your maid of honor?"

"Yes. She's pretty excited about it."

I'm nodding eagerly. "I remember Julie from when she shadowed you during a few of your med student shifts here. How's she doing?"

Rachel tucks her short hair behind her ears. "She's loving her first year of med school here in the Lakewood area." She pauses, and her smile becomes mischievous. "Of course, part of the reason she's enjoying things so much may be due to the fact that she recently started dating Zach O'Cain, who treats her like an absolute queen."

My mouth drops open. "Hang on. Julie is dating Zach O'Cain? The same Zach O'Cain who rotated through here as a fourth-year med student last year? The same Zach who's now one of Lakewood's first-year internal medicine residents?"

"That's the same Zach." Rachel giggles again. "And since Zach and Austin are residency colleagues, Austin has already made it very clear to Zach that he better not do anything to break the heart of his future sister-in-law." She keeps laughing and shakes her head. "Not that Zach would. It was so obvious to me that Zach fell head-over-heels for Julie the moment he laid eyes on her last year. He worships the ground she walks on."

Something that feels a lot like longing tugs at my heart, and I become particularly aware of Grant standing by my desk. Trying to distract myself, I hurriedly clear my throat and go on talking to Rachel:

"I can't wait to hear all about your plans. I love weddings, so please feel free to keep me posted on anything and everything: flowers, dresses, venues, and anything else. I even want to hear about the napkin color and the appetizers."

"You got it." Rachel grins. She appears like she's about to say more when her eyes shift past me. Her blush deepens. "Hi, hon."

Following Rachel's love-struck gaze, I spot Austin sauntering toward us. I grin all over again. Not only is there an adorable height discrepancy between Rachel and Austin—he towers over her by a foot—the differences in their personalities are even more pronounced. Yet, somehow, their differences are precisely what make them so compatible. They're perfect for each other.

My heart aches again. My eyes flick Grant's way. If only . . .

No. I'm not going to do this to myself. There's no point in dwelling on what can't be.

"Hey, everyone. I heard talk of appetizers, so I figured I would join the conversation," Austin quips as he reaches Rachel's side. He kisses the top of her head, and then he says to Grant and me, "Good to see you guys."

"Great to see you, too." Grant gives Austin a friendly man-clap on the shoulder. He and Austin live in the same apartment complex, and they've become pretty good friends. "And congratulations. Rachel just told us the news. I'm really happy for you."

"Yes, congratulations!" I spring back to my feet. "I'm thrilled for you both!"

"Thanks." Austin gives Rachel's hand a gentle squeeze while he smiles at Grant and me. "I feel like the luckiest guy in the world."

"Aww, thanks, hon." Rachel is blushing again.

Austin's pager goes off. He pulls his adoring gaze from his fiancée to check his new message.

"Sounds like I need to go admit another patient. Dr. Godfrey has someone over in Fast Track with acute pancreatitis." Austin puts his pager back into the holder on his belt. He gives Grant and me another nod. "I'll see you both soon."

Austin doesn't say anything else to Rachel before he departs, but he doesn't need to; the look he shares with her says everything. My inner romantic nearly melts into a puddle as I observe them. I love when couples are so in tune with one another that they have a silent language all their own.

Rachel has a dreamy smile upon her face as she watches Austin head toward Fast Track.

Once he's gone, Rachel seems to snap back to attention, and she spins to face me.

"I'll go introduce myself to Mr. Benyon." Rachel gives Grant and me a fast wave and begins scurrying away. She calls over her shoulder, "Have a good evening, you guys."

As Rachel disappears from view, I move to sit back down. At the same time, Grant happens to shift his stance closer to my desk. We nearly collide and then we both freeze, so now we're suddenly standing face-to-face with only a tiny amount of space between us. Our gazes meet. I suck in a sharp breath while my heart starts flying around inside my chest.

Curse Grant and his stunning blue eyes.

I clear my throat and take a clumsy step backward. I bump into the desk, causing the computer mouse to fall off and hit the floor with a jarring clatter. Cheeks igniting, I bend down to retrieve the mouse from off the floor, but Grant does, too, so we both have to stop again so our heads don't knock. We're each bent at the waist, our faces nearly touching once more while our hands hover together near the floor.

"Allow me," Grant says calmly. As unruffled as ever, he picks up the mouse and places it on the desk.

I shakily stand up straight and then lower myself onto my chair, pretending to be as unaffected as he is. "Thanks."

"Good evening, Grant," a man says over the din. "I'm sorry for being late. I was in a meeting that ran longer than expected."

I exhale with relief at the welcome interruption. Grant and I turn to see Dr. Gary Priest, attending physician and the director of the emergency medicine residency program, walking toward us.

Dr. Priest—whose looks, I've always thought, somehow seem very appropriate for his name—is a tall, thin man whose age is somewhere in the upper fifties. His thick hair and epic mustache are a mid-tone brown sprinkled with gray. He has round glasses, and as usual, he's dressed in a button-up shirt, suit pants, and tie. Dr. Priest has a compassionate, insightful aura about him. There's usually a humorous gleam in his eye, but when needed, he can flip into an almost intimidating degree of seriousness. I think everyone agrees that Dr. Priest is a perfect person to direct one of the busiest, highest-acuity emergency medicine residency training programs in the country. In fact, back when I first met him during residency interviews, Dr. Priest immediately struck me like a coach whose team I wanted to play on. I've respectfully called him "Coach" ever since.

"Good evening, Doctor Priest." Grant offers his hand.

Dr. Priest shakes Grant's hand and then looks my way. "Hi, Elly. How did your shift go?"

I jokingly cringe. "Twenty-one patients tonight, Coach. Eleven admits, including seven to the ICU. And no time to complete a single chart. You know, a typical day around here."

Dr. Priest chuckles. "I do know. I can't wait until we get the new department open so we at least have a little more room to work." He looks Grant's way once more. "I appreciate you coming. As I mentioned in my email, something has just come up that I wanted to chat with you about." He unexpectedly pins his eyes back on me. "I would like to meet with you, too, if that would be all right."

My eyebrows rise before I can stop them. "You do?"

Dr. Priest nods. "Yes. If you have a few minutes, since your shift is now over. This matter involves you, too."

Grant and I exchange a glance.

"Um, sure. No problem," I tell Dr. Priest, sounding more nonchalant than I feel as I push myself to my feet.

"Great." Dr. Priest glances around the department. "Let's head up to my office, so we can talk somewhere that's quiet."

Dr. Priest begins striding toward the back exit, clearly expecting Grant and me to follow. I hurriedly log out of my computer and collect my things while shooting another questioning glance Grant's way. His eyes meet mine, and the look on his face tells me that he's as baffled as I am.

My stomach twists as Grant and I leave the department. A resident doesn't get called into Dr. Priest's office without good reason. What could he possibly need to talk with Grant and me about?

Three

After walking through the labyrinth of windowless corridors that connects the outdated, undersized emergency department with the spacious, state-of-the-art rest of Lakewood Medical Center, Dr. Priest, Grant, and I reach the elegant main lobby. There are still some hospital employees and patients around, but the area isn't nearly as busy as it is during peak business hours. It's a striking contrast to the ED, which typically gets busier, louder, and even more crowded as the night comes on.

The three of us pass by the unoccupied information desk to reach the elevator bay. Still without a word, we ride an elevator up to the eighth floor of Prescott Tower. When the elevator settles to a stop and its doors open, Dr. Priest steps out into the foyer first. Grant lightly puts a hand on the small of my back while motioning with his other hand for me to exit the elevator next. My insides dance at his touch. Grant has no idea how the simple feel of his hand upon me has the power to launch fireworks inside my core.

Scurrying out of the elevator, I trail Dr. Priest down the long hallway to our left, which leads to the offices of the emergency medicine attendings and administrative staff members. I start peering through the huge windows at my right, taking in the view of the city as the sun is going down. Far below, the streets are nearly at a standstill with rush-hour traffic. Pedestrians fill the sidewalks. There are five ambulances lined up at the emergency department's EMS entrance, and another ambulance is pulling in with its lights flashing.

While I watch the scene outside, the clouds shift around the sun, abruptly changing my view to one of my own reflection in the window—and to a view of Grant, who's striding down the hallway behind me. Still feeling the lingering memory of his touch, I avert my gaze and stare straight ahead once more.

I huff out a breath and roll back my shoulders. Okay, I need to get a handle on my emotions. I need to focus on . . . well, on whatever it is that Dr. Priest wants to talk to Grant and me about. I cannot get incapacitated by my feelings for Grant, the way I used to do when I was a brace-faced, frizzy-haired teenager in high school. Grant and I are just friends. We've always been just friends. We'll only ever be friends.

Dr. Priest reaches his office, unlocks the door, and gestures for Grant and me to go inside. I cross the threshold and glance around. Dr. Priest's domain is actually made up of two large, brightly lit offices connected by an internal door. Both offices are painted a soothing shade of tan with white trim. Several healthy-looking plants adorn the space. The front office belongs to Leslie Yamada, the assistant coordinator for the ED. Leslie's office is vacant at the moment, undoubtedly because she has gone home for the evening.

I proceed through the shared doorway to enter Dr. Priest's tidy office, and I take a seat on one of the two big leather chairs that face his desk. I'm hit with more curiosity and nerves, and my eyes start searching the room for clues about what this meeting is regarding, but I spot nothing. So I settle my attention on the framed diplomas that are hanging on the wall behind the desk. The impressive display of Dr. Priest's academic achievements doesn't come across as snooty or intimidating, though, since he also has photos of family members and his travels around the globe displayed with equal prominence. Studying the pictures, I realize this is the first time I've had a chance to look at them closely. Though I've been in Dr. Priest's office several times before, it has been to briefly drop off an assignment or mention an interesting case. I've never been called in here to discuss a mystery issue before.

Grant takes the chair beside me. I sense his eyes shift my way, and I meet his gaze. Grant quirks an eyebrow, letting me know that he still has no idea what this meeting is about. I mirror Grant's facial expression, indicating to him that I remain equally clueless. Grant nods once in reply, readopts his unreadable expression, and proceeds to fix his attention on the wall behind the desk.

I smile a little. I cherish the fact that Grant and I are able to read each other so well. Considering we've been friends since we were fourteen, I suppose it's not surprising that we're able to understand each other's silent communication, yet it still makes me happy. Usually, a glance or a slight tip of his head is all I need in order to know what's going through Grant's mind—except when he adopts that impossible-to-read expression of his, that is. When Grant does that, I have no idea what he's thinking.

Of course, I'm aware that Grant is able to read me as easily as I'm usually able to read him. For this reason, I've had to perfect my I'm-not-in-any-way-shape-or-form-madly-in-love-with-you look and demeanor, which has allowed me to keep my deepest emotions concealed from him for all these years. It's also precisely why I have to remain so vigilant around Grant. If I let down my guard even once, I know Grant will detect how I really feel about him. If that ever happens—if Grant ever even suspects I'm in love with him—it would wreck our friendship, completely and forever. We could never go on being friends in the way we've always done. Nothing would ever be the same. And I couldn't handle the agony of losing Grant as a friend; it was devastating enough to know I would never have a chance for love.

Dr. Priest enters his office, leaving the adjoining door propped open behind him. Taking a seat at his desk, he says:

"Thanks again for being here this evening. I wanted to chat because an issue has recently arisen regarding scheduling that impacts both of you, and I wanted to explain what's going on."

Grant and I swap another glance. A scheduling issue? I'm not sure what that means, but it doesn't sound good.

Dr. Priest props his elbows on the arms of his chair. "As you two well know, thanks to the accelerated pace that the new ED is being built, the facility is opening much sooner than originally anticipated."

I continue studying Dr. Priest closely, trying to get a better read on things. He doesn't look upset, at least, so I guess that's encouraging.

"Obviously, getting our new ED running sooner than originally expected is wonderful, for us and for our patients." Dr. Priest smiles, causing his stellar mustache to look like it's waving. "However, because the ED will be opening sooner than originally planned, we need to speed up the process of orienting and training the new ED attending physicians we recently hired."

My eyes get big with surprise and interest. I've been hearing rumors that Lakewood would hire more emergency medicine attendings to help staff the bigger ED, and while I didn't know if the rumors were true, they certainly made sense to me. A bigger ED means more patient beds; more patient beds means there will be more patients waiting to be seen at any given time; and more patients obviously means more staff is needed. So the speculation that Lakewood would hire more ED providers seemed logical to me, but up until right now, I had no idea a batch of new attendings had already been selected.

"Given the updated opening date for the ED, we need to start orienting our new attendings next month." Dr. Priest straightens his legs, crossing them at the ankles. "Therefore, starting in October, we're having the newly hired attendings work many of the shifts that are usually covered by our residents or rotating med students. This will allow the veteran ED attendings to supervise the new hires, in the sense that they'll help our new attendings get familiar with policies, procedures, and personnel here at Lakewood. That way, all our attending physicians will be up-to-speed as much as possible when the new ED opens early next year."

While I process Dr. Priest's words, all I can think to do is nod. Out of the corner of my eye, I see Grant nodding, too.

Dr. Priest sits up taller. "Now this is where both of you—and all our residents, really—come into play. Because our new attendings will be covering many shifts that are usually designated for residents and rotating med students, there will be fewer available shifts for the residents and med students to cover on any given day. As a result, I need to modify the residents' schedules, and Dr. Kent needs to modify the med students' schedules, to ensure everyone still works the same total number of monthly shifts in an ED as they normally would." He pauses to glance at his computer monitor. "For the foreseeable future, our residents will work more ED shifts over at University Hospital, and the med students who are on their emergency medicine rotation will do all their shifts there."

The news slowly sinks in. Usually, Lakewood's emergency medicine residents cover one or two shifts per month at University Hospital, which is only a few miles away. This allows residents to get the unique experience of working in an academic-based environment. Truth be told, each time I'm there, I'm amazed at how two EDs that aren't very far apart geographically can feel so vastly different. For one thing, University Hospital's ED isn't quite as busy as Lakewood's. For another, University Hospital isn't designated as a Level One Trauma Center, so the trauma patients who are brought there aren't typically as critically injured. Most notably, many of the patients at University Hospital have rare, you'll-only-see-this-once-in-your-career types of issues, like complications after a multi-organ transplant, or problems from an unnamed inborn error of metabolism that's only one of six known cases in the entire world.

Anyway, if I understand Dr. Priest correctly, until the new ED opens, I'll be working more shifts per month at University Hospital. It's not a humungous change, but I admit that I have mixed feelings about it. I enjoy working at University Hospital, I learn a lot, and the attendings are top-notch. Yet Lakewood is my home. I love the high acuity, varied patient population, and the complete insanity that abounds within Lakewood's walls.

"In addition to sending residents and med students over to University Hospital more often," Dr. Priest continues, "we'll be making additional changes to the residents' schedules."

I snap out of my thoughts. *More* changes?

"Obviously, University Hospital doesn't have enough attendings to supervise more than a few additional residents or med students at any given time, so we can't send over all our personnel at once," Dr. Priest notes with a chuckle. "Therefore, we're also rearranging schedules so more of our residents will be doing their off-service electives on any given month. For example, we usually have one second-year resident away from the ED each month to do the EMS rotation. However, for the time being, we'll be sending away two residents each month to do it."

Little alarm bells are now going off in my head, telling me that something bad is brewing. I try assuring myself that I'm just being paranoid—that because my EMS rotation is the rotation I'm most excited about, I'm being overly protective—yet I can't quite convince myself this is the only reason I'm uneasy. Interestingly, in the periphery of my vision, I notice Grant run a hand through his hair in a restless way, which tells me that he, too, is starting to grow unsettled. Yes, this is definitely not good.

"So let's talk about how this pertains directly to the two of you." Dr. Priest focuses on Grant. "You were originally slated to do your EMS rotation next month, right?"

"That's right," Grant replies, back to appearing as unfazed as ever. "In October."

Dr. Priest shifts his eyes to mine. "And you were originally scheduled to do your EMS rotation in April?"

"Correct," I eke out.

"Well, here's the change I propose," Dr. Priest says. "Leslie and I reviewed everyone's schedules, and it appears it will work well to have both of you do your EMS rotation next month. In other words, you would spend October together, working with one of our local EMS agencies." He shows Grant and me another pleasant smile. "Would that be acceptable to you?"

I stare at Dr. Priest's gigantic mustache. I'm not moving, and I'm barely breathing. Though I may appear still on the outside, however, my mind is whirling as I finish calculating what this proposed schedule change will mean. Instead of having a few weeks away from Grant—a chance to catch my breath while he's off doing his EMS rotation—I'll be spending all of October working alongside him.

Is my poor heart going to be able to handle this?

"The change is fine with me," I hear Grant tell Dr. Priest in a steady tone. "I realize that's easy for me to say, though, since the adjustment doesn't alter my schedule. I'll still be doing my

EMS rotation next month, like I was previously slated to do."

"Fair enough." Dr. Priest puts his concentration on me. "What about you, Elly? I know how much you've been looking forward to your EMS rotation, so I figured you wouldn't mind doing it sooner versus later. What do you think about the plan?"

My stomach clenches in protest. My palms get sweaty. It's not like I can tell Dr. Priest how I'm feeling, though. So I'm trapped. I'm simply going to have to act like everything is okay. Like I've always done.

I clear my throat. "Sure. That sounds fine, Coach."

Out of the corner of my eye, I see Grant glance at me. I pretend not to notice.

"Great." Dr. Priest checks something on his computer. "As for the details: the two of you will be spending your rotation with Lakewood Fire and Rescue. Like you've come to know from working in the ED, Lakewood Fire and Rescue is set up in a two-tier system. The majority of their EMS providers—about eighty-five percent of their crew members—are firefighters who also have training in basic life-saving skills and on-scene medical care. These BLS providers work in crews of three, and they're dispatched to all EMS calls. If the patient is stable and lower acuity, the BLS crews treat the patients themselves and transport if indicated."

Though I'm reeling, I'm also scrambling to re-engage objectively in the conversation. We're talking about the EMS world, and I need to hear what Dr. Priest is saying. It's not exactly easy to concentrate, however, considering I can see Grant in the edge of my vision, and his stunning blue eyes keep flicking between Dr. Priest and me.

Dr. Priest goes on, "The other fifteen percent of Lakewood Fire and Rescue's EMS providers are firefighters who were selected to go through two years of additional training in advanced life-saving skills to become paramedics. These ALS crews work in pairs of two. They're dispatched to assist the BLS crews for high-acuity patients, and they control the scene when they're there."

I'm just starting to get over my shock of learning I'll be working with Grant when more alarming realization hits me: with my EMS rotation being sprung upon me so much sooner than I expected, I'm totally unprepared. I would have normally spent several weeks before the rotation getting ready for it, devoting time to researching the fire department, visiting stations, doing ride-alongs with crews, attending the fire department's open-to-the-public meetings, and studying the agency's policies and procedures. While such extensive preparation isn't necessary to get through the rotation, the EMS month is immensely important to me and might affect my long-term career, so I would choose to start the rotation as prepared as possible. Now, though, I won't have that chance. Instead, I'm going to have to scramble.

Plus, there's still the glaring issue of how I'm going to stop myself from getting distracted by the fact that Grant is on the rotation with me.

"During your month with the fire department, you'll each spend your shifts riding along with an ALS crew." Dr. Priest pauses to stroke his mustache. It really is an impressive mustache. "This is by design, since the ALS crews provide the more advanced medical care in the field, and they're the ones who call the ED to get direction and orders when managing high-acuity patients. Also, in addition to learning more about what the paramedics do in the field, spending time with the ALS crews will allow you to teach them as you debrief after patient encounters and discuss the care you observed them provide."

For the first time since this conversation began, I experience a flicker of excitement. I'm looking forward to the teaching aspect of this rotation very much. Teaching opportunities arise all the time in the ED, when med students, fellow residents, or nurses pose a question about a patient or a case. Both providing and learning from "bedside teaching" moments are some of my favorite parts of the job. It's invigorating to know that in addition to learning more about what the paramedics do, I'll have chances to teach them, too.

Dr. Priest motions to his phone. "I just spoke with one of the fire department's battalion chiefs, and he notified me that they've arranged for you to be assigned to different ALS crews for the month. You'll work all your shifts with your individually assigned crews."

Relief washes over me. Grant and I will be working with different crews, riding in different ambulances, and going on different calls. We'll have different shift schedules. We may even be based out of different stations. In other words, the amount of time that I'll spend in close proximity to Grant will be much less than I initially feared.

My posture relaxes a little bit.

"Finally, as a last initial piece of info about your rotation," Dr. Priest prefaces while clicking his computer mouse a couple of times, "like always, residents on this rotation are expected to complete some sort of academic project on an EMS-related topic. Unlike prior years, however, since you'll be doing your EMS rotation during the same month, we're asking that you work on your EMS presentation together."

And just like that, my relief vaporizes. Rather than having distance from Grant next month, I'm going to have to work on a project with him. I suddenly begin having flashbacks to all the group projects we did together in high school. Back then, I was so awkwardly love-struck around Grant that I was barely able to utter a word to him. I'm surprised Grant noticed me at all—then again, my peri-pubescent frizzing hair and mouthful of braces were pretty hard to miss.

"Well, I think that's everything I need to tell you tonight." Dr. Priest gets to his feet. "I know you both have a lot to do, so I'll let you get out of here. Again, I appreciate you meeting with me on such late notice, and thanks for your cooperation and flexibility. I'm glad this worked out so well for both of you."

Grant stands up. I also get to my feet, keeping a strained smile on my lips.

"Tomorrow, Leslie will email you your individualized schedules, as well as more info about the rotation and the academic project." Dr. Priest comes around the desk to join Grant and me. "Please feel free to reach out if you have any questions." His mustache smiles again. "For now, though, unless there's anything else I can answer for you, I'll let you go enjoy your evening."

Grant steps back from his chair, motioning for me to move past him to exit the room first. My mind is distracted with thoughts of the EMS rotation as I move Grant's direction, but as soon as I slide by him, I'm hit by the heat of nearness and inhale another faint whiff of his incredible cologne, and suddenly all my senses awaken fully. It requires everything I have to ignore the spell Grant has upon me as I continue moving by him.

Walking fast out of Dr. Priest's office, I continue past Leslie's desk and reach the hallway, where I finally stagger to a halt. As I work to catch my breath, part of me wants to flee down the hall and get to the elevators before Grant catches up with me, so I can have more time to collect my thoughts. Instead, though, I turn around and wait until Grant emerges from the office and strides to my side. Without speaking, Grant and I walk to the foyer and get on the elevator.

The elevator door slides shut, and things get extremely quiet. As always, being in Grant's presence unleashes a war within me. On one side of the battle is the fact that Grant is one of my best friends. He and I have known each other for years. We understand each other better than anyone else does. I can confide in Grant about (almost) anything. I know he'll always have my back. Meanwhile, on the other side of the battle is the fact that I must keep my love for Grant a secret. I know Grant doesn't love me, and I vowed to swear off love, anyway. So the end result of the clash inside me is that being with Grant is both agonizing and exhilarating. I can be myself around Grant, yet I have to conceal my truest feelings from him. He knows everything about me, but he knows absolutely nothing about me. Day after day, year after year, the war has continued. My relationship with Grant is exhausting, invigorating, confusing, comforting, heart-wrenching, and uplifting all at the same time.

"I'm sorry your EMS schedule got changed."

Grant's remark yanks me to attention. I lift my eyes from my feet and discover that Grant is watching me with his brows pulled together. Before I can reply, the elevator pings, and the door slides open. With a light cough, I step out. Grant follows. The lobby is vacant now, the lights are dimmed, and the music has been turned off. As we start heading in the general direction of the empty information desk, I look Grant's direction, put on a smile, and reply:

"Thanks, but it's no big deal. I don't mind . . ."

I trail off. Who do I think I'm fooling? I won't be fooling Grant, that's for sure. Grant knows better than anyone how much I've been looking forward to my EMS rotation and how important it is to me. He undoubtedly knows that rushing into the month isn't how I would have chosen for things to play out.

With a sigh, I tug the elastic out of my hair, causing my hair to land freely around my shoulders. "Actually, I'm pretty disappointed. I wish I could have more than a few days to prepare."

Grant's eyes shift to my hair. He blinks, and then he looks straight ahead. "I know you would have. This rotation means a lot to you. I'm really sorry things got shuffled around at the last minute."

"Thanks." I sigh resignedly. "I guess there's nothing I can do about it now, though."

Grant turns his head and shows me a smile. "Well, the good news is that if there's anyone who will be able to pull off an amazing rotation on such short notice, it's you."

"That's nice of you to say." I can't stop my cheeks from warming under his praise. Grant's smile somehow makes everything a little bit better. "However, if roles were reversed, I'm certain you would do a stellar job conquering a last-minute rotation, too."

Grant's smile morphs into a playful grin. "I appreciate your vote of confidence, Doctor Vincent. However, if I did manage to successfully pull off a rotation with just a few days to prepare, it would only be because I was putting in immense effort to try to keep up with you."

I do a double take. "What?"

Grant chuckles and uses one hand to casually ruffle his hair. "Elly Vincent, I realized long ago that if I was going to have any chance of keeping up with you, I would have to stay on my toes. From the moment I met you, I knew I would have to bring my A game each and every time."

I nearly trip. "Wait a sec, are you serious?"

Now it's Grant's turn to appear surprised. "Of course I'm serious." He slows his pace, and his expression takes on a serious hue. "You can't tell me that you didn't know this." He smiles again and nudges me. "I mean, did anyone else compete with you for all the best grades in high school? Or for the title of valedictorian? Or for the top grade in each of our pre-med college courses?"

"You do have a point." I laugh at the memories. "It was only and always you, Grant. I . . ." I trail off, my throat unexpectedly becoming thick with more emotion. I avert my gaze.

There's a beat of quiet, and then Grant and I resume walking across the lobby without a word. Eventually, Grant breaks the silence by asking:

"So are you heading back to the ED to chart?"

I come to a stop, causing Grant to do the same. I glance in the direction that would take me to the emergency department, and then I look the other way, viewing the door that leads outside.

"You know, I think I'm going to head home and chart from there instead." I rub my forehead, which is starting to ache. The effects of a long, exhausting shift, combined with all the emotions I've experienced over this past hour or so, are definitely catching up with me. I'm weary, both in mind and heart. "It has proven to be a long day, for several reasons, so I think I'll work from home, where it's more peaceful." I drop my arm to my side. "I'll see you in a few days."

I make a move to go, and once again, Grant starts walking alongside me.

"Why are you going this way?" I shoot him a confused look. "You never park in the main garage."

Grant returns my side-glance with one of his own. "I'm walking you to your car, El."

My chest warms with affection and gratitude. Of course Grant is walking me to my car. Because that's the kind of man Grant is. He always walks me to my car when we leave the hospital together.

We head to the main door and venture outside. There's a wet chill in the air, and the sky has grown dark. I can see my breath. Rain-soaked, autumn-colored leaves litter the ground, and a few puddles have collected on the concrete, confirming that rain was recently falling. I shiver and throw on my jacket.

Grant and I cross the road that's directly in front of the hospital to enter the gigantic, multi-level parking garage. I hear the echoing sounds of cars being driven toward the gated exit, and there's a loud buzz coming from the blinding lights that illuminate the stairwell. Slowing my pace, I start racking my fatigued brain, trying to remember where I parked this morning. My mind is pretty much nothing but mush now, though, and I can't recall where I left my car. With a sigh, I halt in my tracks yet again.

"What's wrong?" Grant stops beside me.

I duck my head and make myself busy fishing through my bag to find my keys. "You're not going to believe this, but I can't remember where I parked." I force a laugh. "I guess today has left me more rattled than I realized."

Grant doesn't reply, but I can feel him watching me closely. Waves of emotion keep crashing into me while the events of the day replay in my mind: an exhausting shift that included having to pronounce a young man dead and later dealing with someone making unwanted advances toward me, hearing a dear friend is engaged and being reminded of my own painful decision to swear off love, the daunting reality of having hours of charting ahead of me, the shock of learning I'll be starting my EMS rotation so much sooner than expected, and the added angst of knowing I'll be doing my rotation with Grant.

This has been a brutal day.

Blinking away the tears that are stinging my eyes, I retrieve my keys from the depths of my bag, lift my head, and show Grant a grin like everything is fine. Based on the way the muscles of his jaw are twitching, however, I don't think Grant is fooled. Before he can say anything, though, I hit the *unlock* button on my key fob, causing a familiar beeping sound to fill the air. Spinning on my heels, I hurry in the direction of my car.

Without missing a beat, Grant catches up with me, steps farther ahead, and opens my car door. I murmur a thanks to him as I slide into the vehicle. I toss my bag onto the passenger seat and shove my keys into the ignition.

"Thank you again for everything," I tell Grant while I reach out to close my door. It's taking everything I have to keep my voice steady.

"You're welcome." Grant lets go of the door and steps back. "Goodnight, Elly."

"Goodnight, Grant."

I shut the door, back out of the parking stall, and drive off toward the exit. I cast a last look in my rearview mirror, and I see Grant striding back toward the hospital. As soon as he disappears from view, I begin to sob.

Four

"I'm so sorry about your EMS rotation getting changed at the last minute, El. How are you feeling about it all? Are you ready to start tomorrow?"

"I think so. At least, I hope so," I reply into my phone with a drawn-out sigh. "I'm as ready as I can be, anyway, under the circumstances."

It's late morning, and I'm chatting on the phone with my other best friend, Mackenna Patterson, while strolling through the park that's not far from my little house. With one hand, I'm holding my phone against my ear. With my other hand, I'm gripping a to-go cup that's filled to the brim with blazingly hot apple cider, which I purchased from my favorite café down the road.

It's great to be catching up with Mackenna; though it has only been a few days since we last talked, it feels like ages have passed. Usually, Mackenna and I communicate via text, phone call, or email every day. This past week, however, I've been so swamped with trying to prep for my rotation that I haven't had a chance to touch base with Mackenna at all. Frankly, I haven't had time to do much of anything, except race around to accomplish in a few days what I would have otherwise done over the course of several weeks prior to my rotation. I've managed to squeeze in brief tours of a couple of Lakewood Fire and Rescue's stations, do one ride-along with a crew, attend a meeting hosted by the agency that was open to the public, and study the BLS and ALS crews' handbooks to familiarize myself with their protocols and procedures. Needless to say, all the last-minute cramming meant I didn't have time to do much else, including talking to Mackenna . . . or to anyone else, for that matter.

Thankfully, Mackenna and I are always able to pick up right where we left off. Mackenna and I met when I was a freshman in college. She was a year ahead of Grant and me, but she was also pre-med, so our paths wound up overlapping in classes, labs, study groups, and pre-med meetings. Mackenna, I discovered, was a high-energy extrovert, and she had an uncanny knack for thinking outside the box. Though our personalities were different in many ways, Mackenna and I became dear friends, and we've remained close ever since. Mackenna is now living nearly two thousand miles away, finishing up the third and final year of her own emergency medicine residency. She's also starting the thrilling process of submitting resumes for her first post-residency job as an emergency medicine attending. In typical, free-spirited Mackenna fashion, she's leaving herself open to going almost anywhere, so she's job hunting across the country. Of course, I'm hoping she'll ultimately decide to return to the Lakewood area to work, hence the reason I've just finished telling her about how Lakewood recently hired several more emergency medicine attendings. I badgered Mackenna to submit her resume to Lakewood, too, in case even more attendings get hired.

"Well, El, you're fearless, perceptive, extremely skilled with people, and ridiculously brilliant, so I know you'll pull off this rotation with flying colors," Mackenna states. "Nonetheless, I'm sorry you had to scramble to get prepared. That's super stressful. It's not cool that you didn't have a lot of warning."

"Thanks. I appreciate that." I sit down on a vacant park bench and place my cup on the bench beside me.

With the mouth-watering aromas of apple and cinnamon from my drink still filling my nostrils, I use my free hand to unbutton the top of my long brown coat and loosen the plaid scarf that I've got tucked around my neck. I glance around the park, which is serene and nearly empty this time of the morning, and I break into a smile. It's the first day of October, and it definitely looks and feels as though autumn has officially arrived. Above me, the sun is shining in a clear blue sky. The air is crisp and cool. Colored leaves are scattered across the ground. A faint smell of campfire is touching the air. Still smiling, I take a moment to bask in the fall-ness; it's nice to have a chance to relax after these crazy past few days.

Mackenna clears her throat. "Hey, have you talked with Grant? That is, have you talked with Grant since the evening you learned that you would be doing your EMS rotation with him?"

I was reaching to pick up my apple cider from off the bench, but I pause. My heart skips. "No," I draw out the word. "I've been so busy that I haven't had a chance to talk with Grant since we were in Doctor Priest's office."

I decide to leave it at that. I don't tell Mackenna that although I haven't spoken with Grant since he walked me to my car, I've been thinking about him—a lot—and wondering what he has been doing to prepare for our rotation. Of course, Grant doesn't need to do nearly as much prep work as I've engaged myself in. I've undoubtedly gone way beyond what any other second-year ED resident has ever done, because this rotation may play a critical role in guiding my future career. Nonetheless, I have no doubt Grant will be ready for tomorrow, and he'll do an incredible job, like he always does.

I sigh.

Grant.

"Oh," Mackenna replies. She seems to pause before going on in a more nonchalant tone. "Well, you'll obviously be working with Grant a lot this month, so you'll be talking to him soon."

I frown. I know precisely what Mackenna is hinting at, but I don't take the bait. Instead, I pick up my cider, blow on it, and enjoy a sip.

Back while we were in college, Mackenna wasn't shy about telling me—boldly and frequently—that she thought Grant and I should date. Whenever she brought up the subject, however, I politely and firmly shut her down. I told her I wasn't interested in pursuing romance with Grant or anyone else. I stuck to the lie that I wanted to focus on my education and career, rather than chase after love.

I'm sure Mackenna thought I was crazy. Or blind. Or both. After all, Grant was the most good-looking, brilliant, kind, gentlemanly guy in the entire pre-med department. The only reason Mackenna herself didn't join the lineup of gals who were constantly vying for Grant's attention was because she was dating someone else at the time. Anyway, over all these years, I've continued hiding behind the same façade, lying to one of my best friends about the other.

I hate lying to Mackenna. I've always hated it, but it has to be done. My feelings for Grant are off-limits; I have to protect them at all costs. How I feel about Grant is the one thing that I will not—I cannot—share with anyone. I cannot risk Grant ever finding out how I feel, because if he did, it would end our friendship.

That's why Mackenna can't know the truth. No one can know. I cherish my friendship with Grant too much for anyone to ever know.

"Whoops, it looks like lunch break is over, and it's time for me to head back into the auditorium for the rest of didactics," Mackenna tells me. She sounds like she's walking fast.

"Good luck tomorrow, El. Give me a call to let me know how your first day went, okay?"

I smile gratefully, as though she can see me. "I will, Mac. Thanks."

Mackenna ends the call. I slip my phone into the pocket of my coat, and I resume sipping my cider. A few minutes ago, I was contemplating going back to the café to get a pumpkin scone, but I'm not thinking about food anymore. I'm too distracted reminiscing about everything. Well, actually, I'm reminiscing about love, but when you really think about it, that is pretty much everything.

I suppose it's interesting that I'm such a devoted romantic at heart. After all, even when I was young, I was forced to acknowledge the devastating heartbreak and vulnerability that can come from loving someone. When I was only eight, my younger brother was diagnosed with acute lymphoblastic leukemia. He passed away two years later. When I was fourteen, my parents got divorced; in the years preceding their official split, it was already evident their relationship was strained and cracking, and finally their marriage fractured beyond repair.

Indeed, during my young and impressionable years, I learned in brutally hard ways that loving someone made you susceptible to overwhelming loss and anguish. Yet, somehow, I became and remain an incurable romantic. Perhaps the reason why is because I understand that not everyone is lucky in love, and so I'm delighted to cheer for those who do find true joy and happiness in matters of the heart.

Anyway, in hindsight, I realize it wasn't any one thing that caused my parents' marriage to shatter. Rather, it was a sinisterly slow, steady destruction, accelerated by the strain of my little brother's diagnosis and the crushing weight that came with both of my parents being physicians, which left them constantly immersed in unforgiving, high-stress, demanding jobs. I was fortunate, at least, that their divorce was amicable. After the split, Dad stayed in California, where I had been born and raised, to continue managing his orthopedic practice, and Mom moved me to the Lakewood area, where she became a pediatric intensivist.

Shortly after Mom and I moved, it was time for my ninth-grade school year to begin. Life at that time was a disaster. Mom and I weren't even close to being unpacked after our move. Mom was adjusting to her new job and to life as a divorcee. I was still reeling from being uprooted and taken away from everything I had ever known, and I was grappling with the sadness of not getting to see my dad regularly anymore. Not to mention, I was in the middle of all things teenage and awkward, which didn't exactly help matters.

Despite the chaos, my first day of school rolled around all the same. So with my teeth covered in braces, and my hair hitting a peri-pubescent frizzy stage, I found myself timidly walking through the door of a new high school, not knowing a soul.

Thankfully, I had brains and a sense of humor.

And thankfully, I soon had Grant.

My first day at my new school began with honors English class. Before the bell rang, while the other students giddily chatted with their friends, I sat alone at a desk in the back corner of the room. Head down and close to tears, I was miserably lonely and convinced I would never get used to life in a new place.

Then, out of the corner of my eye, I noticed some guy taking a seat at the desk next to mine. After a moment's pause, the guy turned my way, and I realized he was waiting to say something to me. I looked over at him through my teary gaze, and in a surreal, slow-motion moment, I found myself staring into the strikingly blue eyes of the most handsome guy I had ever seen. He was tall. He had thick, jet-black hair. His build made it clear he was athletic. He smelled good. He had the aura of someone who hung out with the popular crowd . . . and yet he was smiling at me in a genuine, welcoming way.

I nearly threw up.

Grant introduced himself and held out his hand to shake mine. For one awkward second, I just stared back at him, trying to decide if the handsome, friendly, good-smelling guy was actually real. The only thing that eventually shook me out of my stunned stupor was the fact that, in a subtle way, despite the calm confidence of Grant's demeanor, I sensed he was feeling a teeny bit shy, too. So I managed to relax enough to shake his hand and eke out my name.

The moment our hands touched, all the air escaped my lungs, and my heart started racing like it was going to explode. The feel of Grant's hand around mine ignited a fire within me that I had never felt before, and all at once, I knew I was in love. It was the most incredible, terrifying, wonderful sensation I had ever felt, and I've carried that flame for Grant ever since.

Grant was confident yet disarming as he asked me questions about myself. I remember not only being stunned that Grant was talking to me, but that he seemed legitimately interested in what I had to say. He introduced me to his friends. He warned me about our teacher's penchant for wearing animal-print outfits, causing me to laugh for the first time since I had heard my parents were divorcing. By the time class began, I dared to hope that maybe, just maybe, my new life wouldn't be too bad.

Class hadn't been in session for more than a few minutes when our teacher (who, I vividly remember, was wearing a leopard-print dress that day) asked if anyone knew which French author had devoted nineteen chapters of his epic novel to a discussion of the Battle of Waterloo. Grant and I both immediately raised our hands . . . and then we paused . . . and then we exchanged a curious glance.

Our teacher called on Grant. He gave the answer of Alexander Dumas and the novel, *The Count of Monte Cristo*. The teacher shook her head and turned to me. Holding back a smile, I said the answer was Victor Hugo and his novel, *Les Miserables*. The teacher confirmed I was correct. Grant's eyebrows rose. The rest of the students gasped. As if our gazes were pulled together, Grant and I looked at each other once more. Our eyes locked more intensely, and then, slowly, we both broke into amused, resolute smiles.

And that was how our academic competition was born.

From that day on, Grant and I were the best of friends and the fiercest of academic rivals, determined to beat each other for the best grade in every class. Our scholastic rivalry swiftly gained fame throughout the school; students placed bets on whether Grant or I would get the highest grade on the next exam. Somehow, the competition between Grant and me solidified our friendship. We studied together, helping and encouraging one another while simultaneously being spurred on by the drive to outdo one another.

One time, when Grant bested me by a single point on a math test, I pulled out an old fifty-cent coin from my wallet—for no particular reason, I had carried it around with me after finding it while unpacking during the move— and I jokingly handed it over to Grant as the "trophy" for his latest win. After that, Grant and I continued exchanging the old fifty-cent piece for years, awarding it to whoever got the latest top score or grade, until at some point near the end of our college years, the coin was forgotten.

High school passed in a blur, but I'm thankful to say they proved to be good years. I developed a solid, supportive group of friends, and I also stayed in touch with my friends in California. Even traveling back-and-forth to California to visit Dad wasn't as awful as I had expected. I stayed contentedly busy with my schoolwork. I enjoyed piano lessons and participating on the track team. I gradually outgrew my shyness, and I became confident in my humor and smarts. And—hallelujah—my braces came off, and I discovered the miracle of a hair straightener.

Meanwhile, Grant was also growing up . . . he was definitely growing up. He wasn't just becoming even more handsome and mature, however. Grant Reed, being the extremely popular, good-looking, intelligent, and kind guy he was, had basically reached celebrity status at school. He was the captain of the basketball team. He played the saxophone, somehow managing to make participating in school band look cool. Grant was the homecoming king. And all along, he kept up his perfect GPA like I did. He was almost too incredible to be real.

And that was precisely the problem.

As Grant became more and more popular, busy, and successful, I feared the friendship we shared would fade away, much like the relationship between my parents had faded. Miraculously to me, though, the friendship that Grant and I shared never wavered. In fact, to my amazement and relief, our friendship got stronger—and as our friendship strengthened, my love for Grant deepened, too. Yet I kept my feelings a secret. I knew that loving someone could lead to heartbreak and that even the most solid relationship could end. Petrified of losing Grant if he found out how I felt, I hid the truth. I told myself to be grateful for the friendship we shared, even if my heart wasn't entirely fulfilled.

That's how I wound up as both a hopeless romantic—delighted to get swept up by the tales of happily-ever-afters in sappy movies and Jane Austen novels—while resisting the pursuit of love for myself. I never confessed to Grant, and I tactfully skirted around the advances of other boys, which occurred with increasing frequency as the years passed.

The one thing that made it easier for me to keep my love for Grant a secret was knowing he didn't love me in return. We were close friends—best friends—but in Grant's eyes, *friends* was clearly all we were. I wasn't like the girls Grant dated or took to school dances. Grant was drawn to girls who were popular, fashionable, and super-model-ish. Grant dated the girls who moved in the premier social circles, like the cheerleaders and homecoming princesses. With my nose in the books, I wasn't one of those gals.

After high school, Grant and I both chose to stay in the Lakewood area for college. I was ecstatic we would be attending the same university. When freshman year began, I found something immensely comforting in simply knowing Grant was there among the sea of otherwise-unfamiliar faces. I loved meeting up with Grant for lunch between classes, and attending athletic events together along with our other friends. And, of course, Grant and I continued our hilariously intense academic rivalry. We studied together, earnestly helping one another while simultaneously maintaining our playfully cutthroat competitiveness.

Regarding the romance department, other than the vast number of new potential dating opportunities that college introduced, things carried on in pretty much the same way as they had always done. Grant was pursued by countless women, a phenomenon I did my best to ignore, and Grant dated, which I tried even harder to ignore. All the while, my heart remained completely, secretly devoted to Grant. So between my love for Grant and my wariness of pursuing romance at all, I turned down each and every guy who asked me out.

Then something seemed to change.

Somewhere late in our freshman year, I found myself growing restless. It was like the dam that restrained my emotions burst wide open, and I suddenly wanted to confess to Grant how I truly felt about him. I had no idea why there was a change. I knew it was crazy. It went against everything I had previously felt and believed. It risked irrevocably harming our friendship. However, upholding the friends-only act was grating on my soul; pretending I didn't love Grant was clashing too severely with my romantically inclined heart. So as our freshman year of college drew near to a close, I resolved to tell him the truth.

I'll never forget the day when Grant and I were studying for finals outside, situated under a birch tree in a quiet corner of campus. As we reviewed notes from English class, we began talking about the day's lecture, which had included a discussion of Victor Hugo and *Les Miserables*. I took that as my sign. Everything had come full circle. It was time for me to tell Grant the truth.

Before I could summon the courage to speak, however, Grant blindsided me with an unexpected announcement of his own: he had decided that he was going to pursue pre-med courses through the rest of college, and he was going to go to medical school after college was over.

For me, time suddenly came to an abrupt, horrible standstill. My heart crashed. My soul shattered.

Unbeknownst to Grant, I, too, had decided to go to medical school. I was going to tell Grant my plan, of course, but my overwhelming desire to profess to him my love had obviously taken priority. I knew that whenever I did tell Grant about my career plan, he would be surprised to learn the medical profession appealed to me at all. Grant understood that I had seen the destructive effects the profession had had on my parents. However, as I intended to explain to Grant, what I witnessed growing up didn't make me loathe

the medical profession or want to avoid it. For all the immense challenges that I had witnessed were part of the medical field, I also witnessed how much fulfillment there could be in serving as a physician. Being a doctor would give me an opportunity to aid people in their darkest hours, alleviate pain and suffering, advocate for those who couldn't advocate for themselves, and steer people's lives in a better direction. In my heart, medicine was my calling and my mission. So after giving the pros and cons of a medical career an immense amount of thought, I decided to join the ranks of the medical profession.

Being aware of the stress a medical career entailed was actually encouraging to me, not a deterrent. I understood what I would be getting into. I wouldn't be going into the medical profession blindly or disillusioned, and I felt that allowed me to make a truly informed decision about whether or not pursuing medicine was right for me. I also knew that I had learned from watching my parents, and I hoped that what I learned would help me avoid making many of the mistakes they did.

And what was the biggest mistake that I believed my parents had made? What was the one thing I was absolutely determined to avoid?

I would never get into a relationship with a fellow physician.

I had seen, first-hand, that the demands of the medical profession made it nearly impossible for two physicians to have a happy, healthy, balanced, successful relationship. I had witnessed the way two physicians conversed with each other about nothing but work. I knew of the trauma, worry, and stress that doctors carried home with them. I knew how the effects of that stress bled over into home life, and I knew how those effects increased exponentially when there were two doctors under the same roof. The combined demands constantly placed upon two physicians made it impossible for them to have meaningful breaks from the oppressive, intense, merciless workplace. Indeed, it was clear to me that a relationship between two doctors was doomed to fail.

So in that horrible, time-stopping, gut-wrenching moment when Grant announced that he was planning to go to med school, my impulsive resolve to profess to him my love vanished. Grant's decision to enter the medical profession changed everything. Instead of opening up my heart, I would have to build an even stronger wall around it.

With my soul aching terribly, I put on a smile and told Grant I was thrilled for him. I disclosed that I, too, had chosen to go the pre-med route. Grant was sincerely thrilled when he heard my news. We spent the next few hours talking about what pre-med classes we would take, where we wanted to go for med school, and what specialties we were potentially interested in pursuing. Every second of that conversation drove the knife into my heart a little deeper, but Grant never knew it.

That night, I returned to my dorm, collapsed onto my bed, and burst into sobs.

Once the tears dried, it was like my soul had nothing left to feel. I vowed never to let myself go through anything so agonizing again. I would do more than just keep my love for Grant a secret; I would lock away my heart completely. I had lost my brother, my parents as a couple, and any chance there might have been to be with Grant. My heart had been crushed too many times, and I wouldn't let my heart get crushed again.

Over our next three years of college, Grant and I had several classes together as we moved along the pre-med track. Though I cherished every moment with him, the pain of being in Grant's presence—the unspoken feelings, the constant reminders of what would never be—ate away at me. It also became harder to act unbothered whenever Grant mentioned a woman he had taken out on a date, or when gals flirted with him in front of me. I came to the conclusion that I needed some real space and time away from Grant. I needed to clear my head and begin healing my heart. So when Grant mentioned he was hoping to stay in the Lakewood area for med school, I applied elsewhere.

I eventually told Grant that I had been accepted into a med school in California. He stared at me, his expression unreadable. Though I burned from the heat of how much I left unsaid, I acted like my plan to leave the area was no big deal, chalking it up to a simple desire for a change of scenery, and to spend more time with my dad and old friends. Grant didn't push the issue, but I sensed he was leaving a lot unsaid, too.

After that, things between Grant and me carried on in almost the same way. Almost. A strain started quietly gnawing away at the bond we shared, and our dynamic wasn't quite the same anymore. The change was subtle but devastating to me. My only consolation was that I knew what I was doing was ultimately for the best, for both of us.

Grant and I graduated from college *summa cum laude*, and in a blink of an eye, it was time for me to move to California for med school. I had already shipped most of my things to my dad's house; he was kindly storing my belongings until I could move into my apartment. So on that early morning when my mom drove me to the airport, all I had with me was a small suitcase and an even smaller carry-on. I was filled with nerves and excitement about my future, and I was harboring excruciating remorse and sadness about my past. I hid my emotions, though, as I told Mom goodbye. After she drove away, I found myself completely alone. Gripping my bags more tightly, I entered the airport and started making my way toward the security line.

That was when I heard him call my name.

Grant's voice reached my ears, perfectly clear and distinct above the noise. With a stuttering gasp, I spun around. My heart came alive when I saw Grant jogging through the crowds to get to me. His hair was disheveled. His t-shirt and jeans were wrinkled. His eyes, however, were vibrant as he kept them locked on mine.

When Grant reached me, he didn't say a word. He just pulled me into his arms and held me in his strong embrace. I dropped my bags and threw my arms around him, letting myself cry. In that moment, I knew that whatever strain there had been between us was forgiven and forgotten.

And only then did the magnitude of what I was doing hit me fully.

I was saying goodbye to Grant potentially—likely—forever. There was no telling where life would take either of us. There was no guarantee I would return to the Lakewood area, or that if I did, Grant would still be there. There was no way of knowing if Grant and I would cross paths again, and there was no promise that Grant would care about seeing me even if our paths did intersect in the future. After eight years of having Grant at my side as my most trusted and truest friend—my confidant, listening ear, and strength—I was choosing to leave him behind. I was letting him go.

All at once, the air left my lungs. My heart ached like it would break. I clung more tightly to Grant as he held me, and my tears fell harder.

I don't know how much time passed before I finally slipped out of Grant's embrace and took a step back from him. Grant's breathing was fast, and his gaze was intense, as he peered into my eyes. My throat was too thick to say anything, but it was just as well; I knew there were no words to convey what I so desperately wanted to tell him. So instead, without bothering to wipe away my tears, I gave Grant a last smile, picked up my bags, and walked off to catch my plane.

Medical school passed for me in much the same way it passes for other med students: four fast-paced, daunting, brutally challenging, amazing years of terrifying, thrilling, intimidating, devastating, wondrous, eye-opening, life-changing experiences. Starting with rigorous classroom studies and then advancing to patient care under the direction of residents and attending physicians, med school wasn't solely about academic learning. In those four years, my classmates and I found ourselves at the bedsides of patients—people—who suffered, triumphed, and succumbed to injury or illness. We held the hands of strangers. We cried and laughed with people from all walks of life. We didn't just learn about medication dosing and treatment protocols; we came to better understand the frailty of the human condition and the simultaneous resilience of the human race. Our perspectives on what it meant to be alive were altered forever. I thought I had been prepared for med school, but nothing could have truly prepared me for the journey it proved to be.

During those four years, Grant and I tried to stay in touch, but the frequency of our calls gradually diminished, and the number of exchanged texts dwindled. I was crushed but not surprised. Grant and I were both busy, and we were living increasingly separate lives. Despite the years and the miles, however, my love for Grant never wavered; while Grant was no longer at the forefront of my mind, he always remained at the forefront of my heart.

At no point did this contrast strike me more than during my fourth year of med school. I had finished the whole residency application process before I realized that I hadn't even told Grant about my decision to go into emergency medicine for my specialty. I also realized Grant hadn't told me what specialty he had decided to pursue. The fact that Grant and I had simply forgotten to share something that important with each other was a harsh reminder of how separate our lives had become.

The infamous Match Day in March arrived, and I was thrilled to learn that I had been accepted into Lakewood's emergency medicine residency program. Another blink later, it was early June and time for med school graduation. The ceremony was exhilarating and poignant, filled with reflection and celebration. I fondly bid farewell to the many professors, residents, and attendings who had guided me through my education, and I sadly said goodbye to wonderful classmates who had become dear friends along the way.

I returned to the Lakewood area to start the rapid-fire process of getting settled in before residency began. With Mom's help, I moved into my little rental house. I bought a car, since my route to the hospital where I would be working didn't include a convenient bus line. I stocked up on groceries. I refreshed my wardrobe so I would have business-appropriate attire for the rotations that didn't approve of scrubs (it's basically blasphemous, for example, to wear scrubs in a dermatology or surgery clinic). And I managed to catch up on much-needed sleep.

The last week of June arrived, which meant it was time for residency to begin . . . sort of. Officially, the various residency programs at Lakewood didn't begin until July first, but in keeping with his tradition, Dr. Priest hosted a week-long orientation beforehand for his twelve new emergency medicine residents. The orientation was designed to help the fledgling ED residents get prepared for the onslaught of their clinical duties, and so the week was scheduled to include refresher tours of the ED and the rest of the hospital, didactics taught by ED attendings, practice using the electronic health record, and time in the mannequin lab to perfect skills like suturing, splinting, and placing a central line.

On the first day of orientation, when I arrived to Lakewood Medical Center, I could hardly breathe under the weight of all the emotions and thoughts that were filling my heart and mind. I also couldn't help reflecting back on when I had started med school four years prior. In some ways, I felt exactly the same: intimidated, lost, petrified, thrilled, excited, and confident all at once. In other ways, though, as I walked through Lakewood's doors, I felt profoundly different. This time, the hospital badge I was issued had "M.D." after my name.

This time, I was given a long white coat to wear. My pager was programmed for messages to come directly to me. I was a doctor, not a student. I was responsible for patients, and I was expected to provide that care in an efficient, intelligent, empathetic, and independent manner. Though I would have supervision by attending physicians, I would be making many critical decisions on my own. And this time, my training would focus on me becoming proficient in my chosen specialty: emergency medicine. It was both daunting and exhilarating to ponder what the three years of residency would bring.

In a daze, I made my way up to the eighth floor of Prescott Tower. As I caught my reflection in a mirror, I once again realized I was staring into the eyes of Dr. Elly Vincent, M.D. I was Dr. Vincent, resident physician at Lakewood Medical Center. Was I ready? Did I know enough? Did I know anything at all?

Lost in thought, I ventured down a long, imposingly quiet hall to reach the doors that led into the Discovery Conference Room. I paused to appreciate the moment. I was about to have my first-ever encounter with the eleven other members of my emergency medicine residency class. I was about to meet the people who would be my closest colleagues and friends for the next three years of my life. These were the people with whom I would experience the intense highs and lows of residency. These people would become my family.

I entered the large, elegantly decorated conference room and scanned the scene. At my left was a robust catered breakfast spread. At the opposite end of the room, a group of people were chatting. Mentally referencing the photos I had seen in the orientation email I received, I was able to identify some faces among the group: Dr. Wesley Kent, Lynn Prentis, Dr. Tammy Sanders, Dr. Jesse Santiago, Leslie Yamada, and Dr. Priest. I felt a fresh twinge of nerves as I took in the sight of so many of the big-wigs in Lakewood's emergency medicine department. I knew I was looking at some of the individuals whose wisdom, encouragement, and mentoring would guide me as I strove to become the best emergency medicine physician that I could be.

Pulling my eyes from the group, I settled my complete attention on the long table in the middle of the room, which had several people seated around it. I smiled. This was my team. These were my new residency colleagues.

Everyone at the table appeared to be about my age. A few of them were eating; others were engaged in that polite type of conversation people make upon first meeting each other. I started surveying the group members more closely, assessing everyone's facial expressions and body language . . . until my eyes abruptly came to a hard stop when they locked with the intense gaze of a guy who was seated at the far end of the table. A guy who was staring back at me. A guy who had strikingly vibrant blue eyes. Unmistakable blue eyes. Unforgettable blue eyes.

There was a whooshing sound in my ears, and a sensation swept over me that momentarily made me feel as though I had become completely disconnected from my surroundings. A blink later, I was back in my body and still staring at the guy who was seated at the table with the other members of my new residency class.

Grant.

Grant Reed.

Grant Reed was seated at the table.

The only man I had ever loved was seated at the table.

Why was Grant seated at the table?

My legs went weak. I sensed myself go pale. My heart started pounding so furiously that I could barely catch my breath. My thoughts raced almost faster than I could keep up with as my brain finished processing what it meant.

Grant had decided to go into emergency medicine. Grant had matched with Lakewood Medical Center's emergency medicine residency program. Grant was going to be one of my residency colleagues for the next three years. I would be interacting with Grant nearly every day for the next thirty-six months.

My throat went dry as the implications of the situation crashed down upon me. I had spent the past four years keeping myself away from Grant, trying to get over him, and now he was right in front of me once more. It took only one more clumsy thud of my heart before my long-sequestered feelings exploded inside of me, bursting out from the place where I had kept them hidden for so long. And I knew that I was as in love with Grant Reed as ever before.

It was Grant who made the first move. Keeping his eyes on mine, Grant pushed back from the table, got to his feet, and began striding toward me with deliberateness in his strides. My body trembled as he approached. In the four years since I had last seen him, Grant had grown taller and even more muscular. His features were chiseled. The curl in his thick, jet-black hair had tamed into an alluring wave. The button-up shirt and dark jeans he wore fit his frame to perfection. And Grant's aura of calm, steady confidence was more potent than ever before.

All I could do was work down another swallow.

Grant came to a stop right in front of me. He searched my face, and then he broke into the most breath-stealing smile I had ever seen.

"Elly."

The sound of Grant saying my name was like dumping gasoline onto the fire of emotions that was already raging inside me. More memories and feelings that I had long suppressed started flaming in my mind, the heat they generated confirming just how greatly I had missed Grant and how much I loved him.

"Grant," I uttered, barely managing to say the word.

Grant glanced down at my hands, and all the items I was carrying, and then he put his eyes back on mine. Still smiling, he drew me into an embrace. Instantly, the fire inside of me raged hotter. I hadn't been in Grant's arms since the day he saw me off at the airport, and I realized just how much I had longed to feel him hold me again.

"Fancy meeting you here," Grant said in my ear, sounding as though he was still smiling.

For one more blissful second, I let myself stay lost in his embrace. I then shook myself to my senses. Grant was a fellow physician, and I had vowed never to get into a relationship with another doctor. Besides, Grant had never loved me like I loved him—in fact, I didn't even know his current relationship status. Four years had gone by since I had last been in his arms. Who had he dated during that time? Was he currently dating somebody? Oh gosh, was he engaged? *Married*?

My body grew cold at the thought, in spite of myself.

I slipped out of Grant's arms, discreetly peeking at his left hand as I did so. No ring. When I exhaled with relief, I had to mentally shake myself to my senses again. Grant had every right to date and fall in love. I was the one who had sworn off romance, not Grant. Nonetheless, I remained immensely unsettled as I wondered, almost fearfully, what I might learn about Grant's relationship status.

Still trying to steady my breathing, I gazed up into Grant's eyes once more. Again, my breath escaped me. How I had missed looking into those eyes!

"It's great to see you," I told him, somehow keeping my voice steady. "I cannot believe we both ended up here."

Grant chuckled, his eyes sparkling. "No kidding. It seems our paths just keep crossing, doesn't it?"

I drew in a breath. "Yes . . . yes, it does."

"Well, how about we get some lunch today so we can catch up?" Grant remained completely unflustered. "It would be awesome to hear what you've been up to all this time and what made you decide to come here for residency."

I fixed him with a playful look. "Well, obviously, I came specifically to Lakewood because I knew there had to be someone to keep you in line. After all, who else is going to humble you by beating you out for all the best scores and reviews on every rotation?"

Grant went still. His gaze grew more focused. Leaning in closer to me, he broke into another smile as he lowered his voice and said, "Challenge accepted, Doctor Vincent."

And that was how my first day of residency began.

What started out as the biggest day of my life and medical career up to that point also became the most emotional day of my existence. Grant and I did go to lunch that afternoon, and the ease and swiftness with which we fell into real, candid, heartfelt conversation made it seem like we had never been apart. We talked openly about everything (except my locked-away feelings for him, of course), and we got caught up on what had happened in each other's lives over the four years. When we wandered into the topic of relationships, I learned Grant had dated during medical school, but he was presently single; we spoke only briefly of my relationship status, or lack thereof, before Grant diverted the discussion to another topic.

By the end of our meal, it was as though the past four years were nothing but a fleeting blip of time. Our friendship was as solid as ever. Grant was still the brilliant, gentlemanly, gorgeous, kind, subtly funny man I had always loved and adored, and his natural maturation over four years only made it so he captivated my heart more than ever before. I wasn't surprised Grant had matured, of course; I knew my looks, opinions, and behavior had matured, too. Yet absorbing the man Grant had become, all at once, after four long years of being apart, unleashed feelings within me like a tidal wave, and I knew I was as completely and devotedly in love with Grant as ever before—and even more so.

That night, I returned home in a stunned haze, with so many emotions burning inside of me that I couldn't see straight. Apparently, my perpetual lot in life was to have the man I loved right in front of me, only to be forced to keep my love for him a secret.

Five

There's an invigorating breeze stirring the maple trees, causing the yellow, orange, and red leaves to flutter to the ground. Inhaling a breath of morning air, I shut my car door and turn toward the sprawling building that's otherwise known as Lakewood Fire and Rescue's Station Fourteen. I draw in another breath and exhale. This is it. This is the first day of my long-awaited EMS rotation. After almost a year-and-a-half of excitedly awaiting this moment, and a few days of frantically racing to prepare for it, I'm actually here. I'm about to start the off-service rotation that will help me determine if I want to pursue an EMS fellowship after residency.

I break into a giddy smile. Despite the mad rush of recent days, I'm still as enthusiastic about this rotation as I've always been. In fact, at this present moment, I would say that I'm about seventy percent thrilled to be here, twenty percent nervous-but-still-thrilled-to-be-here, and ten percent distracted by the fact that I know Grant will be on this rotation, too.

Okay, Elly. Get it together. Focus.

I shake my head, like doing so will rattle the lingering thoughts of Grant out of my mind, and I channel all my concentration toward what I'm supposed to be doing. In the email I received from one of Lakewood Fire and Rescue's battalion chiefs, I was instructed to arrive here just before eight in the morning. Station Fourteen is where the two paramedics whom I'll be shadowing work their shifts, so this station will be my home base for the month.

I didn't get a chance to tour this particular station yet, and this is my first time ever laying eyes on it in person, but I did some online research about it last night. Per what I read and saw online, I clearly lucked out in terms of location for the month. Station Fourteen was built only a couple of years ago, and it's placed strategically smack in the center of the Lakewood region to help meet the area's population growth and associated increase in nine-one-one calls. In stark contrast to the many fire stations that were built decades ago, this is a huge facility, and it's constructed in an airy, modern style, with extra-high ceilings and big windows. Also, this mammoth station is equipped with top-of-the-line everything, from the fire-fighting tools and medical equipment, to a sprawling gymnasium, a kitchen to rival the most expensive restaurant, spacious sleeping quarters, and a vast lounge area that includes an enormous television and plush recliner chairs.

This place is so nice that I almost don't know what I'm going to do with myself. Compared to the dilapidated state of Lakewood

Medical Center's current-and-soon-to-be-demolished emergency department, this fire station is like Buckingham Palace.

Pulling my eyes from the station, I glance down at myself, confirming that my blue cable-knit sweater and black slacks didn't get wrinkled during the twenty-minute drive here. Per the agency's policy, individuals doing ride-alongs are to wear business attire rather than scrubs or any other identifying uniform. This policy exists for a couple of reasons. First, when acting solely in the capacity of an observer, which is what I'll be doing while on calls with the crews, a physician isn't "running" the scene. The EMS crews still go through their regular channels of authority as they follow treatment protocols and procedures, including radioing the receiving hospital's ED if they need real-time direction from a physician. Yes, a physician who's doing a ride-along could take command of the scene, if he or she felt compelled to do so, and thereby accept all liability for the medical treatment the EMS crew provides until the patient is accepted by the receiving ED. However, such a drastic intervention is an extremely rare occurrence. So while on scene, to avoid confusing patients and bystanders about who's in charge, or causing questions about why the doctor who's standing right there isn't providing help, a physician who's doing a ride-along wears plain clothes, essentially going incognito.

The other reason for the policy about business attire is more simple: everyone associated with Lakewood Fire & Rescue is expected to uphold the highest degree of professionalism when interacting with the public, including in their standards of grooming and dress, which is why the EMS crew members wear such crisply ironed uniforms despite the gritty duties their work entails.

Deciding my outfit will meet approval, I cinch my ponytail tighter and adjust my cross-body bag on my hip. Ready, nervously excited, and determined, I make my way across the parking lot to the fire station's main entrance. The huge, bullet-proof glass door that leads inside is locked by an automated system, but there's a gigantic red button next to the door marked with an equally gigantic sign that tells visitors to use the button like a doorbell. After another steadying breath, I push the button. Immediately, I hear a loud chime echo through the station, announcing my arrival. The intercom on the wall momentarily turns on. I glance up at the security camera that's high above the door. I clear my throat, knowing I'm on the grid now.

Motion inside the station catches my attention. Peering through the door to see into the foyer, I see a guy emerge through a door on the opposite end of the room and jog toward the entrance. I put on a professional smile and take a step back, making room for the door to swing outward as the guy pushes it open.

"Hi, there," the guy greets me. "How can I . . ."

The guy trails off. I do a double take and freeze. There's a palpable beat of I've-seen-you-before communication exchanged between us. The guy who answered the door just happens to be the super-hot paramedic who brought the CHF patient into the ED the other day. The paramedic with the humungous muscles. The one who grinned at me while I was staring into the resuscitation bay.

And I have to admit: my second viewing is even more impressive than the first time around.

Like before, the guy is dressed in his paramedic uniform, which consists of a white button-up shirt tucked into black pants that have cargo pockets on the sides. He's got a pager on his belt and hefty boots on his feet. There's a patch with the fire department's emblem on his shirt's left shoulder, and he has another patch above his right breast pocket that shows his last name: *Blackrock*. His dark hair is cut short, military-style. Up close, his light-brown complexion proves to be as flawless as it appeared from across the ED the other evening. His piercingly dark eyes are glinting in the sunlight while he observes me as closely as I'm studying him. If I had to guess, the guy is a couple years older than me, perhaps in his early thirties.

"Well, good morning." The guy's eyes are now sparkling with something that seems a lot like amusement. He breaks into a dashing grin, revealing perfectly straight, white teeth. "You must be Doctor Vincent." His smile widens. "It's nice to see you again, Doc."

"It's . . . nice to see you again, too." I manage to collect myself enough to say. "Please call me Elly."

"Paramedic Jonathan Blackrock." The guy extends his hand and keeps peering right into my eyes. "Please call me Jonathan."

As we shake, Jonathan's hand seems to engulf mine. My insides tumble.

Jonathan releases my hand and holds open the door for me. "Come inside, Elly. I'll introduce you to my partner and show you around the station."

"Thank you."

I step past Paramedic Blackrock and enter the foyer. Not surprisingly, the interior of this place is as clean, spacious, and high-tech as the outside would suggest. Directly across from the entrance is a receptionist's desk, currently unoccupied, behind more bullet-proof glass. Security cameras are mounted near the ceiling. There are plush chairs throughout the space, clearly intended for visitors to use. A locked and alarmed cabinet with see-through doors is situated against the wall at my left; the cabinet contains a few medications, such as epinephrine, and basic medical equipment like an oxygen saturation monitor and sphygmomanometer. Mounted on the wall next to the cabinet are an automatic external defibrillator and a phone. I presume the equipment and meds are meant to be used on civilians who come to the station in need of immediate help.

"Right this way," I hear Jonathan say from behind me.

I look over my shoulder at him. Jonathan makes sure the front door locks as it closes, and then he meets my gaze. His lips remain turned up into a suave smile as he continues by me and heads for the door that's adjacent to the receptionist's desk. With the rapid movements of someone who has performed the same motions countless times before, Jonathan briskly types in a code on a numeric keypad. Once the door clicks to indicate it's unlocked, Jonathan pulls it open.

"After you." Jonathan gestures to the doorway.

Under Jonathan's charismatic smile, my stomach flips again, and my eyes flick to his left hand before I've even realized it. He doesn't have on a wedding ring.

Interesting.

As soon as I realize what I'm thinking, I snap my eyes back to Jonathan's face. I draw in a silent, sharp breath as the awful realization hits me: I think I might be a little bit *attracted* to this man.

I cough and stand up straighter. No. No way. Nope. Absolutely not. This is my EMS rotation, and I must remain focused on the work. Besides, even the most innocent I-just-met-you-and-yes-you're-obviously-hot type of attraction is dangerous. I vowed to swear off romance completely, and I intend to stick with that vow.

I give Jonathan a polite nod and walk through the doorway to enter a long corridor beyond. Jonathan secures the door behind us, and then he comes to my side. As we walk together, the only sound is that of our footsteps echoing on the concrete floor. I flick my eyes around the space. Daylight is pouring in through windows that are so high up they're almost at the ceiling. The corridor's walls, which are painted a shade of rusty red, are decorated with award certificates, plaques, and photos of EMS crews in action. I keep myself silently occupied with viewing the pictures as Jonathan and I venture farther down the hall.

Jonathan leads the way around a corner. The corridor opens up to a spacious, modern, restaurant-worthy kitchen. My attention sweeps the space and lands on the large island in the middle . . . more specifically, my attention lands on a man who's seated on one of the island's industrial-style stools. The man is dressed in a paramedic uniform that's identical to Jonathan's. He appears to be in his mid-to-upper forties. He has sandy blond hair and a trim goatee. Currently, he's munching on what appears to be a freshly made breakfast burrito. When he sees me, the man puts down his food and gets to his feet while wiping off his hands with a napkin.

"Good morning." The man smiles warmly. "Are you Doctor Vincent?"

"I am." I return his smile, instantly at ease in his presence. "Please call me Elly."

"Will do. It's great to meet you, Elly. We're looking forward to working with you this month." The man gives me a friendly, almost fatherly type of nod. "I'm Paramedic Steve Falco." He motions to Jonathan, and something humorous flashes in his gray eyes. "I have the misfortune of working with Paramedic Blackrock."

Jonathan laughs. "Right back at you, man." He looks my way, still chuckling. "Falco and I have been working together for about two years, ever since I graduated from paramedic training. He's an awesome mentor, even though his goatee is a disgrace."

Steve snorts and takes his dishes over to the sink. "At least I can grow a goatee, Blackrock."

Jonathan's grin widens as he watches his partner. "At least I don't have to hide my ugliness with a goatee, Falco. I actually look good when I'm clean-shaven."

"Only your mother thinks so," Steve replies without missing a beat.

Jonathan leans casually against the wall and crosses his arms over his chest. "And your wife and kids are the only ones who think your goatee looks good."

Steve shrugs. "Well, last I heard, you didn't actually get honorably discharged from the Army when your service concluded all those years ago." He loads his dishes into the dishwasher and turns to Jonathan once more. "I heard they thought your face was so embarrassing that they kicked you out of the armed forces altogether."

Jonathan tips back his head and laughs again. "How did you find out?"

"Your most recent parole officer mentioned it when he stopped by to make sure you were wearing your ankle locator." Steve now cracks a grin.

My eyebrows are steadily rising while the rapid-fire banter between Jonathan and Steve plays out before me. I make my first mental note about the EMS world: apparently, the more you like and respect your partner, the more you insult them.

Jonathan shifts my way. "Okay, now that you've had the bad luck of meeting Falco, how about I take you on a tour of the station so—"

A deafeningly loud alarm starts blaring out from overhead speakers, as does the equally loud sound of an automated, monotone female voice making an announcement. Jonathan and Steve's pagers start going off. Lights in the room begin flashing. The monstrous television in the adjacent lounge area powers down.

Before I've even finished processing what's happening, Jonathan is already in motion. He puts one hand on the point of my elbow and starts leading me at a jogging pace down another corridor. Steve follows right behind us, checking his pager.

"BLS is requesting backup for a sixty-nine-year-old female with palpitations," Steve calls above the ruckus, his affect all-business now.

"Copy." Jonathan shoots me a side-glance. "Ready for your first call, Doctor Vincent?"

I nod. Adrenaline is pumping through my body. "You bet."

Jonathan pushes open the heavy door at the end of the corridor. Without breaking stride, the three of us rush into the station's gargantuan garage. I have only a blur of a second to take in the sight. Bright lights are shining high overhead. The air is colder in here than it was in the station, and the alarm is echoing even more loudly. Tools, supplies, and equipment fill the shelves that line the walls. A gigantic, shiny, bright red ladder truck is parked at the far end of the garage with its front end facing the huge garage door. The ladder truck's doors are open, and firefighters' bunker gear is laid out on the ground next to the truck. I realize that's done intentionally to allow crew members to get ready as quickly as possible if they're called to fight a blaze.

The garage's middle three parking stalls are empty; I'm guessing one of stalls belongs to the rig being driven by the BLS crew that's already out on the call we're being asked to assist with. Meanwhile, closest to the doorway that Jonathan, Steve, and I just ran through, there's an ambulance that's painted red with a thick white stripe running down the middle. *Lakewood Fire & Rescue Paramedics* is written on the ambulance's side in bold white writing. The driver- and passenger-side doors of the rig are open, as if the vehicle is just waiting for launch.

Steve jumps into the driver's seat, puts on a headset, closes his door, and turns over the ignition, causing the ambulance's engine to roar to life. Jonathan jogs around the passenger side, but instead of getting in the front cab with his partner, he shuts the door and continues around to the back of the ambulance.

"I'll ride in the back with you," Jonathan yells so I can hear him over the commotion.

Jonathan tugs open one of the ambulance's back doors, and then he turns my way and holds out a hand. Taking that as my cue, I dash to Jonathan's side and place my hand in his, allowing him to help me up into the back of the rig.

An empty stretcher runs lengthwise down the middle of the space, braced securely to the floor. There's a bench built into each side wall, giving crew members a place to sit while they're tending to a patient. Supply carts are hooked to the walls, and several pieces of equipment are mounted on shelves higher up. At the front of the space, there's a big window that provides a view of the driver's cab and out the windshield. Through the window, I can see Steve pulling up a map on the rig's state-of-the-art GPS unit while he speaks to someone through his headset.

I breathlessly plunk myself down on the bench to my left. Jonathan hops into the ambulance with me, shuts the doors with a resounding slam, and takes a seat on the bench opposite me. The garage door rises. Steve navigates the ambulance out of the garage as its siren begins to wail. There's another roar from the ambulance's engine as Steve merges out onto the road and starts navigating around the morning's rush-hour traffic.

I glance out the back windows, getting a last glimpse of the fire station. My best guess it that from the moment the alert first sounded to now, no more than ninety seconds have passed.

And now we're en route to my first-ever EMS call as a resident physician.

I look over at Jonathan. He's swaying slightly with the movement of the ambulance as he holds his phone to his ear. His brow is furrowed with a look of concentration while he listens to whatever the person on the other end of the call is saying. Jonathan says something in reply before ending the call. He returns his phone to one of his cargo pockets and picks up the headset that was on the bench beside him; the headset is connected by a long cable to a power source in the ceiling. After Jonathan adjusts the headset's microphone so it's near his lips, his eyes meet mine. He grins and gestures to the left side of my bench. I look down and discover there's a headset beside me, too. I quickly don the bulky piece of equipment and get it situated around my ears. Now the noises of the engine and siren are muffled, and I can hear the faint sound of static through the headset.

"Do you copy, Doc?"

I hear Jonathan's voice in my ears, loud and clear, and I return my eyes to his. I give him a thumbs-up.

"I copy, Paramedic Blackrock."

"Great." Jonathan smiles before he glances between Steve and me while saying, "I just got off the phone with the BLS crew. Cell phone coverage is terrible where they are, but as best as I could hear, they were initially dispatched for a woman who was reporting generalized fatigue. While the crew was doing their initial assessment, the patient developed a sensation of palpitations as well as chest pain. The patient's vitals are currently stable."

"Copy," Steve replies, his voice coming through on my headset.

I lean forward on my bench to see into the driver's compartment and watch out the windshield. Steve continues skillfully guiding the ambulance through the streets, and he slows while giving an extra blast of the siren each time we're about to proceed through an intersection. Within another minute or two, we're pulling into a residential neighborhood, and I spot a two-story house up ahead that has an ambulance parked in front of it. The ambulance is painted all red, and it says *Lakewood Fire & Rescue* on its side.

Steve brings our rig to a stop behind the other ambulance, shoves open his door, and hops out. As Steve jogs toward the back of our rig, Jonathan yanks off his headset and gets to his feet. Steve opens the back doors for us, causing a rush of fresh, brisk autumn air to fill the back of the ambulance. Squinting in the sunlight, I hurriedly pull off my headset and climb out, moving aside while Jonathan and Steve grab the equipment they need. The next thing I know, the three of us are charging up the leaf-covered driveway that leads to the home's front door.

The door is slightly ajar. Steve uses his foot to push it open all the way, and then he heads inside at a fast walk, carrying a bright orange bag that contains the crew's supplies. Jonathan follows behind Steve, bringing the cardiac monitor. I scamper through the doorway after them.

The foyer is clean and tidy, and I can smell a faint hint of cinnamon in the home. No one is in sight, but there's an abrasive sound of non-stop radio chatter filling the air, undoubtedly coming from the BLS crew members' radios. Following the radio chatter, Steve, Jonathan, and I quickly cross the entryway and barge into the living room.

By the light that's streaming in through the large, curtain-framed front window, I see a woman seated on the carpeted floor. The three members of the BLS crew are down on their knees around her. The BLS crew members' shirts are dark blue, not white, but otherwise their uniforms match what Steve and Jonathan are wearing.

Immediately, my brain flips into analytical-physician mode. The woman—the patient—appears her reported age. She's dressed in a sweatshirt and jeans. Her gray hair is trimmed short. She's mildly overweight but otherwise looks like someone who is generally healthy. Right now, though, her eyes are wide, her respirations are fast, and she's unnaturally pale. My pulse ticks up with apprehension.

"What do we have?" Steve asks the BLS crew.

One of the firefighters gets to her feet and backs up, making room for Jonathan and Steve to move around a recliner chair to get closer to the patient, while she begins giving report:

"Mrs. Kader is sixty-nine. History of hypertension controlled with medication. No allergies. Over the course of the day, she has been feeling increasingly weak. She eventually felt so poorly that she called nine-one-one. Upon our arrival, her vitals were stable and non-orthostatic. As we continued our assessment, Mrs. Kader reported the sudden onset of palpitations and a squeezing discomfort in her chest. At that time, we radioed dispatch to get you guys here."

Steve drops down on one knee and unzips the orange supply bag. Jonathan assists the patient with lying flat on her back, and then he begins putting stickers on her chest so he can obtain an ECG. One of the other firefighters starts to get a new set of vitals on the patient.

I take a step closer to the action, but then I catch myself and stop in my tracks. I have to remember that I'm not a treating physician today; I'm here only to observe. Though it goes against all my natural instincts, I retreat from the patient and stand by the coffee table.

It only takes a couple of seconds for me to realize that while you can take the girl out of the emergency department, you can't take the emergency department out of the girl. I'm watching as intently as if I were caring for the patient myself. My eyes are hopping between the patient, the ECG machine, and the monitor that displays patient's vital signs. I note the patient's pallor is getting worse, as is her ominous, wide-eyed stare of silent panic. Everything inside me is yelling that this patient is on the verge of decompensating. I restlessly shift my stance as I watch the crews continue to work. In all the time I spent thinking about what this rotation would be like, I never once considered how hard it would be to observe without helping. It's completely unsettling.

"Sinus rhythm with PVCs," Jonathan announces as he reviews the patient's ECG.

"Blood pressure ninety-eight over palp," reports the firefighter who's checking vital signs. "Pulse one-eleven. Sat ninety-two."

My apprehension rises another notch. This woman's heart is flicking extra beats. Her blood pressure is drifting down, and her heart rate is creeping up. Everything indicates badness is brewing. I glance at Steve to confirm he's putting an IV into the patient's arm; IV access will be crucial if the patient's blood pressure continues to drop and fluid or medications become necessary. My attention next shifts to the BLS crew, and I confirm they're addressing the patient's hypoxia by providing her supplemental oxygen via a nasal cannula. Lastly, I look at Jonathan. He's speaking to the patient, explaining that she needs to be transported for further evaluation. The patient agrees, speaking in a voice that's hoarse and distant.

Suddenly, almost subconsciously, I notice out of the corner of my eye that there has been a change in the waveform that's tracing across the ECG machine, which is still tracking the patient's cardiac activity. I snap my head toward the machine to view it directly.

Mrs. Kader has just gone into the dangerous, unstable, potentially lethal heart rhythm of ventricular tachycardia, otherwise known as "v-tach."

My chest constricts. I immediately look back at the patient. To my relief, she remains conscious, but she's peering up at the ceiling with a glazed-over stare. I clench my hands at my sides as I wait for one of the crew members to notice what's happening. I see Jonathan glance down at the ECG machine. He does a double take, and then his brows snap together.

"We've got v-tach," Jonathan announces.

The intensity in the room ratchets up. Steve gets a bag of fluid infusing through the patient's IV, and then he begins checking the airway equipment in case it becomes necessary to intubate Mrs. Kader. The lead BLS crew member announces that she and one of her partners will go retrieve the stretcher from the back of the ALS rig. As the two firefighters hurry out of the room, the remaining BLS crew member checks the patient's vitals again.

"Blood pressure eighty over palp," the firefighter says with an edge to his words. "Pulse one-sixty."

My own heart rate is probably going even faster than the patient's. Mrs. Kader is now officially hemodynamically unstable, and she's still in v-tach. She needs to be cardioverted. The crew needs to apply a shock to her heart to get the heart back into a normal perfusing rhythm. Otherwise, the patient's blood pressure will likely continue to drop, and she'll go into full-blown cardiac arrest.

Jonathan gets to his feet and snatches his phone from his pocket. "I'm calling the doc at University Hospital to get authorization to proceed from here," he tells Steve.

"Copy," Steve replies briskly.

I literally bite the insides of my cheeks to stay quiet while I watch the events playing out in front of me. The crews are doing everything they should, and they're doing it well, yet it's torturous to just be standing here and staring at them.

Jonathan presses a button on his phone and then puts it to his ear. Steve slides closer to Mrs. Kader and explains to her what's going on, but I can't gauge how much the patient comprehends anymore; Mrs. Kader's gaze is becoming increasingly empty while the haunting evidence of ventricular tachycardia keeps tracing across the ECG machine.

"Hello?" Jonathan suddenly says loudly into his phone. His jaw clenches, and he uses his free hand to cover his other ear, like he's trying to block out all the other noise in the room. "Hello, Doc? Doc, do you copy?"

"Cell service has been bad for us here, too," the lead firefighter explains as she and her partner return with the stretcher.

I put my attention back on the patient and the monitor. The patient's skin is gray. Her blood pressure has dropped even more. She's about to go into cardiac arrest. She needs to be cardioverted. Now. Right now.

"Doc?" Jonathan barks into the phone. "Doc, we're . . . Doc? Hello? Do you copy?"

"Use the radio," Steve tells Jonathan above the din, speaking fast.

"Blood pressure seventy-two over palp," the firefighter announces.

Another bolus of adrenaline hits me, and my mind comes into total focus. I can't just observe any longer. I have to try to help.

Stepping into the middle of the room, I call out over the commotion, "Everyone, listen up. I'm Doctor Elly Vincent, emergency medicine resident physician at Lakewood Medical Center, and I'll be taking control of this scene."

There's a micro-second pause as Jonathan, Steve, and the three BLS crew members stop what they're doing to look over at me. I'm not rattled, though. This may be my first day of a new rotation, and we may be inside the patient's house instead of in an emergency department, but the medicine doesn't change. This is still what I do. This is what I've trained for.

I meet Jonathan's gaze. "Prepare the biphasic defibrillator to perform synchronized cardioversion at one-hundred-fifty joules."

Jonathan's eyebrows rise for a fleeting moment, and then he jams his phone into his pocket, drops back down on one knee, and starts readying the machine.

I look at Steve. "Draw up twenty-five micrograms of diluted fentanyl and one milligram of midazolam to administer through the patient's IV. Follow this with intubation, including protocol medication for paralysis and post-intubation sedation."

"You got it, Doc." Steve starts pulling what he needs from the bag of supplies.

Though it's only a matter of seconds, time seems to pass with excruciating slowness as Jonathan and Steve get prepared, their skill and competence evident as they work. The paramedics then look up at me. They're ready. It's time to do this.

"Administer the initial medications and perform synchronized cardioversion at one-hundred-fifty joules," I direct. "Then secure the patient's airway."

Steve administers the first two meds through the patient's IV. Jonathan promptly hits a button on the defibrillator that ensures the shock will be applied at a specific moment during the patient's cardiac cycle, and then he pushes another button to charge the device. The defibrillator emits its piercing, eerie sound, which rapidly rises in pitch, and then the sound changes to a two-toned alarm.

"Everyone clear," I order above the noise, scanning the group. I put my eyes back on

Jonathan. "Proceed with synchronized cardioversion."

"Everyone clear," Jonathan repeats, doing another check to make sure no one is in contact with Mrs. Kader.

Jonathan pushes the red button on the machine. The machine lets out a buzzing sound, and the patient's body arches as the blast of electricity hits her chest wall. There's a split-second pause. All of us have our eyes fixed on the monitor. The BLS crew members are waiting to pounce in and do chest compressions, if CPR is necessary. Steve has already positioned himself above the patient's head, and he has the intubation equipment in his hands.

An instant later, a new waveform begins traveling across the defibrillator's screen. I exhale with relief. It looks like a normal sinus rhythm.

"Do we have a pulse with that?" I ask.

Jonathan palpates the patient's wrist while one of the firefighters feels for the patient's femoral pulse.

"We have a pulse," Jonathan confirms, looking up at me.

I nod to Steve. "Secure the airway, Paramedic Falco."

Steve bends down close to Mrs. Kader's head, and within moments, he has the patient intubated. Steve then leans out of the way, and one of the firefighters attaches the bag-style oxygen delivery device to the end of the endotracheal tube that's sticking out of the patient's mouth. The firefighter starts squeezing the bag, causing the patient's chest to rise and fall in a slow, steady way as she's given the oxygen her body needs.

"Sat ninety-nine," the lead firefighter states. "Blood pressure one-ten over palp, pulse ninety-four."

"The patient is still in a normal sinus rhythm," Jonathan adds.

The tension in my muscles starts to dissipate. We prevented Mrs. Kader from going into cardiac arrest. She's back in a normal heart rhythm, and her vitals have stabilized. We have control of her airway, to get her adequate oxygen while she remains comfortably sedated.

"Nice work, everyone," I say. "Let's get this patient transported for further evaluation and care."

Everyone jumps into action, and now I do find myself a bit out of my element. Managing a patient in v-tach is in my wheelhouse. Overseeing the care of a v-tach patient who has just been cardioverted and intubated in her living room, however, is not part of my typical work day. It's also not my norm to be managing a patient who's being transferred onto a stretcher, pushed through her living room and out the front door, and wheeled down a driveway to the back of a waiting ambulance, all while being stared at by crowds of curious people who've come out of their homes to see what's going on. Thankfully, the crews are clearly comfortable with the process and the crowds, so I let them do their thing.

Once Mrs. Kader's stretcher is secured in the back of the ambulance, Steve hops into the driver's seat, dons the headset, and turns over the ignition. Jonathan stays in the back of the rig, and a BLS crew member joins him to help with caring for the patient while we're en route to the hospital. I climb into the back of the ambulance with the others, still officially in charge of overseeing care until we've handed off the patient to the ED team.

The lead firefighter, who's standing outside the back of our rig, states that she and her other crew member will follow behind us in their ambulance, in case further assistance is needed. I give her a nod while I don my headset. The firefighter shuts our ambulance doors.

"Doctor Vincent, do you copy?" I hear Steve ask from up front.

I look through the window that separates the back of the ambulance from the cab, and I meet Steve's eyes in the rearview mirror. "I copy. Patient remains hemodynamically stable. We're ready for transport."

"Copy that."

Steve hits the siren and drives away from Mrs. Kader's house, leaving the flocks of neighbors behind.

Using one hand to brace myself as the ambulance races down the road, I turn toward Jonathan. "I'll call the hospital to give report, if that would help."

Jonathan glances at me briefly and then starts adjusting the patient's IV fluid. "Sure."

The firefighter pulls a phone from his shirt pocket, pushes a couple buttons on it, and hands it over to me.

"Cell coverage is better now," the firefighter tells me. "The call should be connecting to the EMS backline at the University Hospital ED. The charge nurse will answer."

"Thanks." I slide my headset away from one ear and press the phone against it.

"Good morning, EMS. This is University Hospital's emergency department," a woman answers the call. "This is the charge nurse speaking. How can I help you?"

"Good morning. This is Doctor Elly Vincent, resident physician at Lakewood Medical Center's emergency department. I'm calling to provide report about an incoming patient."

Six

"After synchronized cardioversion at one-hundred-fifty joules, the patient converted back to a normal sinus rhythm. She has remained in normal sinus ever since. Vitals stable throughout transport."

I finish giving report while University Hospital's resuscitation bay is ablaze with people, noise, and motion. Jonathan, Steve, and the BLS crew members transfer Mrs. Kader over to the stretcher that's in the middle of the room, and the ED team jumps into action. Nurses get to work placing a second IV, drawing labs, and hanging more IV fluid. Techs are connecting the patient to the cardiac monitor and setting up to obtain a new ECG. The respiratory therapist is getting the patient hooked to the ventilator. Cassandra Barlow, one of the ED's great social workers, is on the phone with the patient's family members. The radiology tech is standing by with the portable x-ray machine, ready to shoot a single-view chest x-ray to confirm proper endotracheal tube placement. The charge nurse is paging the on-call cardiologist, in case the patient is deemed to need to go to the cath lab.

Dr. Lucy Arroyo, one of the emergency medicine attending physicians here at University Hospital, comes to my side. Dr. Arroyo is in her mid-thirties, so combining her relatively young age with her short stature and sweet facial features, I'm guessing a lot of patients are stunned when they discover Dr. Arroyo packs a hefty punch of authority. Her clinical care is efficient and spot-on, she never gets rattled, and she can lay down the law with unruly patients unlike anyone else I've ever seen.

"Nice job out there, Elly." Dr. Arroyo gives me a fast nod and resumes watching the team work on Mrs. Kader. "Sorry about the bad cell coverage you had on scene. Really glad you happened to be with the crew so you could direct care." She pulls her stethoscope from the pocket of her long white coat and puts it in her ears. She takes a step toward the stretcher but pauses to add with a hint of a smile, "And I can't wait for word of this to get out. There's going to be a lot of talk once people learn you took command of an EMS call."

Before I can reply, Dr. Arroyo disappears into the crowd that's surrounding Mrs. Kader's stretcher. I'm not sure whether to laugh or cringe. Dr. Arroyo is right: there's definitely going to be fallout from this. Hearing a resident physician took command of a scene, especially on her first day of her EMS rotation, isn't exactly what Dr. Priest or the leadership at Lakewood Fire & Rescue were probably expecting to hear.

Actually, I take that back. Dr. Priest definitely knows about my ED black cloud, so maybe he won't be surprised to hear about this. However, Lakewood Fire and Rescue had no idea about me. I suppose Dr. Priest should have warned the agency that I do tend to be a magnet for high-acuity chaos.

I blow a strand of loose hair from my eyes and survey the room. The cardiologist has joined the care team. The patient's vitals remain stable, and she's still in a normal sinus rhythm. Though she'll undoubtedly be admitted to the ICU for further workup, I'm optimistic Mrs. Kader will make a good recovery and eventually get to go back home.

I see that Jonathan has migrated over to a desk in the corner. He's using the ALS crew's laptop to finish the documentation about the call. Meanwhile, Steve and the BLS crew members are gathering up their equipment and supplies so they can take everything back out to the ambulance bay for cleaning, inventory, and restocking.

"Steve, can I be of help?" I ask, walking toward him.

Steve smiles at me. "Thanks for asking, Doc, but we've got it. You've definitely pulled your weight with this call already; we can take care of the grunt work."

Steve gives me another smile before he exits the room with equipment in-hand. The firefighters follow, hauling the backboard and the rest of the EMS supplies out of the resuscitation bay. As I watch them go, I observe one of the firefighters pause beside the ED's clean-linens cart. The firefighter glances over his shoulder, snatches a clean pillow off the cart, and hurriedly continues out the door.

I can't help chuckling at the firefighter's instinct to escape before someone on the ED staff notices that he has taken a pillow. It's all part of the ongoing pillow war between EMS and the ED, which has been raging since long before I got to Lakewood.

One would reasonably assume that when an EMS crew restocks their ambulance after a call, doing so should include taking a new pillow to replace the pillow they left behind in the ED with their last patient. However, things are not this simple. This is because there's a mysterious pillow vortex in the Universe that leaves emergency departments perpetually low on their pillow supplies. Obviously, when one pillow enters the ED because an EMS crew brings in a patient, and then that same EMS crew subsequently takes one clean pillow from the linens cart as a replacement, it should mean there is an equal and unchanging number of pillows in the Universe. However, this is not the case. EDs never have enough pillows. No matter what. The phenomenon defies all mathematical calculations and philosophical understanding. The ED staff blames EMS crews for taking more pillows than they need; the EMS crews insist they only take a replacement for the one they leave behind. And so the pillow war continues, and disappearing pillows remain one of the greatest mysteries in emergency medicine.

Still chuckling, I exit the resuscitation bay and sit down at an unoccupied workstation that gives me a view of the EMS entrance, so I can watch for when my crew is ready to depart. I then lean back in my chair and look around the department. This place seems as busy as would be expected for late morning on a Friday. Emergency departments typically ramp up with patients over the course of any given Friday, especially as it grows late in the afternoon, when outpatient clinics get close to shutting down for the weekend and they send more of their patients to the ED for the workup they need. Predictably, EDs remain extremely busy on Saturday, experience a temporary lull in the early hours of Sunday, explode with patients over the course of Sunday afternoon and evening, reach peak numbers on Monday, and then taper back down to the mid-week levels of insanity on Tuesday, Wednesday, and Thursday. Then Friday rolls around again, and the cycle starts over.

"Hey, Elly!"

I check behind me to see who called my name. To my delight, Savannah Drake, another of the awesome first-year residents in Lakewood's emergency medicine residency program, is weaving through the throng to reach me. Savannah is dressed in hospital-issue scrubs. Her light-brown hair is pulled up into a high ponytail, and as always, her blue eyes are shining with a friendly and slightly humorous gleam. She takes a seat at the desk next to mine.

"I have a couple minutes before my shift starts so I wanted to say *hi*." Savannah smiles in her warm, disarming way. "What are you doing here this morning?"

I tip my head toward the EMS entrance. "First day of my EMS rotation."

"Oh, that's right!" Savannah's eyes get big. "Priest put both you and Grant on the EMS rotation this month, didn't he?"

"Yep." I make sure my smile doesn't falter. "Apparently, they're adjusting most of the residents' and med students' off-service rotations to accommodate the orientation schedules of the new ED attendings."

"That's what I heard." Savannah is nodding. "That's also why I'm doing a shift here instead of at Lakewood today. About half my shifts this month have been moved to University Hospital." She shrugs. "I don't mind too much. I learn a lot working in this department." She pauses, shows a more sheepish grin, and lowers her voice. "Admittedly, though, I like working at Lakewood better."

"Me, too." I also keep my voice down in a conspiratorial way. "So your secret is safe with me."

"Good." Savannah laughs. "Anyway, other than doing your EMS rotation earlier than you were expecting, how are you doing?"

I cinch my ponytail, giving myself a microsecond to decide how to reply. "Pretty well, all things considered. How about you?"

Savannah sighs happily. "I definitely can't complain, since I just enjoyed two weeks of vacation."

That's when I register the fact that Savannah is sporting an out-of-season tan. In a blink, the realization smacks me.

"Oh my gosh, you were out of town for Danielle Gillespie's wedding, weren't you?" My inner romantic begins bubbling over with excitement. "How was it? Amazing? Incredible?"

Savannah's eyes are dancing merrily. "It was wonderful. The event was exactly the type of beautiful, destination beach wedding Danielle had always dreamed of." She sighs again, this time reminiscently. "Of course, I'm a little biased because she's my best friend, but I think Danielle was the most gorgeous bride I've ever seen, and Joel was just *so completely in love* with her, you know what I mean?"

I work down a swallow. "I . . . know exactly what you mean."

Savannah readopts a playful grin. "And I'm proud and a little relieved to say that I performed my maid-of-honor duties without any catastrophes. We did have a couple close calls with snags in nylons, but we managed to pull through."

"I'm glad to hear it," I laugh. I glance around us and then lower my voice once more. "Okay, I know you keep things very discreet in the workplace, but since you're not officially on-duty yet, you can tell me: did you happen to have a certain extremely attractive date accompanying you at this particular destination wedding?"

Savannah blushes, and her eyes shine even more brightly. "Yes, Wes was my date."

I squeal softly and give her a playful nudge. "And did being in the midst of all the marriage bliss trigger any wedding talk between you and Doctor Kent?"

Savannah's cheeks go a darker shade of red, and she again breaks into laughter. "No comment."

"Fair enough . . . I can't wait to hear all about it, though." I wink. "In the meantime, I'll keep myself content with learning the details about Rachel and Austin's upcoming nuptials."

"Oh, I know! I'm thrilled for them!" Savannah is beaming. "Admittedly, though, I have no idea how the two of them will agree on anything wedding-related. Rachel's ideas will undoubtedly be the polar opposite of Austin's."

"I wouldn't expect anything less from them," I laugh. "Somehow, though, I have a feeling . . ."

I trail off as I look toward the EMS entrance again. The BLS crew members are nearly finished packing up their rig. Steve also looks like he's done restocking the paramedics' ambulance.

"Hmm. If I'm not mistaken, my chariot is about to depart, which means I need to go." I sigh as I get to my feet. "It was really great seeing you, Sav, and I hope our paths will cross again soon."

"Likewise." Savannah stands up and checks the clock. Her jaw drops. "Whoops, it looks like I also should get moving so I'm ready for signout." She gives me a playful salute. "Good luck with your rotation."

I salute back. "Good luck with your shift."

Savannah waves and dashes away. I whip around to rush for the ambulance bay, but I wind up crashing into Jonathan, who was approaching me from behind. I stumble from the impact, the collision practically knocking me off my feet. For goodness' sake, crashing into Jonathan is like hitting the Great Wall of Muscle.

"Whoa, sorry about that, Doc." Jonathan grabs my upper arm with his free hand while keeping his laptop secure in the other. "I was just coming to tell you that we're ready to head out."

"No worries." I gather my footing, acutely aware of the feeling of Jonathan's strong hand around my arm. "Thankfully, I'm still in one piece."

Jonathan laughs as he lets go of me. "Glad to hear it."

A pause follows while Jonathan and I look each other in the eyes. A sense of piqued curiosity seems to hover in the air. As quickly as it came on, however, the moment passes. We break eye contact. I clear my throat, and he backs up a little. Without another word, we turn and start walking together toward the ambulance bay. When we step outside, I squint in the autumn sunlight, and my nostrils get filled with the potent odor of diesel fumes. The BLS crew is already driving away, the engine of their rig letting out an emphatic roar as it disappears down the road. Steve is standing by our ambulance, checking his phone. He looks up at Jonathan and me.

"The BLS crew is headed to the grocery store to buy food for dinner," Steve tells us. He looks at me and explains, "We try to eat dinner together, and we rotate who makes the meal for the group." He puts away his phone. "Thanks to the fact that firefighters and paramedics are extremely competitive about almost anything, there's an ongoing battle for who's the best chef in the station, which means we always end up eating pretty darn well." He gestures in the direction the BLS crew departed. "Someone is whipping up pork chops tonight, so I hope you brought your appetite."

"That sounds delicious," I tell him. "I'm happy to pitch in for the food. Who do I pay?"

"Don't worry about paying." Jonathan leans into the front of the ambulance to secure the laptop in its bracket. "I've got you covered."

Steve snorts a laugh and shoots me an amused look. "I never would have guessed it possible, but it's good to know my moron of a partner is occasionally able to act like a gentleman."

"Well, I definitely didn't learn how to be a gentleman from you." Jonathan turns around, gives Steve a roll of his eyes, and then concentrates on me. "Please go ahead and ride in the front with this idiot during the ride back to the station. I'll take the back."

"Yeah, get in the back where you belong," Steve quips as he hops into the driver's seat and shuts his door.

Jonathan laughs, shakes his head, and puts his gaze back on mine. We both break into smiles. My stomach flutters a little, which triggers the alarm bells to go off in my head once more. I cannot get charmed by the hulky, hot paramedic guy. No way. Absolutely not.

"Thanks for covering dinner," I tell Jonathan in a friendly-but-not-too-friendly way before I scurry around to the passenger side of the rig and pull myself up into the cab.

I put on my headset, and Steve starts the engine. I hear Jonathan get into the back of the ambulance and shut the doors. As we pull away from the hospital, I'm grateful Jonathan and Steve resume their ruthlessly hilarious banter, since it gives me a chance to gather my thoughts. The conversation then switches gears, and the paramedics ask me some medical-related questions about the call we just completed. Like always, as I answer their questions, I enjoy the opportunity to do some teaching.

We soon pull up to the fire station, and once the mammoth garage door rolls up, Steve skillfully backs the rig into its parking stall. I hear Jonathan hop out of the back. I open my door and jump down from the cab, watching with curiosity as Jonathan grabs a super-long, gigantic yellow cable that's hanging down from the ceiling. Jonathan plugs the cable into what basically looks like an oversized outlet on the side of the ambulance. I deduce that's how they must charge the vehicle's gadgets and gizmos between calls.

"While you give the doc a tour of the station, I'll go update the battalion chief," Steve tells Jonathan as he gets out of the driver's seat.

Jonathan's eyes dart to me, and then he gives his partner a nod. "Sounds good."

Steve heads inside. As the door shuts behind him, the garage gets quiet. Jonathan and I share another look before he continues prepping the ambulance for the next call. I'm not sure what to do, so I make myself busy analyzing the various types of equipment that fill the shelves lining the walls, trying not to pay too much attention to the hot paramedic while he works. Eventually, the awkward silence is broken when Jonathan comes to my side, peers right into my eyes while showing me another smooth smile, and says:

"How about I take you on that promised tour of the station now?"

Stay focused, Elly, the voice in my head reminds me. *Do not get distracted by the hot paramedic guy.*

I adjust my cross-body bag on my hip. "Sounds good. Thank you."

Jonathan steps past me, pulls open the door that leads into the station, and goes inside. I follow, and Jonathan and I begin making our way down the long corridor toward the kitchen.

"So you're kicking off this rotation with quite a bang," Jonathan remarks, turning his head and giving me a probing look. "You're on your first call, and you're already taking control of a scene?"

I decide to infuse some lightheartedness into the conversation. "Before my rotation started, I guess I should have warned everyone about my black cloud."

"Your what?" Jonathan blinks a few times, and then he breaks into a half-smile. "Are you telling me that you're bad luck or something?"

I laugh. "Not exactly bad luck, but I . . . "

I trail off as we enter the kitchen and I notice there's someone on the other side of the room. I glance over at the person and do a double take, and my heart skids to a stop.

It's Grant.

Instantly, a very familiar, exhilarating sensation erupts within my chest, and I'm momentarily rendered breathless by Grant's unexpected appearance. Grant is dressed in a green fleece pullover and dark jeans. He has his car keys in one hand and some papers in the other. His hair is combed. He's cleanly shaven. And his spell-binding gaze is alert and deliberate as his eyes shift between Jonathan and me.

"Grant," I recover from my daze enough to find my voice. "Why . . . I mean, how come you're . . . I mean, what are you doing here?"

Grant glances Jonathan's way once more, and then he settles his attention fully on me. "Paramedic Falco let me in. I stopped by to drop off the forms we needed to fill out before our first ride-along." His serious expression fades, and the corners of his lips twitch upward. "I know this will shock you, El, but when I tried to email the forms to the battalion chief from my apartment, the email never got through."

I laugh. "Ah. Let me guess: the infamously bad Internet service at your apartment complex struck again?"

"Apparently so." Grant chuckles along with me. "Would you expect anything less?"

"Nope." I shake my head. "To be honest, I'm surprised you tried emailing anything from your apartment at all. I . . ."

I break off when I remember that Jonathan is also in the room. Shifting Jonathan's way once more, I discover that his brows are pulled low, and now his gaze is sliding from Grant to me and back to Grant again.

I sense the beginnings of a strange tension filling the room.

"Jonathan," I quickly say while attempting another smile, "this is Grant Reed. Grant and a few of the other residents at Lakewood happen to live in an apartment complex that has notoriously bad Internet service. It has become something of a legend among the hospital's residents."

Jonathan peers at me and nods once. "I see."

Grant's expression is all-business as he rolls back his shoulders, takes a step forward, and addresses Jonathan directly. "Please allow me to further introduce myself. I'm Doctor Grant Reed. I'm an emergency medicine resident physician, and I work with Doctor Vincent in Lakewood Medical Center's emergency department." He extends his hand. "I'm also doing my EMS rotation here this month."

I gulp. Grant was also assigned to work with a crew that's based here at Station Fourteen? This means Grant and I will cross paths even more frequently than I anticipated. I'm not sure whether to be thrilled or dismayed by the news.

Jonathan's lips press into a straight line as he shakes Grant's offered hand. "I'm Paramedic Jonathan Blackrock."

Grant's expression doesn't change as he lowers his arm back to his side. "It's nice to meet you."

Jonathan's eyes are narrowing slightly. "It's nice to meet you, too."

There's another pause.

Grant's stare seems to stay on Jonathan for a protracted beat, and then he looks my way once more. His relaxed smile returns. "Hey, El, how about I text you later today so we can figure out when to meet to start working on our project?"

"Sounds good." I give Grant another smile.

Jonathan loudly coughs and faces me, too. "Well, what do you say, Elly? Should I take you on your official tour of the station now?" He flashes a confident grin. "A private tour courtesy of Yours Truly?"

I snicker and turn toward Jonathan. "That would be great."

Jonathan steps right next to me, and then he stops to look again at Grant. "Those papers of yours need to go to the battalion chief. Did

Paramedic Falco already tell you where the chief's office is located?"

Grant puts his eyes back on Jonathan. His face and tone reveal nothing. "He did, thanks. I'll drop off the forms and show myself out."

Jonathan nods once before he puts his eyes back on me. With another smile, Jonathan motions toward a door on the far side of the kitchen and says:

"Let's start our tour by heading that way. It's our radio room, and I'll show you how all the equipment works."

Jonathan crosses the room and pulls open the door. I follow after him. Before stepping through the doorway, I look over my shoulder to give Grant a final wave. But Grant is already gone.

Seven

I sense that distinctly autumnal feel to the air as I get out of my car and hold up a hand to shield my eyes from the morning sun, which is shining vibrantly in the blue sky above. Despite the sunlight, however, I can see my breath, and there's a hint of frost upon the grass and fallen leaves at my feet. Deciding both gloves and sunglasses are necessary for a day like this, I reach back into my car and gather up what I need. I slip on my sunglasses and mittens, button up my blue coat, tug my black beret a little lower on my head, and lock my car. Finally, I turn to look across the street. I draw in a breath.

Okay, I'm ready to go.

I think.

I'm meeting Grant for brunch this morning, and we arranged to eat at one of our favorite breakfast joints. The restaurant is smack in the middle of the many amazing eateries that fill both sides of the lamppost-lined street in this fun, hip part of town. Like all residents, med students, and attendings at Lakewood Medical Center and University Hospital, I know this area extremely well. A group of us will often go out to dinner around here after a long shift, or we'll come to enjoy a celebratory breakfast after a long run of overnight shifts is done. Needless to say, many hilariously good times, as well as a lot of much-needed emotional decompressing, have taken place in this neck of the woods. Without question, though, the most epic dining-out experience occurred a little over a year ago, at O'Flanagan's Irish pub not far down the street. While a group of us were having dinner there, Rachel Nelson inadvertently ingested a marijuana-laced cookie, and then, in her ensuing mental haze, she downed an alcoholic beverage by mistake. The poor gal got pretty delirious, and Austin Cahill literally had to scoop her up and carry her home.

That's the kind of stuff from which Lakewood emergency department legends are made.

Today, however, I don't think anything quite so noteworthy will happen. At least, I hope not. Grant and I are meeting to decide about our project for the rotation. Thankfully, since I've had plenty of experience working on scholastic-type projects with Grant in years past, and because we planned this meeting a couple days ago, which has given me time to prep to be in Grant's presence, I shouldn't get too flustered around him today . . . not like our last couple of encounters when I've unexpectedly run into him, at least. Today, I should be able to easily maintain my I-like-you-as-a-best-friend-and-nothing-more façade, especially since this isn't even close to the first time Grant and I have met up at a restaurant. We've probably gone out to eat together hundreds of times over the years, so I'm well-practiced at staying one step ahead of myself and keeping my truest feelings a secret.

As these thoughts pass through my head, I'm once again struck by the juxtaposition the situation presents: when Grant and I are together, I feel completely safe, relaxed, and able to be myself. I can tell him anything. We talk and laugh about everything. There's no one else with whom I would rather spend my time. He's my best friend. We understand each other perfectly, and Grant knows me better than anyone else does. However, one could also argue that Grant doesn't know me at all. And although I *could* tell him anything, I actually don't. I'm keeping my most powerful feelings hidden, and in so doing, I'm hiding who I really am. So I suppose it's not surprising that even as I stand here on the street curb, peering at the restaurant from the other side of the road, my heart and mind are already revving up for the next round of the never-ending battle between them.

I step off the curb and scurry across the road to reach the charming entryway of the restaurant, which has an adorable brick façade and huge front windows. Pushing open the door, I step into what should probably be called Queen Elizabeth Central. This restaurant is a vibrant celebration of all things Great Britain. The flags of England, Scotland, and Wales are waving proudly in the breeze outside the front windows. Inside, the walls of the restaurant are decorated with framed photos of some of Britain's most beautiful castles, lakes, and cottages. Other wall adornments include posters of members of the royal family that date back several decades, and other vintage memorabilia. There are lovely little teapots on the dining tables. British candies, pastries, and chocolates are in display cases near the door for patrons to purchase. As always, this place makes me feel as though I've transported to a delightfully charming Edinburgh-Cotswolds hybrid village.

With the aromas of freshly baked scones and hot tea filling my nose, I pull off my sunglasses, hat, and gloves, and I slip my things into my purse. As my eyes adjust to the indoor lighting, I smooth down my hair while scanning the dining tables. My heart does a wee jig inside my chest when I spot the *braw laddie* himself seated at our favorite table by the window. As we make eye contact, Grant smiles. I exhale softly, warmed from head-to-toe simply by the sight of him. I hastily force myself to get my emotions back under control, and then I head toward him.

"Good morning, Doctor Reed." I reach the table and begin unbuttoning my coat.

Grant stands up, comes around to my side of the table, and pulls back my chair. "Good morning, Doctor Vincent."

I hang my coat over the back of my chair and sit down. Grant helps push my chair closer to the table, and then he returns to his seat. As it always does, Grant's gentlemanly gesture brings me extremely close to blushing. I realize I need to divert our attentions to something else. STAT.

"How did your first EMS shift go yesterday?" I quickly ask.

Grant takes a drink from his water glass and puts it down. Unexpectedly, an amused smile takes over his face. "It was rather . . . *enlightening*."

My eyebrows rise. "Uh-oh. Do I even want to know what you mean by that?"

Still grinning, Grant leans back in his chair and crosses his muscular arms over his broad chest. "Let's just say that everyone in the station happened to be talking about how a certain Doctor Elly Vincent took command of a scene the day before. According to the chatter, this same Doctor Elly Vincent successfully directed a resuscitation in the field that included a synchronized cardioversion of a patient in unstable v-tach."

"Ah. That." I cringe and laugh at the same time. "Yes, I admit the gossip is true. I should probably warn everyone at the fire station that my black cloud has apparently followed me out of the ED and right into the back of the ambulance." I shake my head. "And *they* should have warned *us* about how fast gossip spreads in the EMS world."

Grant chuckles. "Agreed. Based on what I witnessed yesterday, at least, I think it's safe to say that scuttlebutt spreads almost as fast within a fire station as it does in an emergency department."

"Yikes. That's no easy accomplishment," I note while snickering. "I thought nothing came close to the speed with which hospital gossip generates and spreads."

Grant continues chuckling as he casually runs a hand through his thick hair. My brain gets foggy as I watch him, and my fingers tingle with the urge to ruffle Grant's hair, too. I promptly drop my hands to my sides and sit firmly upon my fingertips. There shall be no hair ruffling in the restaurant. Or anywhere. Absolutely not.

"Anyway, since I'm extremely familiar with your black cloud, as soon as I heard the story about the field resuscitation, I knew it had to be true." Grant leans in, and his expression gets serious. He lowers his voice. "Running a field resuscitation on your very first call of the rotation? That's incredible, El. And brave, frankly. I'm really proud of you, if you don't mind me saying so."

Now I know I'm blushing. "Of course I don't mind you saying so. Thank you."

Grant continues watching me closely, and I'm dangerously close to getting completely lost in his hypnotic gaze. So I make myself sit up taller, clasp my hands together on the tabletop in front of me, readopt a humorous tone, and add:

"Regardless, I think it's safe to say that between the two of us, I won the award for the wildest first day of our EMS rotation."

The corners of Grant's lips twitch upward once more. He sits back in his chair. The humorous gleam returns to his eyes, which are sparkling in the sunlight that's streaming in through the window.

"I won't argue with that, Doctor Vincent." Grant holds up his water glass. "Congratulations on winning the wildest-first-day-of-the-rotation award."

I laugh, lift my own water glass, and clink it against his. After taking a sip, I put my glass back on the table and jokingly go on:

"Too bad we don't still have that old fifty-cent piece we used to exchange years ago. If we did, I would insist on receiving it as the trophy for winning the first-day-of-the-rotation award."

Grant pauses only long enough that I notice. He then takes another long drink before setting his glass on the table. "You definitely earned it," he says, not grinning anymore.

Silence follows; it's an awkward silence. I groan inwardly, and if I could kick myself underneath the table, I would. It was a mistake for me to bring up our old tradition of exchanging the fifty-cent piece to the latest academic "victor." I have no idea what happened to that coin, but mentioning it after all these years makes it sound like . . . well, like I think about every moment Grant and I shared together. It makes me sound like I care too much. And Grant can't know how much I care.

Time for some damage control.

I pick up my menu and pretend to read it. "Have you given any thought to what our project for the rotation should be?"

"I have, yes," I hear Grant reply. "I suspect, though, that you've given the project even more thought than I have, so I wanted to let you have the floor first."

Before I can answer him, a waitress approaches and cheerily inquires if we've decided what we want to eat. Grant makes eye contact with me, and I answer his unspoken question with a nod. Understanding me perfectly, Grant looks back up at the waitress and gives her my order and then his own. Not surprisingly, we're both getting the same thing we always do when we have brunch here: a ham and cheese quiche, a side of fruit, and an orange spice herbal tea for me; a double order of the spinach, cheese, and bacon quiche for Grant. The waitress enters our orders on the electronic order-placing gizmo she has in her hand, and then she gathers up our menus and strolls away. No longer with a menu to hide behind, I meet Grant's gaze across the table.

"Yes, it's true," I tell him, resuming the conversation where we left off. "I've put a lot of thought into our project for this month . . . far more thought than is necessary."

"I figured as much." Grant nods. There's no judgment in his tone or features. "I know how important this rotation is to you, El, so I'm happy to defer to whatever you would like to do." He shows me a grin. "Of course, I realize that if we were still in high school, you would be accusing me of trying to make you do all the work on the group project. Rest assured, I intend to pull my weight. I just want to make sure we do what you feel will help you get the most out of the rotation, especially since you may apply for an EMS fellowship."

I laugh. "You're probably right about the group project in high school. I definitely would have teased you about being a slacker in that situation." I run my thumb along the condensation that has formed on my glass. "However, in this scenario, I really appreciate you letting me take the reins."

Grant nods again, appearing satisfied. "So tell me what you were thinking."

I tuck my hair behind my ears. "I haven't ironed out all the details yet, but I was essentially envisioning something like this: in the next few days, we'll do a retroactive review of all calls for patients with stroke-like symptoms that the ALS and BLS crews responded to over the past six months. As we review those calls, we'll collect baseline data on how often the crews met five important on-scene metrics for managing potential stroke patients: performing a FAST exam, getting a LAMS, finding out the patient's last known well time, checking the patient's glucose, and obtaining at least two sets of vitals."

Grant pushes up his sleeves and rests his forearms on the edge of the table. "Okay. I like where this is going."

I glance down at Grant's sculpted forearms, which are now in full view before me. For a second or two, I completely forget what I was saying. Blinking fast, I quickly put my eyes back on Grant's face. With a cough, I go on:

"We'll then put together and record a short video, in which we'll teach about those five on-scene metrics and why they're important for optimizing care of potential stroke patients. We'll upload the finished video to the Lakewood Fire and Rescue's online portal so all the crews can watch it."

Our conversation is interrupted when the waitress comes back to our table. She places a tray in front of me that has upon it a beautiful teapot with matching teacup and saucer. I give the waitress a smile before she departs, and then I pour myself a cup of the tea, letting the delicious aroma of orange spice fill my nose. After inhaling a few breaths, I go on with explaining to Grant my idea:

"For the rest of the month, you and I will review the charts of all calls for potential stroke patients that the crews respond to. We'll review each chart within a day or two of the call, and we'll provide the involved crew members with feedback and teaching as indicated. At the end of our rotation, we'll graph out the data from the prior six months of stroke calls and compare it to the data from the month we spent teaching the crews about on-scene stroke care. Hopefully, we'll show that the percentage of calls where the crews met all five metrics for on-scene stroke care improved as we provided teaching and feedback. We'll present this data to Doctor Priest and the fire department leadership for review."

Grant remains quiet, so I take my first sip of tea. At last, Grant sits up straight and replies:

"That's an awesome idea, El."

"Really?" I break into a smile and put down my teacup. "You mean that?"

Grant smiles in return. "Of course I mean it. I'm in. Let's do it."

Grant's smile is making my heart dance. I sigh to myself. Only Grant could manage to make me swoon while I'm talking about cerebrovascular accidents.

The waitress returns again and places our meals in front of us. Grant and I promptly dive into our food without another word. Thankfully, we've always shared the critically important belief that meals are best enjoyed while they're hot, so we never interrupt our first all-important bites of food with conversation.

After a while, I put down my fork and peek at Grant. He appears calm and content as he continues eating, which is precisely how I would expect him to appear under the circumstances. Meanwhile, as I'm loving my food and (secretly, literally) loving my company, I still haven't managed to completely settle into "friends-only" mode around Grant this morning. I'm not sure why. For whatever reason, my heart continues drumming a little too fast, and electrical-like sparks are intermittently shooting down my spine.

It's not fair to be in love with the one person you can't be in love with.

If I'm being honest, part of me wishes Grant would just fall head-over-heels for someone and get it over with. Grant has dated plenty over the years, and he has had serious girlfriends, but he obviously hasn't yet found "the one." Frankly, I kind of wish he would find her. If Grant fell madly in love with someone, he would devote all his time and attention to her. She would rightfully take my place as Grant's best friend. I would get pushed to the sidelines, and that would help me get the closure I need to move on and heal my heart. As it is right now, though, seeing Grant often, especially with both of us being single, is a painfully constant reminder of what theoretically could be, and yet what cannot and will not ever be in real life.

The more I ponder my theory as I sit across this little table from Grant, the more I know I'm right. Grant needs to fall in love. If he would stop focusing entirely on work and start noticing all the women who are constantly vying for his attention, surely there would be someone in the crowd who would win over his heart. There must be that gorgeous, kind, sweet, intelligent soulmate Grant has always seemed to be searching for. Indeed, Grant needs to fall in love. Grant would be happy, and I could move on.

Unfortunately, there's a catch: I can't force Grant to fall in love.

So maybe the next-best solution is for you to fall in love with someone else.

As soon as the thought flashes through my mind, I drop my fork with a gasp. The utensil hits my plate with a startling clatter. Grant whips up his head and looks at me. His brow furrows.

"El, are you all right?"

All I can do is stare back at Grant while my own earth-shattering thought replays in my head. What if I opened up my heart to someone else? What if I abandoned my fears about the vulnerability that comes with loving someone? What if risking my heart is actually the way to heal it?

My stomach begins churning. My neck flushes. My palms get sweaty.

Would taking the chance of falling in love with another man allow me to finally move on from Grant?

My mind is racing now. Is it possible that I've been going about this completely wrong all these years? After all, I am a hopeless romantic; that's never going to change. So in denying my inner romantic—by choosing to close off my heart entirely—have I inadvertently been making it impossible for me to move on from Grant? Has hiding away my heart been the reason my love for Grant has continued burning? When I vowed to give up on love all those years ago, did I unknowingly trap myself into a state of perpetually pining away for Grant?

If I freed myself to consider pursuing romance with another man, would I actually discover a chance for love with someone else in this world?

I inhale a shaky breath. My whole body is trembling.

Grant pushes back from the table and stands up. "El, you're pale, and your eyes are really dilated." He's speaking calmly, though there's an edge to his words. "How about we get you home, okay?"

Without waiting for my reply, Grant scans the restaurant, makes eye contact with our waitress, and politely signals for her to come over. Meanwhile, I'm still staring at nothing while I flounder to wrap my mind around the shocking ideas that are going through my head. I'm vaguely aware of Grant speaking to the waitress and giving her his credit card, which she runs through the little electronic gadget she's holding. The next thing I know, Grant has a hand firmly around my upper arm, and he's helping me to my feet.

Grant puts his free hand on my other arm. "Elly, talk to me. What's going on?"

I can't tell Grant what's going on, of course. Besides, the truth is that I barely know what's going on myself. So all I can do is clear my throat and weakly reply to him with:

"Nothing serious. I'm just tired. I've . . . had a lot on my mind, and I haven't been sleeping well. Like you said, it would probably be best if I went home."

Moving fast, Grant retrieves my coat from the back of my chair and my purse from the floor. Putting a stabilizing hand back on my arm, Grant guides me to the exit. As we emerge from the restaurant, I draw in breaths of the cool, fresh air, which helps clear my head and bring me back to awareness. Grant guides me across the road, and when we get to my car, he puts himself in front of the driver's door and faces me.

"I think I should drive you home," he says.

"Thanks for offering, but I swear I'm okay." I manage a reassuring smile. "What happened in there was a combo of sleep deprivation, sunshine coming in through the window, and a cheesy quiche filling my stomach. I promise I feel better now, though. Honestly, I'm lucid." I laugh a little. "Trust me, I wouldn't drive if I didn't feel safe doing so. The last thing I want is to end up as a trauma patient in our own emergency department, especially if there's a chance I would get transported there by the EMS crew I'm working with this month."

"Fair enough." Grant's expression remains etched with concern as he hands me my purse and coat. "If it's okay with you, though, I'll follow you home to make sure you get there all right." He finally puts on something like a smile. "Besides, this way, if you do wind up needing ambulance transport, I'll be there to help you fend off your EMS fan club. After all, you're pretty much a legend at Station Fourteen now."

I groan as I pull my keys from my purse. "Gee, thanks."

Grant seems to wait a moment before stepping back from me. He readopts his serious expression. "I'm parked one block over. I'll drive here to meet you."

"Sounds good." I pull open my car door. "Thanks again."

Grant strides away at a fast walk. I get into my car, and as soon as I shut the door and find myself alone, I'm crushed by another tidal wave of emotion.

It is possible that this is the answer? Should I really take a chance on love? After all these years—after all I've been through—do I really want to open up my heart to the idea of romance with someone else? If I allow myself to become vulnerable, will doing so be worth the risk? Will it let me heal my heart and move on?

I catch a glimpse of Grant's vehicle coming down the road. Putting on a smile, I give him a wave, drive out of the parking lot, and begin navigating down the street. The trip passes in a haze, and the next thing I know, I'm pulling into my driveway. With quivering hands, I tug the keys from the ignition and get out of my car. I turn to give Grant another wave while mouthing, *Thanks.*

Grant gives me a nod, and then he drives away.

Eight

I tuck in a few wispy hairs that got loose from the base of my bun, make sure the hem of my red shirt is straight, and start walking toward the entrance of Station Fourteen. I'm about halfway across the parking lot when an eardrum-rattling alarm fills the air, causing me to spin in the direction of the station's garage. The huge light near the peak of the roof has started flashing, and the garage's massive middle door is rolling up. The next thing I know, the BLS crew's aid car emerges from the garage with its own lights flashing. The two firefighters who are seated in the front of the rig give me quick waves, and then the driver hits the ambulance's siren as he pulls out of the parking lot. Once the ambulance disappears down the road and the wail of its siren fades away, I hear someone behind me say:

"Mornin', Doc."

I turn around. Steve is holding open the station's front door and showing me a friendly smile.

"Hi, Steve." I smile back at him. "How are—"

"Falco?" someone else calls out. "From what I'm hearing over the radio, I'm guessing that . . ."

The guy trails off as Steve and I look his way. It's Jonathan. He's coming outside via the still-open door of the garage. As he draws closer, Jonathan becomes backlit by the ethereal glow of the sunlight that's bouncing off the morning clouds, so between the perfect lighting and how hot Jonathan looks in his uniform, the man basically looks like a superhero in a blockbuster movie making his entrance.

I realize Jonathan has his eyes zeroed in on mine.

"Hi, Doc." Jonathan breaks into his charismatic smile.

There's a distinct twisting sensation in my abdomen; it's the same sensation I've felt before in Jonathan's presence. This time, however, I don't ignore it. Instead, I dare to allow myself to analyze it a little bit. Because although it utterly terrifies me, I've come to the staggering conclusion that the epiphany I had last Sunday while eating brunch with Grant was correct: I need to take a different approach to romance. A vastly different approach.

After Grant made sure I got home safely last Sunday, I spent the next two-and-a-half days sequestered inside my house. In a restless, often-tearful state, I fought to work through all the painful, stunning, powerful emotions and thoughts that had exploded to the surface in that shocking moment of epiphany I had had in the restaurant. I forced myself to do a deep dive into my most raw and honest desires, fears, dreams, and hopes. The days were long, and the nights I spent tossing and turning were even longer.

At times, I took a logical, practical approach to the situation, methodically weighing the pros and cons of my options. Other times, I released all my clashing feelings simultaneously, letting them battle it out freely. Ultimately, I discovered, the approach I took really didn't matter. After the nearly three days of contemplation, I found myself circling back to the same life-changing realization that I first experienced during brunch: I had two choices for how I could move forward in life, and though both choices came at a potentially devastating cost, I had to pick one.

My first option was simply to keep doing what I had been doing for years: avoid romance, thereby keeping my heart protected from getting hurt but leaving me pining away for Grant, the only love I've ever known, and the one love that can't and won't ever be.

My second option—an option I never would have expected myself to consider—was to pull a complete one-eighty. I would erase the vow I made to myself years ago. I would let myself pursue romance, if and when an opportunity came along. The thought of doing so utterly terrified me, though, for it obviously meant I would have to allow myself to become vulnerable. I would have to accept the risk that by pursuing love, my heart could get crushed, much the same way my heart had been crushed before.

Late last night, I finally made my choice. No matter how I tried to spin the facts, I had to acknowledge that what I've been doing for the last several years wasn't working. By avoiding romance altogether, I've been keeping myself stuck in a rut, loving Grant without being loved in return. So as petrifying as it was to fathom, I made the drastic decision to end my romance boycott. I would no longer hide my heart. I would let myself pursue a relationship, if the right person came along, despite the potential for heartbreak that romance might bring. I knew my soul needed to heal and move on, and I decided that letting myself experience the possibility of loving someone else was the only way for that healing to happen.

Steve clears his throat, causing me to jump as I emerge from my thoughts. I look his way, and I see his eyes shifting between Jonathan and me.

"What were you saying, Blackrock?" Steve prompts, focusing back on his partner.

Jonathan turns from me to face Steve again. "I was saying that I anticipate we're going to get a call to assist the BLS crew. Based on the radio chatter, the patient is probably getting upgraded to altered mental status secondary to hypoglycemia."

Before Steve can even reply, both of the paramedics' pagers start going off. At the same time, the light near the roof starts flashing once more, and the alarm again pierces the air. The automated announcement from dispatch starts echoing out from the garage's speakers. Jonathan and Steve check their messages and start walking with brisk steps toward the ambulance.

"Let me help you into the back of the rig, Elly," Jonathan says over his shoulder to me. "I've got to sit up front with Falco for this one."

I nod in reply, a familiar sense of adrenaline launching inside me. As Steve pulls himself up into the ambulance's front seat, Jonathan meets me at the back of the rig. He tugs open a back door with one hand while holding out his other hand to me. I put my hand in his. My stomach flips again, and my eyes flick up to Jonathan's face. Jonathan seems to pause for a microsecond, and then he shows me a quick smile. He assists me up into the back of the ambulance, releases my hand, and closes the door. I'm suddenly breathing fast as I make my way to one of the benches, sit down, and don the bulky headset. Jonathan hops into the cab with Steve, and an instant later, we're underway.

I scoot to the edge of my bench, keeping my head turned to the left so I can watch out the windshield. Steve is maneuvering through an intersection that's bogged down with traffic, and Jonathan is answering a call on his phone. Once the call is over, Jonathan relays to Steve and me an update via the headset:

"The patient is a twenty-something-year-old male with a history of type-one diabetes. His work colleagues called nine-one-one because he was acting confused. Upon BLS assessment, he was found to be severely hypoglycemic."

"Copy that," Steve replies.

No more than another minute passes before Steve brings our rig to a stop in front of a coffee shop, which is situated in the middle of a long lineup of quaint storefronts. Still peering out the windshield, I see the BLS crew's ambulance parked across the road. The glass door leading into the coffee shop is propped open. Several people are clustered outside, talking amongst themselves while making animated hand gestures and jockeying for position to get a view of what's happening inside. A few of the onlookers are shop employees, based on the aprons they're wearing, and the rest of the crowd members—the ones holding recyclable to-go cups of various sizes—are clearly patrons who will now have to finish consuming their beverages outside.

In what became a well-rehearsed routine during my last shift, as soon as our ambulance is brought to stop, I tug off my headset, get to my feet, shove open the back door, and hop out of the rig, making room for Jonathan and Steve to collect the equipment they need. Once the paramedics are ready, we charge into the shop together, leaving the growing throng of curious onlookers in our wake.

As soon as we're inside, I zero in on our patient. He's seated at a table next to a window, about halfway toward the back of the room. The young man is wearing a black t-shirt and black-jeans, and like his coworkers outside, he has on an apron that displays the coffee shop's logo. His black baseball hat, which also is decorated with the shop's logo, is on the table in front of him. The young man is hunched to one side in his chair. His face is pale. He's staring at the BLS crew members with the distinctly muted expression of someone who isn't mentating clearly.

Jonathan and Steve hurry forward, equipment in-hand, to join the three firefighters who are surrounding the patient. This is a different BLS crew than the one we crossed paths with the other day, so I don't yet know the crew members' names, but it's clear to me that they're well-experienced in what they're doing.

Jonathan gets to the patient first. He introduces himself, and then he starts listening to the patient's heart and lungs with his stethoscope. Steve gets down on one knee near the table and unzips his bag of supplies while asking the BLS crew:

"So what do we have?"

"Twenty-four-year-old male," the lead firefighter replies. "History of type-one diabetes, which is usually well-controlled with insulin. Noted by coworkers to be acting sluggish and confused this morning, so they called nine-one-one. Upon our arrival, the patient had a GCS of thirteen. He reported feeling clammy and shaky. As further history, the patient said he had breakfast this morning, and he had his regular morning dose of insulin. When he started feeling unwell at work, he checked his glucose level with his home glucometer, and it showed a glucose level of one-fifteen, which would be normal for him. However, when we checked the patient's glucose level with our device, it showed his glucose was significantly low at thirty-four. So we're suspecting the patient's home glucometer isn't reading accurately. The patient is feeling too nauseated at this time to attempt oral glucose replacement."

Steve nods and gets up on one knee to work on placing an IV. Jonathan finishes his exam. One of the firefighters begins cycling a fresh set of vitals. Soon, Steve has the IV placed, and Jonathan gets down on his haunches in front of the orange supply bag to draw up a dose of IV dextrose, which will raise the patient's glucose level.

"Hey," the patient says in a moan, looking around at all of us with his glassy-eyed stare. "I don't feel too good. I think—"

The patient vomits all over the floor.

There's only a split-second pause, and then everyone goes back to what they were doing. Flashbacks of my last ED shift go through my mind. Clearly, EMS providers are as unbothered by working around piles of emesis as are those of us who treat patients in the ED.

Jonathan is now drawing up a dose of anti-nausea medication. He glances at the monitor and puts his focused gaze on Steve. "I vote we transport this gentleman for symptomatic hypoglycemia, inability to keep down PO, and ongoing tachycardia."

"Agreed." Steve accepts the syringe of medication from Jonathan, and he administers it through the IV along with the dextrose.

Two of the firefighters hustle out of the shop to get the stretcher from the back of our ambulance. The remaining firefighter does another finger-stick check of the patient's glucose level.

"Repeat glucose one-seventeen," the firefighter reports.

In what is a predictable turn of events, and is always gratifying to see, the patient swiftly becomes more alert and interactive as his glucose rises. While the patient speaks with the paramedics, the two BLS crew members return with the stretcher and help the patient get up on it. Jonathan secures the stretcher's seatbelt-like straps around the patient and covers him with a blanket. Steve cleans up the supplies and gets to his feet while slinging the orange bag over his shoulder. One of the BLS crew members props the cardiac monitor against the stretcher's side railing so it will be visible during transport. Once everything is ready, Jonathan pushes the stretcher out the door while the rest of us follow.

The crowd on the sidewalk is steadily growing as more people wander out of the nearby stores to observe what's happening. About half of the people in the crowd are using their phones to film the scene, so I'm guessing we'll wind up on numerous social media sites by lunchtime . . . if we're not being live-streamed already.

The patient is put in the back of the rig, and his stretcher is secured. Steve heads for the driver's seat. I climb into the back of the ambulance with Jonathan, introduce myself to the patient and explain I'm acting as an observer, and sit on the vacant bench. One of the firefighters shuts our back doors with a hefty slam. Steve brings the ambulance's engine to life, and within seconds, we're en route to the hospital.

"I'll call Lakewood to give report," Jonathan says through the headset.

While Jonathan makes the call to the ED, I shift my attention back to the patient to continue observing him. The young man is now resting with his eyes closed. I squint, making sure it's not simply due to the lighting in the rig, before deciding the patient's skin really is looking pale again. I glance at the monitor. His vitals remain within normal limits, but his heart rate is creeping up. I feel a prick of unease. I—

"So, Elly, how do you think that went?"

I hear Jonathan's voice in my ears, and my eyes snap his way. He's putting his phone back into his pocket while grinning at me.

"What do you mean?" I ask, speaking low like Jonathan is doing, so the patient can't hear what I'm saying.

"Nothing specific." Jonathan is still smiling in his confident, charming way as he adjusts his headset back into place. He leans casually against the side wall, letting his body sway to the rhythm of the ambulance. "I just want to find out how you think this call went."

I glance at the patient again. I focus on Jonathan once more. "Well, I don't think the care is over. I actually have a suggestion to make."

Jonathan's smile fades. "Oh."

"Great, Doc. Feedback from you is always appreciated," Steve interjects from the front seat. He glances in the rearview mirror and breaks into a grin. "Besides, Paramedic Blackrock needs every bit of help he can get."

I snicker at Steve's humor. I'm getting used to the harsh style of EMS banter, but I know I can't let it rub off on me too much. I guarantee it wouldn't go over well if I sauntered up to one of my colleagues in the ED and said, *Oh, hey, buddy. You're the most incompetent excuse for a physician I've ever worked with. Great to see you, though.*

Yes, something tells me the humor would get lost in translation.

I look to Jonathan again. To my surprise, Jonathan isn't laughing at Steve's quip. Instead, Jonathan is observing me with his lips pressed into a slight frown. When my eyes meet his, Jonathan exhales and asks me:

"Okay, so what are you thinking?"

"I would advise checking another glucose level, to ensure it's not trending down again." I do another check of the cardiac monitor. "Type-one diabetics usually know their bodies extremely well. They're typically very in-tune with their glucose level and if there's something they need to do to correct it." I return my attention to Jonathan. "So for this gentleman, who reportedly has well-controlled diabetes, to wind up with such severe hypoglycemia without a clear preceding incident or change in routine is notable. It warrants close evaluation and workup, especially since the clinical picture is complicated by the fact that his home glucometer probably hasn't been reading accurately for a while, which means we have no idea what his sugars have actually been running lately."

Jonathan peers a me a moment or two longer. He then exhales another breath and reaches for the equipment he needs. "Will do," he states.

I sit back on my bench and avert my gaze, sensing it's better to give Jonathan some space as he works. I keep tabs on what's going on out of the corner of my eye, though. I see Jonathan explaining to the patient what he would like to do and the patient weakly nodding in apparent agreement. Jonathan then proceeds to obtain another finger-stick sample of the patient's blood, and he applies it to the glucometer. A few seconds later, the machine chirps. Jonathan checks the number displayed on the device. He pauses.

"What's the word, Blackrock?" I hear Steve ask after a few seconds of silence.

I turn my head toward Jonathan once again. He still has his eyes on the machine in his hand.

"Glucose is low again at forty-four," Jonathan answers flatly.

"Wow. Good call on that, Doc," Steve tells me.

Saying no more, Jonathan puts down the glucometer, draws up another dose of IV dextrose, and proceeds to administer the medication through the IV. In real-time, the patient's pallor resolves, and the awareness returns to his eyes. He sits up and starts speaking with Jonathan in clear, coherent sentences.

There's a resounding, final blip from the ambulance siren. I lean forward and check out the windshield. Steve is pulling into the familiar covered ambulance bay at Lakewood Medical Center's emergency department. I break into a smile. This kind of feels like coming home.

Jonathan starts explaining to the patient what's going to happen next. Steve gets out of the ambulance, comes around to the back, and opens the doors. I climb out and slide aside, making room for the paramedics to get the patient's stretcher removed from the ambulance. Steve starts pushing the stretcher toward the sliding door that leads into the ED. Jonathan follows on Steve's heels. I scurry to catch up with them.

As the door slides aside with its recognizable, high-pitched squeak, I cross the threshold and enter the ED. I'm instantly immersed in Lakewood's never-ceasing storm of commotion, which I know so well. Yet I find there's a distinctly different vibe when viewing this place from the perspective of an EMS crew rather than as an ED provider. I can tune out a lot of the ED chaos today, since all my attention is centered on one patient rather than spread out across several people at the same time.

I'm greeted by members of the ED staff, and I begin returning their welcoming smiles. Meanwhile, Laura, who's working as the charge nurse, as she so often does, looks over from her standing-only desk and asks in her typical no-nonsense way:

"Hypoglycemia patient?"

"Yep," Steve replies.

"Room Twelve." Laura points down the corridor.

Steve commences driving the patient's stretcher down the crowded corridor toward Room Twelve. Jonathan and I trail behind him, weaving around the throngs of people in our route. Once we get near to our destination, Jonathan steps in front of Steve, draws aside Room Twelve's ugly, faded, floral-patterned curtain, and holds it out of the way while Steve pushes the patient's stretcher into the room. Jonathan then shifts his eyes to mine. Our gazes catch and hold a moment, causing my cheeks to grow warm, before I enter the room. Jonathan steps in after me, letting the curtain swing closed behind him.

I dart over to a corner of the undersized room to observe while the others get to work. I wave to the nurse, Tom, and the tech, Finn, who were in here waiting for our arrival. Tom and Finn help the paramedics transfer the patient over to the stretcher in the middle of the room. After the patient gets settled, Tom starts entering information into the computer, and Finn gets the patient connected to the cardiac monitor that's mounted on the wall.

The room's curtain is pulled aside by someone on the outside. Dr. Wes Kent, emergency medicine attending physician, director of the ED rotation for med students at Lakewood, and—most importantly, in my opinion—Savannah Drake's long-term boyfriend, enters the room. Like Savannah, Dr. Kent is currently sporting a nice out-of-season tan, which was undoubtedly earned during his recent trip to attend Danielle's destination wedding.

Dr. Kent glances my way and shows me his handsome, professional smile. I'm in the process of smiling back when I realize there's someone else entering the room along with him: a woman who's dressed in scrubs and a long white coat. She appears about my age or perhaps a few years older. She has long, straight, dark-brown hair, which is pulled back in a ponytail. Her eyes, which are darting about the room with a perceptive gaze, are a striking shade of green. There's a stethoscope poking out of one of the pockets of her white coat. Curious, my gaze homes in on the hospital-issued photo ID that the woman has clipped to the pocket of her scrubs top. Under her photo, it reads:

Irene Thatcher, MD
Emergency Medicine Attending Physician

I pull in a breath of realization. Dr. Thatcher must be one of Lakewood's new ED attendings, and it looks like she's doing an orientation shift with Dr. Kent today. I finish my split-second assessment of her, and I almost nod to convey my approval. Dr. Thatcher already strikes me as someone who's smart, hard-working, difficult to faze, and good-natured. I can tell I'm going to like working under her direction.

As if she senses me watching her, Dr. Thatcher looks my way. We only have time to exchange a friendly look before Steve begins giving the ED team report on the patient. Dr. Thatcher immediately shifts her eyes back to Steve, and she listens to him with a look of calm concentration.

Once Steve finishes giving report, Finn exits the room, Tom begins drawing blood from the patient's IV, and Dr. Thatcher starts conversing with the patient. With care of the patient now officially transferred over to the ED team, Steve begins pushing the EMS stretcher out of the room. Jonathan again pulls aside the curtain, allowing Steve to pass through. Also as before, Jonathan keeps holding the curtain back for me. This time, though, when our eyes meet, Jonathan adds a playful wink. There's a pulsation deep down in my abdomen as I pass Jonathan to return to the corridor. I keep walking as I attempt to make sense of what just happened and how I'm reacting. Instead of successfully sorting through my thoughts, however, I'm growing increasingly puzzled, awkward, and uncertain. It's like the romance part of my brain is an outdated, long-abandoned computer that I've just turned on for the first time in years, and I'm stuck using vastly outdated software to calculate information about what's going on.

Is Jonathan flirting with me?

Am I attracted to Jonathan?

I have no idea.

I would laugh, if I didn't feel so pathetic. I mean, I'm a resident physician, for crying out loud. I aced four years of brutal undergrad work and four even more brutal years of medical school. I successfully handled biochemistry, anatomy, nephrology, pharmacology, and just about every other subject under the sun. I can still sketch out the Krebs Cycle from memory. I know how to place a thorocostomy tube, resuscitate an infant in respiratory arrest, diagnose a posterior-wall myocardial infarction, perform a lumbar puncture, titrate pressors, adjust ventilator settings, and suture massive wounds.

Yet I have no idea if the way I'm feeling means that I'm attracted to the hot, buff, charming man I'm working with.

I emerge out of my thoughts when I notice Tara Hess across the department. Tara is one of the internal medicine residents here at Lakewood, and I'm guessing she's currently in the ED to admit a patient to her service. I really like Tara. She's one of the sweetest, most bubbly people I know . . . and her hair has this miraculous ability to stay perfectly curled even when she's on-call. It's amazing. Anyway, Tara and I exchange grins before I resume weaving through the throng to follow Steve toward the ambulance bay. I pretend not to notice when Steve snatches a pillow from the ED's cart of clean linens before he heads outside.

Jonathan seems to appear out of nowhere beside me, and the next thing I know, we're walking together in the direction of the ambulance bay. I try to think of something to say to him, but the ancient computer inside my brain shorts out, leaving my mind totally blank.

We get outside, and as usual, Jonathan and Steve refuse my offer of help as they clean and restock the rig. Once we're ready to depart, Jonathan insists that I ride up front with Steve for the drive back to the station. The two paramedics banter between themselves during the ride, and before long, we're pulling into the station's garage. I hop out of the ambulance, leaving my door ajar so it's ready for the next call. Steve jumps out of the driver's seat, leaving his door open, too. Jonathan gets the huge cable plugged into the rig so it can charge, and then he tells his partner:

"I'll go finish up the documentation for the call."

"Sounds good." Steve checks his watch. "Let me know if you need any help with the big words."

I snort a laugh. Jonathan laughs, too, and he shoots me a glance with eyes that are dancing with amusement. I smile in return. Jonathan seems to let his gaze linger on mine before he heads inside. I watch in the direction Jonathan went for a second or two, my face feeling a little flushed, and then I focus on what Steve is doing, observing while he finishes prepping the rig. Once he's done, Steve and I enter the station and make our way down the hall. When we reach the spacious kitchen, Steve surprises me by letting out a groan.

I turn Steve's way. He faces me in return. He's grinning.

"What are you moaning about?" I inquire with a laugh.

Steve gestures to the lounge area. "It looks like the planning committee for the firefighters' gala crashed the station while we were gone."

"Huh?" I laugh again, my eyebrows rising in unmasked confusion.

Steve simply points past me. I spin around to see what he's gesturing at, and my eyes come to a stop on a gigantic poster that has been placed on an easel in the most conspicuous corner of the room. The poster is quite professional-looking. Its background is designed to look like a starry sky. Big gold stars are scattered along the poster's borders. In the center of the poster, in large, elegant font, it reads:

Lakewood Fire & Rescue's
Annual Gala & Silent Auction
Friday, October 30th
Regency Hotel Ballroom
Dinner at 7:00 pm

Dancing at 9:00 pm
Formal Attire

"A gala? Really?" I re-read the poster, still in disbelief. I then look back at Steve. "That's cool, though I admit that I wouldn't have guessed you guys would be the types to host a formal event like a gala, or do anything that involves decorating with glitter or wearing tuxedoes, for that matter."

Steve tips back his head and howls with laughter. Once he gathers his breath, he replies:

"I don't blame you for assuming we aren't capable of cleaning up well enough for an event that involves a live band, a multi-course meal, and the like." Steve's eyes shift past me, and his grin broadens. "Thankfully, some of us do manage to clean up well. Blackrock, however, remains an embarrassment."

"I heard that," I hear Jonathan say from behind me.

I pull in an unexpectedly stuttering breath, and I check over my shoulder. Jonathan is strolling into the kitchen with a grin on his lips, his dark eyes shifting between Steve, the poster, and me.

Steve chuckles as he grabs an energy drink from one of the four industrial-sized refrigerators that line the kitchen's far wall. As he takes a seat at the kitchen island and opens his beverage, he resumes explaining to me:

"The gala is put on every year by the agency. The money that's made from ticket sales and the silent auction goes toward things the agency needs to help us provide better care to the community. For example, the funds earned from last year's gala were allocated toward buying AEDs for the area's elementary schools."

"That's a really great idea." I take a seat on one of the other island stools.

"Well, it's for a good cause, and my wife enjoys going, at least." Steve shrugs before he guzzles down his drink. He smacks his lips. "Of course, though I'm able to make myself dashingly presentable for the event, I would still prefer to stay at home and watch—"

Steve's pager goes off. I get back to my feet, ready to head out for another call, but then I realize Jonathan's pager hasn't started alarming like his partner's. I shift my eyes back to Steve, who's still seated on his stool and calmly reading his new message. When he's done, Steve lifts his eyes and focuses on Jonathan.

"The chief is here, and he's asking if I want to do my annual in-person eval now." Steve puts his pager back into the holder on his belt. He stands and finishes off his drink. "I'll go get that taken care of, if it would be all right with you."

"Sure. That's fine." Jonathan pulls a bottled water from the fridge. "Hope you don't get fired."

Steve heads for the stairwell. "If anything, they should give me a raise for having to put up with an imbecile like you."

Steve exits the kitchen, and then the room gets quiet. Very quiet. I continue staring in the direction that Steve departed, my chest tightening in a funny way as I become particularly aware that it's now only Jonathan and me in here.

Is this what being attracted to someone other than Grant feels like?

"Would you like something to drink, Elly?"

Hearing Jonathan address me by my first name makes my heart thump an extra time. I certainly don't mind Jonathan doing so—I invited him to call me by my first name when we met, and he has done so often—but suddenly it feels more personal. More purposeful.

Or am I misreading this entire situation? The romance computer in my brain is still trying to reboot after the last time it shorted out, so it's not giving me any help whatsoever.

Feigning calmness, I get back on my stool. "One of those flavored waters would be great. Thanks."

"You got it."

Jonathan gets another drink from the fridge. With a water in each hand, he comes toward the island, sets a bottle in front of me, and takes a place on the stool directly across from mine.

"It's the finest grocery-store water there is," Jonathan tells me with a humorous gleam in his eyes.

I giggle. "Yes, I was going to say it looks very top shelf."

"Absolutely. Very top shelf." Jonathan raises his water to me. "Cheers."

I snicker again before taking a sip. As I put down my water, I observe Jonathan, admiring the way his perfectly proportioned Adam's apple bobs while he swallows. Once Jonathan is done with his drink, he puts his beverage down on the island. There's a pause. Everything suddenly feels . . . *intense.*

Jonathan clears his throat. "Hey, Elly, there's something I want to ask you."

Jonathan's deliberate tone and concentrated look catches my attention, but I maintain an unflustered expression while I wait for him to go on. Peering at Jonathan, to my shock, I realize he looks *nervous.* This is the first time I've ever witnessed Jonathan appear even remotely unsure about anything. Jonathan goes on:

"Elly, I realize that for several reasons I probably shouldn't do this, but I'm going to go out on a limb here."

My body gets hot, and somewhere in the recesses of my brain, dusty memories of the various guys who've asked me out and flirted with me over the years start seeping to the surface. The romance computer in my brain may be outdated, but even it's able to compute what path this conversation with Jonathan is on. I can only pray there's something coded in the computer's outdated software that will help me figure out what to say and how to react this time.

"All right," I say to Jonathan in reply.

I groan to myself. *All right*? Really? I couldn't come up with anything better than that?

Stupid computer.

Jonathan tips his head slightly to one side. "Admittedly, I don't even know if you're single, but if you are, I was wondering if you would like to go out with me some time."

It feels as though everything around me, including Jonathan, gets put on pause. I replay Jonathan's words in my head, and I work down a swallow.

Jonathan Blackrock—the hot, buff, nice paramedic guy—has just asked me out on a date.

What am I supposed to do? The last time I was asked out was a month ago . . . by a patient who promised to literally fly me to the moon for a basketball game. Prior to that, I was asked out by a resident in the radiology program, but I politely turned him down. Just like I've turned down other residents who've asked me out. Just like I turned down the man who used to live across the street from me. And like I declined dates during med school. Like I've turned down each and every guy who has ever shown romantic interest in me.

Now, though, things are different. I've made the decision to keep myself open to romance. Therefore, one would think the situation would be pretty straight-forward: I'm single, and Jonathan has just asked me out on a date. There's absolutely no reason why I should turn down Jonathan's offer.

If I go out with Jonathan, however, it means I'm really taking the leap. I'm really going to walk my talk. I'll be letting myself get to know a guy in a potentially romantic way. I'll be risking vulnerability and heartbreak. I'll be opening myself up to possibly growing legitimately attached to Jonathan while knowing there's a risk that everything might blow up in my face.

And there's the fact that I work with Jonathan right now, and although there's no rule that says we can't go out, it is an additional layer of complexity that would be added to the equation of my very first dating experience right out of romance hibernation.

Yet I'm also acutely aware that I just spent the last three days absorbed in intense self-deliberation on this topic, and after immense soul-searching, I did decide to give romance a try. Hiding from love hasn't worked. I need to meet guys, go out on dates, and pursue romance if the situation is right. It's the only way I'll ever get my heart to move on. It's the only way my romantically-inclined heart might find happiness elsewhere one day.

"Thank you for asking, Jonathan. I would like to go out," I hear myself state.

I freeze at my own words. I just agreed to go out on a date with someone. Specifically, I just agreed to go out with Jonathan, the hunky paramedic.

Jonathan's smile relaxes. "That's great. How about—"

The shrill sound of Jonathan's pager going off interrupts him. An alert begins radiating out from the PA system, followed by the automated dispatch voice announcing a new call.

Jonathan and I share a final look before we both hop off our stools and charge toward the garage. Jonathan shoves open the door and lets me pass through first. There's a clamor from the other side of the garage as Steve appears through another doorway and jogs over to meet us.

Jonathan helps me into the back of the rig, and he shows me another grin. "I hope we can pick up this conversation as soon as the call is done."

"I would like that," I tell him, aware that I'm smiling, too.

Jonathan lets go of my hand, gives me a tip of his head, and shuts the ambulance doors.

Nine

"Elly Vincent, if we ever have to make another video at any point in our lifetimes, you are more than welcome to be the star. While I like video production and video editing, being on camera remains a form of slow torture for me."

I snicker at Grant's dryly spoken remark and shift how I'm sitting to look at him. Grant is seated beside me at my dining room table, which we've been using for the past few hours almost like it's a news anchor's desk. Behind us, Grant's portable green screen is hung to the wall. Across the table from where we're seated, Grant has his point-and-shoot camera—complete with an attached boom mic—mounted to a tripod. There's also a blindingly bright ring light above the camera, and his laptop is nearby and running some sort of elaborate video-editing software. Basically, Grant turned this part of my house into a film studio for the afternoon, and I have to say, it's an impressive set up.

I'm still eyeing Grant's profile, which is illuminated by the late-afternoon sun that's streaming in through the dining room window. Though Grant has always hated being on camera, his looks are most certainly film-worthy. His thick hair, which was combed when he first arrived to my house this morning, has become increasingly disheveled over the course of the day as he has repeatedly run his hands through it while bemoaning the fact that he has to be on camera at all. Grant cast aside his black, zip-up fleece jacket a while ago, leaving his long-sleeved gray shirt—and the way it just happens to highlight his muscular physique—on full display. There's a hint of facial scruff lining his jaw in an immensely alluring way. And his blue eyes are glinting in the sunlight as they flick around the room.

Grant shifts his gaze back to me, and as our eyes meet, I become extremely aware of how closely Grant and I have been sitting to one another while we've been filming. Every ounce of me is drawn to him, yet in what has become a well-practiced move over the years, I make myself lean back to put more space between us.

Grant blinks a time or two, and then he pushes away from the table. Getting to his feet, he twists his torso to stretch. "Anyway, it's a good thing you're such a natural teacher when it comes to medical topics, El. You're great with this type of thing. The video would bomb if I was the only one doing the teaching."

I'm about to disagree with him when Grant's shirt rises slightly while he continues stretching, giving me an unexpected glimpse of his abs. His profoundly well-defined, chiseled abs. I gulp. My eyes get wide as I stare, and my respirations get kind of shallow.

Holy smokes.

I knew Grant was extremely fit, but . . .

Holy, holy smokes.

I look the other way, resisting the urge to fan air past my face. The romance computer inside my brain has the audacity to promptly boot up, as though it's completely up-to-date and at the ready, as if it hasn't ever given me any trouble whatsoever . . . as though it didn't leave me completely hanging yesterday when Jonathan asked me out.

I pause.

I'm going out with Jonathan.

I'm going out with Jonathan because I've decided it's time for me to start meeting other guys and stop dreaming of what can't ever be with Grant.

I clear my throat, keeping my eyes on the tabletop. "Well, it's a good thing you have the tech savvy to make this video happen." I take a drink from the water glass that's beside me. My throat is parched, though whether it's because we just finished shooting the third take of our twenty-minute video, or because the image of Grant's abdominal muscles remains forefront in my mind, I'm not entirely certain. "Without you, none of this would be possible. I definitely don't have the equipment, editing software, or know-how to put anything like this together."

"You mean, you're not as nerdy as me to have the know-how to put anything like this together." Grant grins as he walks around the table, turns off his camera, and starts disassembling his equipment. His grin broadens. "It's too bad we didn't have this stuff back in high school, huh? Especially for that video we had to make about Act Three of *Hamlet*. A few explosions via a green screen definitely would have made that production even more amazing."

I break into laughter as vivid recollections of the Shakespearean spoof we did for our twelfth-grade English class fill my head. Still laughing, I stand, straighten my cream-colored sweater and leggings, and gather up the pages of the script that we used for today's video. Grant and I wrote the script this morning, and I think we did a good job putting together some informative, applicable teaching points about the five metrics we want crews to perform when caring for potential stroke patients. Now with our video recorded, Grant is going to edit the footage and upload the final version this evening, so it will be available for the crews to watch.

"Can I get you anything else to eat or drink?" I take the script and our water glasses into the kitchen, set them on the counter, and head toward the pantry. "There's a ton of leftover pizza from lunch in the fridge; you're welcome to as much as you want."

"Thanks, but I'll let you keep it. I know how much you love pizza leftovers." Grant strolls into the kitchen and starts rinsing the dishes that are piled up in my sink. "However, I may take a few of the remaining cake-mix cookies home with me."

"Don't worry. I read your mind on that one." I back out of the pantry and show Grant the gallon-sized plastic baggie that I've already got in my hands. "I was going to pack up the cookies for you to . . ."

The rest of my words get lost somewhere in my throat when I witness Grant dry his hands on a dishtowel and then casually slap the towel over one shoulder. Leaving the towel hanging there, Grant begins putting the rest of the dishes into the dishwasher. For reasons I cannot entirely explain, the sight of muscular, manly Grant working in my kitchen causes something deep, deep down inside of me to stir and awaken. The feral sensation fills my chest with a pulsating heat, causing my face to flush.

Okay, either this man needs to get out of my kitchen, or I need to vacate before I lose all control of myself.

"Um, here's the bag for the cookies."

I toss the plastic baggie onto the counter with enough abruptness that Grant looks over at me with his eyebrows raised. I ignore him and dart into the living room while adding over my shoulder:

"Take as many cookies as you want. There's no way I'll ever be able to eat them all. Besides, you'll need the extra fuel while you're editing the video tonight."

There's a slight break in the conversation before I hear Grant reply:

"Thanks."

With the sounds of Grant working in the kitchen still filling my ears like a siren's song, I make myself busy fussing around the living and dining rooms, tidying up after the long day spent working on the video. In many ways, everything feels like the countless times Grant and I worked together on projects in high school or studied together in college. In other ways, however, this is drastically different. My feelings for Grant are stronger than ever before, and . . .

No. I can't do this. I have to stop dwelling on Grant. I'm recalibrating my approach to romance, and I can't go back now, no matter how heart-racingly, swoon-worthy it is that Grant is *in my kitchen doing the dishes*. The fact remains that I'm going out on a date with Jonathan, and I—

"So what's your schedule like for the next few days?"

Grant's voice shakes me to attention, nearly causing me to drop the autumn-themed decorative pillow that I'm in the process of returning to the living room couch. I toss the pillow where it belongs and whip around, watching as Grant strides from the kitchen into the dining room. He starts pushing in the chairs around the table.

"I don't have a shift tomorrow," Grant continues, turning my way. "So if you have the day off, too, it might be a good time to meet up to work on the next step of our project." He grins. "I don't think there will be any filming required, thank goodness."

"Indeed, I don't think there's any more torturous filming you'll have to endure." I manage to gather my wits enough to reply with a laugh. "Unfortunately, though, I have a swing shift tomorrow, so that will pretty much eat up the whole day." I twist my lips as I think through the schedule. "I agree, though, that we need to meet up soon, especially since we have to determine how we're going to track the data for the stroke calls that crews respond to this month."

Grant is nodding. "What about Saturday? I've got a morning shift, but I would be done by late in the afternoon. We could meet up afterward."

"Sure. As long as you don't mind working on the project after a long day of . . ."

I trail off. Saturday. This Saturday. This Saturday evening. I'm going out with Jonathan this Saturday evening.

"Actually, I, um, have to take that back." I flinch. "I can't meet up Saturday evening either."

Grant's eyebrows rise. "Did they schedule you for back-to-back shifts over the weekend?"

I exhale a long, silent breath. I can't hide the truth from Grant any longer.

"No, I'm not scheduled to work." I avert my gaze. "I'm . . . well, I'm going out on a date."

There's a pause.

I dare to look at Grant again. His expression has gone totally blank, and he's peering at me closely with his blue-eyed gaze. I cough and shift my stance, waiting for him to stay something while the awkward vibe in the room continues to rise.

I can't blame Grant for being caught off-guard by my announcement, and I'm certainly not offended by his reaction. Considering I've been on a romance boycott all these years, Grant has never heard me talk about guys I'm attracted to, except for when I joke about movie-star crushes. Grant also hasn't heard me say much about the men I declined to go out with. And he definitely hasn't ever heard me announce that I'm going out on a date. Come to think of it, while Grant and I have frequently talked on a superficial level about the women he has shown interest in over the years, we've barely ever spoken about my love life—or lack thereof—at all. I know Grant has simply tried to be respectful and sensitive about my single status; I suspect he avoids bringing up a subject that he thinks might sadden or embarrass me. Anyway, I'm not surprised at Grant's current silence. I might as well have just announced that I'm joining the Olympic synchronized swimming team.

The moment seems to pass. Grant's expression normalizes, and he takes a seat on one of the living room chairs.

"Oh, okay. That's cool. What about meeting up on Sunday, then?"

I exhale with relief. Grant isn't upset about my surprise announcement, and he isn't going to interrogate me for details. Considering I'm still getting used to the idea of going out on a date myself, I'm grateful Grant isn't going to push for more info; that would only make me feel even more awkward and nervous.

In a way, I suppose Grant's approach is similar to how I've approached his dating life all these years. Like I said, we've typically kept our discussions of Grant's dating life pretty simple and shallow, too. I've always been willing to listen whenever Grant wants to chat, but I've never pushed him for more information than what he offers. It's as though there has always been an unspoken understanding between Grant and me that we won't talk too much about our love lives.

"Sunday works great." I sit on the couch, making sure not to smash the cute autumn pillows that I just finished rearranging. "How about meeting here at noon?"

Grant pulls his phone from the pocket of his jeans and taps the screen a couple of times. "Sounds good."

Grant gets back to his feet. He returns to the dining room and gathers up his equipment, somehow managing to carry it all as if it collectively weighs no more than a piece of paper. It suddenly dawns on me that Grant is getting ready to leave.

I scramble to my feet. "Hey, wait. Don't forget the cookies."

I jog past Grant and head into the spotlessly clean kitchen. Using a spatula, I shovel all the remaining cookies into the baggie, and then I scamper back into the living room. Grant has already made his way over to the front foyer. I head across the living room to join him.

"Thanks again for doing the editing." I smile while placing the cookie bag on top of the equipment he has braced in his arms.

"No problem. I'll get the video uploaded tonight." Grant adjusts the way his camera bag is slung over his shoulder.

I open the front door, and a rush of cold evening air swirls into the house. Grant makes a move to leave, but he stops in the doorway and looks at me again.

"I hope you have a really good time on Saturday, El. I'll see you on Sunday around noon."

There's an unexpected lump of emotion in my throat. "Thanks," I eke out.

Grant heads outside. With steady strides, he makes his way to his car while using one hand to retrieve his keys from a pocket of his jeans. I remain in the doorway, getting hit by the cold outside air from the front while the heat from my house warms me from the back.

Once Grant has his equipment secured in his car, he gives me a nod. I wave. Grant gets into his vehicle, turns over the ignition, and drives off. I stay on the porch, an ache expanding in my heart, listening to the sound of his car fade away.

Ten

"So what made you decide to leave the Lakewood area and go elsewhere for med school?"

I take a sip of the apple cider that's in the to-go cup I'm cradling in my hands, giving myself time to decide how I want to reply to Jonathan's politely posed question. Jonathan and I have just finished a delicious (and undoubtedly expensive) dinner at one of the region's fanciest restaurants. Now, after a stop at a cozy café to grab a drink, we're strolling the lamppost-and-park-bench-lined street that runs through the fun part of town where the British restaurant and so many other outstanding venues are located. As expected, this area is alive with Saturday-night energy: music is being performed in several restaurants, the string lights that crisscross over the road high above are sparkling brightly against the nighttime sky, autumnal decorations adorn the front windows of the shops and eateries, and people are everywhere, laughing and chatting as they enjoy the evening.

Though I'm a dating novice, I would dare to say that tonight's outing with Jonathan is going well . . . really well, actually. Of course, I could be way off in my assessment, since I have no personal dating experience to use for comparison. Also, as someone who relies heavily on analyzing people's unspoken communication, I'm aware that I don't know Jonathan well enough to pick up on all the subtle clues that would allow me to know what he's truly thinking. That being said, it still strikes me that Jonathan is enjoying our date as much as I am. Frankly, I'm both relieved and pleasantly surprised by how well things are going.

Earlier this afternoon, thanks to the wonders of modern technology that allowed Mackenna to be "with" me to offer advice via an online video call, the process of getting ready for tonight's date went smoothly. With Mackenna's assistance, I decided on wearing a blue, v-neck fitted top, a black pencil skirt, and black boots, paired with a coordinating walker-style coat. I had fun putting on more makeup than I typically do. I even donned one of the few pairs of hoop earrings that I own (I have no idea when I last wore hoop earrings; they're definitely not something I wear in the ED, since they can become a hazard if a violent or disoriented patient tries to grab them). As the final touch to my look for the night, and at Mackenna's suggestion, I left my hair down, styled in loose curls.

Jonathan arrived right on time to pick me up. When I opened my front door, I had this surreal moment when I wondered if I was simply dreaming. Jonathan looked so hot in his suit coat, button-up shirt, and slacks that I almost laughed like everything was just some sort of charade. However, the other-worldly moment passed as quickly as it had come on, and I knew without a doubt that everything was real. Jonathan was actually standing on my front porch, and his gray pickup truck was in my driveway. As unbelievable as it seemed, the hot paramedic guy was really taking me out on a date.

Our conversation started off polite, cautious, and a little bit awkward. I wasn't surprised. I think Jonathan and I were both figuring out how to recalibrate the boundaries of our interactions, now that we were on a date rather than racing to a call together in the back of a noisy ambulance. So I wasn't rattled by the situation until Jonathan navigated his truck into the ritzy restaurant's valet parking area, and I realized where he was taking me for dinner. I hadn't expected that we would dine in such an exclusive, high-end place, and I feared the formal atmosphere would only exacerbate the already-delicate situation between us.

However, I quickly came to appreciate the wisdom in Jonathan's choice: the restaurant's sophisticated ambience proved to be an ideal contrast to the fast-paced, deafeningly loud, full-of-interruption EMS setting where all our previous interactions had taken place. Instead of trying to talk over alarms, or through headsets in the back of a swaying ambulance, Jonathan and I had the opportunity to sit in a quiet corner table of the restaurant that provided stunning views through floor-to-ceiling windows of the region's famous lake, which was beautifully illuminated by the shimmering lights of the buildings on the shore and the boats that were floating upon the water. For the first time, Jonathan and I were able to talk without a tornado of chaos around us or the unspoken pressure of being watched by coworkers. It didn't take long for our dinner conversation to become more comfortable and open, and I felt as though we were actually starting to get to know one another.

One of Jonathans' first questions was a simple, broad inquiry about how I ended up as an emergency medicine resident in the area. Keeping things to what I felt was an appropriate first-date level of detail, I provided Jonathan with a summary of my life's journey and key moments up to that point. As I spoke, I was also silently assessing how Jonathan was reacting to my story. I decided he was either an extremely skilled actor or he was legitimately interested in what I had to say. Jonathan's attention was both appreciated and sort of intimidating. Only Grant listens to me with unfailing, total focus, no matter what. In fact, ever since I met Grant, he . . .

Never mind. Grant and I are only friends. I can't use him for comparison.

After I shared with Jonathan enough about my life to demonstrate I was willing to let him get to know me better—while simultaneously avoiding sharing every detail of my existence—I turned the conversation spotlight onto him. Essentially bouncing his own question back his way, I asked Jonathan how he wound up as a paramedic in the region. Jonathan provided me with an equally open-without-TMI overview of his life: born and raised in the area, a college graduate, in the military, married at age twenty-four, hired by the fire agency after being honorably discharged from the armed forces, blindsided when his wife left him at the age of twenty-eight, accepted for paramedic training, and finished with paramedic training at the age of thirty. He has been working as a paramedic for almost two years now.

Jonathan also disclosed that he hasn't done much dating since his divorce, in part because he has been busy with work, and in part because he wanted to take some time to adjust after his wife left him. Now, Jonathan explained to me, he has reached a point in his life where he's ready to return to the dating scene, and he's looking forward to finding that special someone with whom he can share a future.

I can't deny that as Jonathan told me his story, I actually found myself imagining . . . envisioning . . . wondering if . . .

Yet while my mind was able to wrap itself around the theoretical possibility of an expanding relationship with Jonathan, my heart wasn't ready to accept it. Once again, though, I wasn't surprised. It's not as though I went into this date believing I would realize without a shadow of a doubt that I had found my soulmate. Not even close.

That's because you've always believed Grant is your soulmate, the voice in my head inconveniently reminds me.

I shove the thought aside.

Regardless, I admit that I was caught off-guard by some aspects of Jonathan's story. I assumed suave, confident, gorgeous Jonathan Blackrock was the type of man who went out on dates all the time. However, while I'm usually good at reading people, I was wrong about Jonathan's dating status. I wouldn't have guessed that Jonathan was guarding his heart, not unlike how I've been guarding mine. In fact, when Jonathan shared that part of his history with me, I could relate so well that I almost explained why and how I understood where he was coming from. But I didn't. I held back. I wasn't ready to talk about those feelings, which I'm just beginning to try to move on from, especially with someone I was only starting to get to know.

I break out of my thoughts when I remember Jonathan is still waiting for my reply to his question. I take another sip of my cider, and then I tell him:

"When it came time to apply for med school, I decided I needed a significant change in scenery." I cast Jonathan a sideways glance as we walk. He's observing me with unmasked curiosity. "I was . . . well, I was trying to get over someone, and putting some physical distance between him and me, and everything that reminded me of him, seemed like a good idea at the time."

Jonathan's eyebrows rise. "And by moving away for those four years, were you able to—"

"Oh my gosh, Doctor Vincent! Hi!"

I hear a gal's cheery greeting above the ambient din, and I snap my head forward, searching the crowds to identify the source of the voice. A second later, I spot Carrie Kennedy, one of the Lakewood ED nurses, waving enthusiastically to get my attention. As I wave back at her, I smile. Even from a distance, Carrie's enthusiasm is infectious. Carrie is a couple years younger than me, and between her young age, bubbly personality, and penchant for fashion, flirting, and manicures even while working in the grimy emergency department, I think some people might assume she's not as skilled or knowledgeable of a nurse as she is. The truth, however, is that Carrie does a fantastic job in the ED, and she does it all without breaking a nail. In fact, Carrie was one of the heroes in the ED during the earthquake that hit the Lakewood region a little over a year ago. Carrie, along with Rachel Nelson, who was only a med student at the time, and another ED nurse, Pete, kept some pretty sick patients alive while trapped in a nearly collapsed part of the building.

Carrie starts weaving a path along the crowded sidewalk to reach me. I see her hospital-issue scrubs under the chocolate-brown coat she's wearing, so I'm guessing she just got off a shift. I also discern that Carrie is wearing even more makeup than usual (which is saying something), and knowing Carrie as well as I do, it's a sure sign she's out with a group that includes the latest guy-of-the-week she's interested in.

Curiosity piqued, I flick my eyes over Carrie's shoulder to spot who she's out with. My heart does a skip of recognition when I see several more people from the Lakewood ED team. Like Carrie, the others in her group are also wearing scrubs, confirming they all decided to go out for dinner after their shift was over. Among the familiar faces, I see Henry Ingram, Maureen, Hadi, Tyler, Xavier . . .

And Grant.

Grant?

I stumble to a halt, nearly dropping my drink in the process, and I'm pretty sure my heart stops, too. Suddenly breathless, I shut and re-open my eyes, praying I'm only imagining things, but when I peer down the sidewalk again, Grant is still there. I gulp. My stomach sinks. My heart wakes back up and gives my chest a vigorous punch.

Yes, Grant really is out with the Lakewood group tonight.

And I'm really out with Jonathan Blackrock tonight.

And our paths are about to collide.

I get totally numb as I continue staring down the sidewalk. Grant hasn't noticed me yet. He's talking with Henry as he walks, every stride he takes bringing him nearer to me. Of course, Grant looks as handsome as ever tonight, dressed in a lightweight jacket, button-up shirt, and jeans. He has a casual air about him but a focused look brewing in his eyes. I can tell Grant is relaxed, yet for some reason, he's not completely so.

Jonathan comes up beside me, snapping me out of my shocked daze. My eyes start leaping between Jonathan and Grant. I then look again at Carrie and the rest of the Lakewood group. I sense myself go pale. My chest tightens.

Forget everything I said about this date going well. This date is most definitely not going well. At least, it won't be going well in five . . . four . . . three . . . two—

"Doctor Vincent, we've been missing you in the ED this month!" Carrie reaches me and gives me one of her smothering hugs. "Grant said you're doing your EMS rotation this month, too, and . . ."

Carrie gets quiet, and she slowly releases me from her hold. I realize that her gaze has shifted from me over to Jonathan, and her lips have formed into the shape of a small circle. Carrie stares at Jonathan for another long moment, and then she looks back at me and flashes a lightning-fast smile that unmistakably says, *Wow! You go, girl!*

Before I can react, Carrie introduces herself to Jonathan with her usual bubbly gusto. While Jonathan and Carrie go on politely discussing how they recognize each another from crossing paths in the ED, I'm rooted in place and completely mute. I'm holding a strained perma-smile on my face. My head is filling up with fog. While to any casual observer, I may look as though I'm enjoying the conversation with

Jonathan and Carrie, I'm not hearing a word of it. Instead, my apprehension is growing as I keep tracking Grant out of the corner of my eye. He and the rest of the Lakewood group are steadily drawing closer, like an approaching tsunami that's about to unleash its destruction.

Members of the Lakewood group start to notice that Carrie is talking to Jonathan and me, and with waves and friendly greetings, they hurry over to join us. As the lighthearted conversation rapidly expands around me, I'm still stealthily observing Grant. It isn't long before I see Grant break off from whatever he's saying to Henry and look over at the group. As soon as his eyes land on me, Grant does a double take and stops mid-stride. I don't move a muscle as I pretend not to be watching him in return. Finally, Grant pulls his gaze from me and scans the others, and his eyes come to a hard stop on Jonathan. I wait, barely breathing. At last, Grant rolls back his shoulders and starts walking over to join us.

I unfreeze. Everyone else is chatting without a care in the world. Meanwhile, I'm filling up with a cringe-worthy sense of dread. This is an epic disaster on so many levels. Even if Grant weren't here, this would still be a monumental mess. Why? Because Jonathan and I are about to become the newest subject of hospital gossip.

This is bad. This is extremely bad.

There's no gossip like hospital gossip. For whatever reason, hospitals breed a special type of rapidly spreading, emotionally charged, drama-filled, never-forgotten, point-of-no-return gossip that makes the scuttlebutt in any other workplace look like child's play. Yes, hospital gossip has no equal, and it's a creature that cannot be tamed. And at this very moment, several of my ED colleagues are discovering that I'm out on a date with one of Lakewood Fire & Rescue's paramedics. The fallout will be huge. The blizzard of gossip that's about to be unleashed in the ED and beyond will be unparalleled—and the rumors will draw even more interest because, up until now, I've been a drama-free gal who has given no one anything to gossip about.

Like I said, this is an absolute disaster.

I groan inwardly as I contemplate the fiasco to come. I'm barely getting my dating feet wet; I'm not ready to be inundated with questions about my love life from curious, nosy coworkers. I'm not skilled at ignoring embellished stories, speculations, and overly dramatic whispers in the workplace. I'm not ready for this at all . . . but it's too late to stop it now.

A nauseating sense of helplessness takes over me. The gossip is going to be awful, but it's nothing but the unpalatable icing on the catastrophe cake. The reality is that while being the newest gossip star is going to be a nightmare, running into Grant tonight is far, far worse. Seeing Grant is unleashing havoc upon my heart and mind.

Remind me why I decided to start dating again?

My stomach churns harder, and I press a hand upon my abdomen to dampen the sensation. I should have thought this through better. I should have asked Jonathan not to take me to a place where we would likely run into people who work in Lakewood's ED. I didn't think it through, though, and now Jonathan and I are smack in the middle of ED Hangout Central on a Saturday night.

Every possible catastrophic scenario of how this might finish playing out is crashing around in my mind. Normally, Grant and I steer clear of talking about each other's love lives too much, but we obviously won't be able to avoid talking about *this*. For crying out loud, Grant has run into me while I'm out on a date with Jonathan. Not to mention, Jonathan, Grant, and I will be crossing paths for rest of this month, and also in the ED in the future. So the mutual understanding that has always existed between Grant and me—the unwritten code that states we don't address each other's love lives in detail—will be impossible to adhere to this time.

My throat thickens. My chest gets heavy. Regret consumes me. This is only my first date since deciding to risk the pain and vulnerability of opening up my heart, and already some of my worst fears are coming true. Once again, romance is proving to be nothing but a set up for heartache . . . at least, that's how it always plays out for me.

Grant reaches the group and comes to a stop near where I'm standing. I keep shooting glances his way, desperately attempting to get a read on what he's thinking, but Grant's face reveals nothing. He doesn't even look at me. Instead, Grant's blue eyes become fixed on Jonathan again, and he calmly extends his hand and says:

"Good evening, Jonathan."

"Hello, Grant." Jonathan arches an eyebrow ever-so-slightly as he shakes Grant's hand in return.

Everyone else in the group happens to choose this particular moment to break off from their own conversations and turn to watch Grant and Jonathan. I moan inwardly, and in an attempt to quickly divert everyone's attention, I immediately turn to Grant and ask:

"How did your shift at the fire station go today?"

Grant seems to take his time putting his eyes on me. "It went well."

I wet my lips as I stare back at him. Grant remains in full-on cryptic mode, so my efforts to read him are futile. Meanwhile, Jonathan has been sucked back into conversation with the others, but his eyes are intermittently leaping over to Grant and me. As I take it all in, I want to curl up in a corner and cry. Everything is so wrong. So mixed up. I'm out on a date with Jonathan, yet every molecule of my being is drawn to Grant. Grant is the man I'm trying to get over, however, which is why I'm out on this disaster-of-a-date with Jonathan in the first place.

I'm flailing mentally as I concentrate on Grant again. "And, um, it obviously looks like you managed to catch up with the Lakewood gang after your EMS shift?"

Grant nods in the affirmative. His posture relaxes a little bit. "On one of our calls, we took a patient to Lakewood. There weren't any new attendings doing orientation shifts today, so more residents were covering the department. Henry let me know that he would be joining several of the residents, nurses, and techs at O'Flanagan's Pub after the ED shift was over, and I was invited to join in, too."

I sense my smile easing into something more natural. "I'm glad you got to go. After all, the pub is one of your favorite spots, and I know you would never pass up an opportunity to—

"Yeah, I'm so glad you were able to join us tonight, Grant!" Carrie unexpectedly interjects. She slides to Grant's side, puts a hand on his arm, and bats her perfectly curled lashes. "Isn't O'Flanagan's, like, one of your favorite places around here?"

Instantly, my expression goes stone-like. My gaze begins shifting between Grant's face and Carrie's hand on his muscular arm. My nostrils flare.

Carrie is flirting with Grant.

I do not like that Carrie is flirting with Grant.

A split-second later, I mentally shake myself to my senses. I have no right to be upset if Carrie or anyone else flirts with Grant. For one thing, Grant and I have never been anything but friends. For another thing, there is the slightly important detail that *I'm currently out on a date with Jonathan Blackrock.* So it's not exactly like I have any sort of claim to get protective about Grant at the moment.

I exhale a silent breath. If I'm going to return to the dating world, I'm going to have to toughen up and accept the angst, twisted emotions, and gut-wrenching difficulties that come along with it.

Maybe I should have entered a convent instead.

Grant turns toward Carrie, and his smile becomes more formal. "You're right: the pub is definitely one of my favorites." He puts his eyes back on mine, and a hint of humor appears in his countenance. "Except they didn't have bangers and mash on the menu tonight," he tells me, the corners of his mouth twitching upward. "So that was a bit of a tragedy."

Completely disarmed by Grant's humor, my smile returns, and I put a hand to my chest in feigned horror. "Oh no! Whatever did you do without your beloved bangers and mash?"

Grant chuckles. "I barely managed to survive by eating something else."

I start laughing along with him, and the familiar, reassuring, wonderful sound of our mixed laughter is music to my ears. Instead of anxious, I become content and thrilled and happy. Because when Grant is with me, I know everything is going to be all right.

My laughter dies away, as does Grant's. Our eyes meet once more. Suddenly, and without warning or explanation, our gazes lock with a new, fiery intensity that's unlike any look we've shared before. My respirations stutter, and something like lightning zings my spine. Grant continues peering directly into my eyes. I sense heat rising up from my core while a magnetic force seems to keep our gazes intertwined. I—

"Well, it has been great to see everyone tonight," I hear Jonathan loudly state. "Glad we ran into all of you."

Jonathan's voice yanks me back to awareness of the world around me. I pull my eyes from Grant to look Jonathan's way. Jonathan glances at me and then over at Grant, and then he focuses on the rest of the group while displaying his captivatingly confident smile.

"Again, thanks for coming over to chat," Jonathan adds.

"Wait a second, Blackrock, are you trying to get rid of us?" Hadi pipes up with a scheming grin. "Are you saying you don't want to hang out while you're out on a date with Doctor Vincent?"

I blush. Everyone laughs . . . everyone but Grant, that is. Grant's expression is back to being totally undecipherable as he observes the exchange.

Jonathan is laughing in a low, rumbling way at Hadi's humor. "Hey, I'm not saying I don't enjoy your company, Hadi, but under the current circumstances . . ."

Jonathan lets himself pointedly trail off. There's another round of laughter from the Lakewood folks as they take the hint, call out farewells to Jonathan and me, and leave us behind while they resume heading down the sidewalk. I force a smile and say some generic goodbyes without actually making eye contact with anyone. As if drawn there, though, my gaze eventually drifts Grant's direction. Grant gives me a tip of his head before he walks off to rejoin the others. Immediately, I long for Grant to be back at my side, but I tell myself to ignore the sensation. I'm out on a date with Jonathan. I can't dwell on Grant.

Jonathan turns toward me. He's still smiling, though there is something pensive in his look. "So now that we've conversed with half of Lakewood's emergency department, may I interest you in some dessert? An ice cream sundae, perhaps?"

His question finishes pulling me out of my distracted state. I'm out on a date with Jonathan, and I must focus on that. I force myself to mentally shift gears, getting my head back in the dating game.

"Ice cream? Really?" I echo, infusing levity into my tone. "Don't get me wrong, I love ice cream, but we already had dessert at the restaurant—and I certainly don't mind mentioning yet again that the pumpkin-cranberry cheesecake was marvelous."

Jonathan's smile takes on new life. "True. However, the fact remains that we haven't had ice cream from the best place in town yet, and I'm pretty sure there's some sort of rule or law that says we have to eat ice cream tonight."

"Hmm." I playfully tap a finger on my chin, as though I'm thinking hard. "I believe you're right about the must-have-ice-cream rule. And I obviously don't want to break any rules."

"Good." Jonathan laughs. "I was hoping you would say that."

Jonathan glances up and down the street, and then he puts a hand lightly on my low back as we dash across the road to reach the ice cream parlor. Jonathan's touch is brief, but based on the searching glance he gives me before he lowers his arm back to his side, I sense there was much his gesture was intended to convey. I might not be a dating expert, but I do read people well, and I believe Jonathan's touch was a careful check to see how I would react to him doing so.

And how, exactly, am I reacting?

My mind speeds up as I attempt to analyze the way I'm responding to Jonathan's unspoken question. How did the sensation of his hand upon my back make me feel?

I can't tell. I don't feel . . . anything, really. Once again, the love-computer in my brain has crashed, leaving me aimlessly drifting on the dating sea without navigation.

Noise from up ahead brings me back to the moment. As always, no matter the weather or the time of day, there's a line of people stretching out the door of the ice cream parlor and running halfway down the block. For good reason, too. This place serves the most delicious ice cream ever created, and the options of flavors include both scrumptious mainstays and rotating seasonal tastes that can't be found anywhere else. Not to mention, the shop's mouth-watering aromas of ice cream and freshly baked waffle cones float out the door like a tractor beam, pulling even more people toward it. On top of all that, the shop itself is adorably attractive, with its trademark, turn-of-the-century pink-and-white motif.

Jonathan and I take our place at the back of the line. I'm thankful the herds of people around us are keeping the ambient noise level so high that it doesn't feel weird that Jonathan and I don't say much while we wait. While Jonathan is a great conversationalist, and I'm genuinely enjoying and feeling comfortable in his company, it's also nice to have a break in the dialogue to collect my thoughts and sort through everything that has happened. However, I still find that I'm not able to make heads or tails of much of anything. My mind is over-analyzing, and my heart is over-reacting. The end result is that I remain a confused mess of thought and emotion.

Jonathan and I make it to the front of the line and enter the shop, where we're greeted by the warmth of the indoors and the heightened scents of ice cream cones, chocolate, and all things sugary. We order, Jonathan pays, and then he and I slip back outside. Soon, we're again meandering along the sidewalk, listening to the music that's being performed inside various restaurants while enjoying our second dessert of the night. Eventually, we find ourselves approaching the sprawling park that's part of this area of town. Like the shops and restaurants we've left behind, the park is filled with people and illuminated by the cozy glow of lampposts that line the pathways.

Jonathan takes another bite of his dark chocolate concoction before asking me, "So what do you think of your pumpkin ice cream?"

I dab the corner of my mouth with my napkin. "It's delicious. Mark this down as yet another reason why I'm going to miss fall once the Christmas season officially rolls around." I sneak another lick of the dark orange deliciousness. "Please don't mistake me, though: while I adore autumn, I love the holidays, too. Including all things peppermint."

Jonathan chuckles. "I'll take that under advisement."

My insides jump, and the effect is so pronounced that I have to wait before taking another bite of my ice cream. I may be reading far too much into Jonathan's last remark, but it sure seems to me like there's future-oriented thinking woven into it. It's like Jonathan is quietly implying—

"I have a question for you, which I hope won't come across as too forward." Jonathan tosses the remnants of his waffle cone into a waste bin, and then he fixes a more serious look upon me.

My eyebrows rise as I continue walking alongside him. "That sounds ominous."

Jonathan's serious expression relents, and he laughs slightly. "No. At least, I hope it's not."

Jonathan is still chuckling as he stops in his tracks. I do the same. We face each other. Jonathan draws in a breath, and his features take on a serious look once more. My insides twist with a strange sense of anticipation and nerves, and my mind is already constructing a list of possibilities of where this conversation is going.

"Elly," Jonathan resumes, "I first want you to know that I've really enjoyed getting to know you while we've been spending time together at the station, and I've also been having a great time with you tonight."

I think there's ice cream melting down the side of my cone and onto my fingers, but I'm hardly paying attention. Instead, I'm replaying Jonathan's words in my mind and deciding how I should reply. There are a thousand things I could say to him, but I want to make absolutely sure that whatever I tell Jonathan is both clear and honest. After observing countless friends' dating exploits over the years, one thing I decided was that game-playing, ambiguity, or dishonesty is not good in any stage of a relationship.

I clear my throat. "I've enjoyed getting to know you, too," I tell him honestly.

Jonathan nods, but his demeanor still comes across as guarded. "And please forgive me for sounding forward, but you're not . . . interested in anyone else, right?"

I was not expecting that. My eyebrows blast upward, and I take a step back from him.

"W-what?" I sputter.

Jonathan's eyes widen. "Wait, that came out wrong. I'm sorry. I didn't mean it like that. I didn't mean to imply . . ." He exhales hard and looks away. After a few seconds, he focuses on me again. There's a deep crease between his brows. "I'm making a mess of this, aren't I?"

I slowly wipe off the melted ice cream from my hand. "No, you're not making a mess of this." I toss my napkin into the waste bin, and I do my best to lighten the mood. "My ice cream, however, is most definitely a mess."

Jonathan ventures another smile. "The reason I'm a bumbling fool right now is because . . . that is, what I'm trying to say is that I would like to continue getting to know you, and I hope you're interested in getting to know me better, too."

I swallow. Now what am I supposed to say? How am I supposed to feel in this moment? Jonathan apparently knows he wants to continue dating me. Should I already know if I want to keep dating him, too? Does the fact that I have no idea tell me something? Is it okay not to be sure? Or is that a bad sign?

I attempt to work though this logically. I like Jonathan, and other than the epic disaster of running into Grant and the Lakewood crowd earlier this evening, I've enjoyed our date thus far. So really, if I think about it, I have no reason why I shouldn't go out again with this hot, nice guy who has a stable job and who's showing romantic interest in me. Is that enough, though? Is that enough to indicate this is potentially the start of something special?

You weren't uncertain when you met Grant. You knew. You knew as soon as you met him that you loved him.

With a silent sigh of frustration, I shove aside the voice in my head once more. I'm not with Grant, and I can't and won't ever be with Grant, so I need to stop holding him up for comparison.

How can you deny your feelings for Grant, though, especially after what just transpired between the two of you a few minutes ago?

My cheeks flush at the memory. My heart stirs. Yes, that look Grant and I shared was . . . well, it was unlike anything that has ever transpired between us before. It was intense. It was real. It was . . . *passionate.*

Wasn't it?

No, it wasn't. At least, it wasn't for Grant. So once again, I face the same choice: either I can continue dwelling on what's never going to be, or I can attempt to learn more about the possibility that's right in front of me.

"I . . ." I pause to steady my voice. "I think I would like to get to know you better, too." I dare to breathe again while I continue choosing my words carefully. "I would like to take things slowly, since I'm newly re-entering the dating scene myself, but if you're comfortable with that, then yes, I would enjoy getting to know you better."

I finish by exhaling another silent breath. I'm getting no help from the love-computer in my brain, but I think my reply was all right. I was honest, I established boundaries, and I didn't play games. At least, that's how I hope Jonathan has interpreted what I said.

Thankfully, the gleam has fully returned to Jonathan's dark eyes. He nods, and with confidence back in his tone, he says:

"That's great. So I want to ask: would you do me the honor of being my date for the Lakewood Fire & Rescue gala at the end of the month?"

My mouth falls open. The gala? I'm not going to lie, the gala sounds like it's going to be amazing. I'm honored Jonathan has asked me. That being said, the fancy gala also seems like something that couples would only attend together if they've reached "official relationship" status. Or am I wrong about that?

There's also the not-so-tiny issue of the politics behind it all. If I go to the gala with Jonathan, nearly all of Lakewood Fire & Rescue's personnel will see us there together. On a date. Looking like an official couple whether we're official or not. In other words, a whole gaggle of EMS providers who regularly bring patients to the Lakewood ED will know there's something developing between Jonathan and me, and this also means there will be more people to stoke the hospital-gossip fire. The rumors will reach inferno levels . . . ironic, really, considering this whole situation started with a trained firefighter to begin with.

What am I supposed to do? Do I let my fears of gossip and rumors interfere? No, I can't let those things stop me. I'm not hiding away my heart any longer. I've made the choice to explore romance, even with the risks and downsides the process will inevitably bring. I need to stop dwelling on what can't be. I have to learn more about my own heart and search out what real, tangible possibilities might be out there. I have to accept that it's impossible to find romance without experiencing some tough stuff along the way first.

"I would be delighted to go with you to the gala," I hear myself tell Jonathan.

Immediately, and in spite of myself, something tugs at my heart.

What have I gotten myself into?

Eleven

"All right, I'm officially finished reviewing my half of the latest batch of charts," I announce proudly as I make a few final, intentionally exaggerated strokes on the keyboard to emphasize my comment. "And I'm done entering the data from those charts, too."

When Grant doesn't reply, I shift in my chair to look his way. We're seated at side-by-side computer workstations in one of Station Fourteen's large, comfortable, high-tech office areas. We've been in here for the past few hours, working on our EMS project. Though neither of us has a shift today, we opted to meet at the station, since navigating the agency's electronic medical record system goes faster from here than when doing so remotely from home. Thanks to the fast connection to the electronic medical record, Grant and I have been plowing through numerous charts of the most recent potential stroke patients that the agency's crews have cared for.

Grant is remaining quiet as he returns my gaze. He blinks at me a few times. He then glances with deliberateness down at his watch, puts his eyes back on mine, and unexpectedly breaks into a grin. "I finished my batch of charts six minutes ago. I win."

"What?" I huff with feigned frustration before I let myself laugh. "Fine. You win this round. If I had that old fifty-cent piece, I would hand it over to you as the trophy."

Grant's grin fades. He pushes back from the desk and gets to his feet. As I observe him, my heart dances. I can't help it. Even when he's dressed casually in a baseball cap, t-shirt, and jeans, Grant still manages to take my breath away. Grant is . . . well, he's simply . . .

I intercept my own thoughts before they run away on me. I need to redirect my mind. I'm working on healing my heart and moving on. I have to accept that Grant and I are only friends. And I most definitely can't keep dreaming about that look we shared the other night when we met on the sidewalk.

"I'm going to go grab a drink from the refrigerator." Grant is all-business now as he motions briskly to the door. "Do you want anything? The BLS crew members told me that we're welcome to anything they have in there."

I sigh to myself when I hear the return of the uncharacteristic edge to Grant's tone. Other than that short, playful exchange we just shared, Grant has been acting strangely all day. It's hard to articulate exactly what's off with him, but something is different. He's acting like himself, yet he isn't acting like himself at all. There's a subtle-but-palpable abruptness about him today, and I don't know why. I'm not even sure when his crummy mood started, since I haven't seen Grant since our paths collided last Saturday while I was out on the date with Jonathan.

"Thanks for asking," I reply, "but I've got a couple drinks stashed in my bag, so I'm okay."

Grant nods once and makes a move for the door.

"Before you go, though," I can't resist calling after him, "are you ever going to tell me what's bothering you today?"

Grant comes to a stop. He keeps his back to me, facing the door. I can see the tension in his muscles, and the way his upper body is rising and falling with his deliberate respirations.

"What makes you think there's something bothering me?" he asks in a low voice.

"Well, for one thing, you're not looking at me," I point out dryly. "So let's start there."

Grant turns around and puts his eyes on mine. "Okay, I'm looking at you."

I adopt an I'm-not-letting-you-off-that-easily kind of expression. Standing up, I cross my arms over my chest. "Seriously, what's wrong? Are you all right?"

The muscles of Grant's jaw start working. He looks away, pulls off his baseball cap, and uses one hand to restlessly rustle his hair. Slapping his hat back onto his head, Grant concentrates on me once more.

"Well, if you insist on knowing," Grant finally replies, "I guess I'm surprised by whom you were out on a date with the other night."

My mouth drops. Grant is upset about my date with Jonathan? I'm so taken aback by this revelation that it takes me several seconds before I'm able to formulate a coherent reply.

"Why is it such a surprise to you?" I demand, my mind buzzing. "More importantly, why does it bother you?"

"It doesn't bother me," Grant retorts immediately. "It's just that . . . well, you hardly know the guy, El."

I stare him. Grant and I are starting to venture onto never-before-treaded ground. We've never dissected or criticized one another's love lives before. This is completely uncharted territory, and I'm swiftly growing uneasy because I have no sense of where this conversation will lead.

"True, I don't know Jonathan well yet," I state, doing my best to sound calm and unruffled. "But isn't the point of dating someone to get to know the other person better?"

Grant sighs and uses one hand to massage his forehead. "In theory, yes. Of course." He drops his arm back to his side and fixes a stern look upon me. "However, that doesn't mean you should rush out and date the first guy who asks you, El. You have to take the situation into consideration. You—"

"Wait, what did you just say?" I cut him off. My eyes get big. "Are you suggesting that I just rushed out to date the first guy who asked me? As if I didn't put any thought into it? As if I'm that pathetic? As if I'm that desperate?" My throat thickens. Hurt is welling up inside me.

"Do you have any idea how completely insulting your comment was, Grant?"

Grant's brows snap together. "You're misinterpreting what I said. What I'm trying to say is that—"

Behind Grant, the door to the office gets opened. I hastily look over Grant's shoulder to see who's coming into the room.

Jonathan appears in the doorway.

"Hey, Doctor Vincent." Jonathan is grinning playfully at me. "I came to help orient a new paramedic, and when I saw your car in the parking lot, I . . ." His eyes shift to Grant. His grin vanishes. "Oh. Sorry, I didn't realize you were in here with anyone."

"It's all right," I eke out. My chest hurts so much that I can hardly speak. "You're not interrupting anything."

I look again at Grant. His jaw is clenched. He holds my eyes with an intense gaze for one more second, and then, in a blink, his expression goes deadpan. Pulling his eyes from mine, he turns around to face Jonathan.

"Hello, Paramedic Blackrock," Grant says, his tone empty.

Jonathan's eyes are slightly narrowed. "Hello, Doctor Reed."

I stare at the two of them. I don't understand the dynamic that's festering in here, but I do know that some tension needs to be released before this whole room explodes. So I hurriedly grab my coat off the back of the chair, and I blurt out:

"Well, I guess it's about time for me to head out." I smile casually at Grant, as though absolutely nothing is wrong. "I think we did a great job getting caught up on charts today. Thanks for all your help."

Both Grant and Jonathan turn my way. Grant looks right into my eyes. Jonathan's narrowed gaze is shifting between Grant and me. Pretending like Grant didn't just drive a dagger of hurt and humiliation into my heart, I turn to my desk and log out of the computer. I pick up my bag, face Grant again, and add:

"This evening, I'll start graphing out our latest data, so we can see how things with the crews are evolving so far."

"Sounds good," Grant replies without emotion. He steps over to his computer and logs out. "In the meantime, I'll start putting together the outline for our written report."

"Great." I make my way to the door. "I'll talk to you later, then."

"Elly," Jonathan interjects, his eyes still tracking Grant, "I'll walk you to your car."

I hesitate before slowing my pace. "Thanks."

I step out of the office with Jonathan at my side. Neither Jonathan nor I say anything as we walk down the foyer and out the station's front door. With every step I take, however, I can feel my emotions rising, and I know I don't have long before the dam will burst. I pick up my pace as Jonathan and I cross the parking lot to reach my vehicle. I hurriedly thank Jonathan for walking me to my car, hop into the driver' seat, close my door, turn over the engine, and drive away.

The dam finally cracks, and tears cascade down my cheeks. Of all the awkward, painful, embarrassing emotions I just experienced, I'm not sure what hurts the most: Grant's humiliating remark about me rushing out to date someone, or the fact that what he said might be true.

Twelve

"Sixty-seven-year-old male. Longstanding history of COPD and hypertension. Developed increased work of breathing with shortness of breath last night, and symptoms have been getting worse ever since." The lead firefighter glances at the patient before continuing report. "Upon our arrival, the patient was able to speak only in short sentences. Respiratory rate in the thirties. Systolic of one-eighty. Tachycardic. Sat of eighty-one percent."

Steve, Jonathan, and I have just entered the tiny basement apartment of our newest patient, and we're making our way through the cluttered front room to join the BLS crew members who are attending to the gentleman. The ceiling is low in here. The stagnant air is saturated with the stench of cigarette smoke. The drapes are pulled shut over the windows, casting everything into shadow, but as I glance around, I can see massive piles of . . . *stuff* . . . everywhere.

I move into the corner to watch the scene unfold. The patient is perched on the edge of his recliner chair, bent forward at the waist and visibly working hard to breathe. The man's lips and the area around his mouth are pale. His eyes are wide. Even though the man's television is on at a high volume, I can hear the patient wheezing with each of his prolonged exhalations.

Jonathan uses a foot to kick aside some of the discarded fast-food wrappers and cigarette boxes that are piled up around the base of the patient's chair, and then he gets down on one knee beside the patient while asking the lead firefighter:

"Meds or allergies?"

"He's supposed to be using an inhaler, but he reports that he ran out of his medication weeks ago and hasn't gotten into his regular physician to obtain a refill," the firefighter replies. "He also ran out of his blood pressure medicine, but he doesn't recall the name of it."

The paramedics get to work, going about their tasks in a fast, coordinated rhythm. This time, it's Jonathan who starts prepping to place an IV in the patient's arm, and Steve is using the stethoscope to ascultate the patient's heart and lungs. Meanwhile, one of the BLS crew members obtains a new set of vitals, confirming the patient's oxygen level remains extremely low at eighty-two percent. As I watch, my sense of concern for the patient grows. His COPD may have flared up simply because he hasn't been taking his regular medications. Or the patient may have an infection that has exacerbated his underlying chronic lung disease. It's also possible he has a clot or fluid in his lungs, or even a cardiac event manifesting in a pulmonary way. His hypertension may also be playing a role here, either as the cause of his symptoms or the end result of something else that's going on. The list of possible issues with this gentleman is long, but one thing is certain: he needs further workup and care emergently.

"IV is in," Jonathan announces, turning on his knee to reach into the bag of supplies. "I'll draw up solumedrol."

"Copy," Steve replies. "I'm starting a first dose of nebulized albuterol now."

Steve dispenses a small amount of the liquid medication into a little chamber that's attached to the bottom of a clear mask. He places the mask over the patient's nose and mouth, which allows the patient to start inhaling the medicine as it's nebulized. Jonathan administers a dose of steroid into the patient's IV, and then he raises his voice to be heard over the hiss of the nebulizer and the commotion of WWF wrestling reruns playing on the television, and he goes on speaking to his partner:

"Once you're done with that first neb, Falco, I'll get this guy on supplemental oxygen so we can get his sat up to at least ninety-five percent."

I snap to heightened attention and open my mouth to say something, but I stop myself. Closing my mouth once more, I retreat back into my corner, nearly stumbling over a life-size cardboard cutout of Don Knotts, stacks of faded magazines that are piled so high they nearly touch the ceiling, piles of garbage, and several long-abandoned litter boxes. Resuming my silent observation of the events playing out before me, I have to remind myself that I'm only here as an observer. I'm not the doctor who's caring for this patient. I shouldn't intervene unless it becomes absolutely necessary.

Steve nods to Jonathan before looking over at the BLS crew members. "We'll transport him to Lakewood."

"Sounds good," the lead firefighter replies.

The other two firefighters take the cue to bring in the stretcher. They start maneuvering around the waist-high mounds of cardboard boxes, broken toys, crinkled newspapers, and dirty clothing that fill the apartment, following the narrow path that permits access to the front door. While the firefighters depart the room, Steve explains to the patient the recommendation for transport, and the patient nods his agreement while adjusting the mask that's sitting on his face. When the dose of nebulized albuterol is done, Steve removes the mask from the patient, glances at the monitor, and tells Jonathan:

"Sat now eighty-six percent."

Jonathan promptly puts a nasal cannula on the patient, securing the thin plastic tubing against the base of the patient's skull while making sure the cannula's two little prongs are situated properly at the lower edge of the patient's nostrils. Moving fast, Jonathan attaches the free end of the cannula to the portable oxygen machine, and he reaches down to turn on the oxygen.

"Excuse me, Paramedic Blackrock," I hear myself calmly interject. "There's one quick clarification to make before turning on the oxygen."

Jonathan pauses, his hand hovering right above the bright green oxygen canister. Just then, the two firefighters return with the stretcher, and more noise fills the room as they begin clearing out a wider path to get the stretcher to the patient. It seems to take Jonathan another beat before he puts his eyes on mine. Steve follows his gaze, also turning toward me. The firefighters stop what they're doing and turn my way, too.

"Yes, Doctor Vincent?" Jonathan asks in monotone.

I pause, surprised to detect irritation radiating out of Jonathan. Then again, perhaps I'm not entirely taken aback by Jonathan's response. After all, I am supposed to be just an observer here. Plus, most people don't enjoy being corrected, especially in front of their peers, and I'm guessing that assertive, confident paramedics who are used to running the scene are no exception to this rule. Not to mention, there's an added layer of complication to the dynamic between Jonathan and me, since our relationship isn't solely professional anymore. I suspect Jonathan wants to impress me with his work, not have me point out suggestions for improvement. So for several reasons, I guess I can understand why there's friction coming from Jonathan's general direction at the moment.

It doesn't mean I have to like it, though. Besides, part of what comes with providing medical care in any setting is being constantly questioned, critiqued, corrected, and even complained about, whether or not the feedback is warranted, timely, necessary, fair, or accurate. For good and for bad, an almost never-ending onslaught of feedback is part of the healthcare gig, and no matter one's role or level of experience, a healthcare provider has to accept this reality and deal with it. Likewise, healthcare providers who are in a teaching or supervising capacity must also learn the art of effectively— yet respectfully and helpfully—providing feedback to others in the profession.

Regardless, I can't worry about drama, ego, or relationship issues right now. I can't worry about the fact that Jonathan and I went out on that date, or that we have another date—a big date to the agency gala—on the books. Right now, I'm acting in the capacity of a physician whose role is to observe, teach, and ensure a patient gets the best care possible.

I take another step closer to the group. "As a quick matter of clarification: do we know what this gentleman's baseline oxygen sat is, and if he's on supplemental oxygen regularly?"

Before anyone else can answer, the patient himself pipes up:

"Ninety percent," the patient tells us. He's still working hard to breathe, but not as badly as he was before he received the first nebulizer treatment. "My sat is usually . . . ninety percent, whenever . . . the doctors check it. I . . . refuse to use . . . home oxygen."

I glance again at the cigarette butts that litter the floor. In one regard, I'm sort of relieved this gentleman refuses to use supplemental oxygen. I'm no chemist, but I'm pretty sure it's not the best idea to inhale concentrated oxygen while simultaneously using an open flame to light a cigarette. The crazy thing, though, is that I've seen plenty of hospital patients doing it. Every day, patients are sitting outside the hospital in their wheelchairs, smoking while also using supplemental oxygen. I'm grateful that I haven't witnessed anyone wind up as a fireball as a result.

"Thank you, sir," I tell the patient. I look at the crew members. "Since his oxygen level improved after that first neb, but he's still audibly wheezing, let's proceed with administering another nebulizer. Also, so as not to delay transport to the hospital, we'll talk more about the oxygen situation while we're in route to the ED."

The BLS crew members get to work helping the patient climb onto the stretcher. Steve gives me a fast smile before he begins prepping another dose of albuterol to administer to the patient through the mask. Jonathan observes me for another second, a deep crease between his brows, and then he starts packing up supplies. I retreat to give everyone more space to work, and then I shift my eyes Jonathan's way, hoping to get a better read on what he's thinking. However, Jonathan doesn't look at me again, so I can't get a sense of what's going through his mind.

Once the patient is secured on the stretcher and Steve has the second neb running through the mask, the BLS crew pushes the patient out the door, guiding the stretcher along the widened path that they carved through the mess. I follow the crews outside. There are now crowds gathered on the sidewalk. Unruffled by the onlookers, the crews move fast, and it doesn't take long for the patient to be safely situated in the back of the ambulance. Steve and I climb into the back of the rig with the patient. Jonathan hops into the driver's seat and turns over the ignition.

"Hey, Doc?"

I look out the back of the ambulance. The lead firefighter is standing there, ready to shut our doors for us.

"I would love to hear more about your thoughts on the treatment of COPD patients sometime," the firefighter tells me.

I smile. "Absolutely. Any time."

The lead firefighter gives me a friendly smile in return before she shuts the back doors of our rig with gusto. Jonathan shifts his headset into place, pulls the ambulance away from the curb, and begins steering past the bystanders. A few seconds later, we've pulled out of the apartment complex, and we're en route to Lakewood Medical Center.

As the ambulance picks up speed, I glance through the window that gives a view of the cab, taking the opportunity to look at Jonathan as he drives. His posture is stiff, and his forehead is creased. I exhale a hard breath. Yes, something about what happened back there in the apartment is definitely bothering him. I'll have to—

Jonathan's gaze unexpectedly flicks to the rearview mirror. Our eyes meet. Before I can react, Jonathan shifts his concentration back to the road.

Pulling my eyes away from the cab, and the extremely hot paramedic who's in the driver's seat there, I return my focus to the patient. He's finishing up his second neb, and he appears much more comfortable. His latest sat shows he's up to eighty-nine percent, so we're getting close to his baseline. All good signs.

Seated on the bench opposite me, Steve is currently on his phone with the Lakewood ED, providing them report about the incoming patient. When Steve ends his call, he puts away his phone, slides his headset back into place, and looks over at me.

"So, Doc, what were you going to say back there about COPD patients?" Steve asks through the headset.

Out of the corner of my eye, I notice Jonathan's gaze dart again to the rearview mirror.

I clear my throat, morphing into teaching mode. "The respiratory physiology of a patient who has COPD is believed to be different than a patient who doesn't have COPD. Some theorize that a COPD patient's body is accustomed to chronically elevated levels of carbon dioxide, and therefore the patient's drive to breathe is triggered by lower levels of oxygen instead. Those who follow this theory teach that giving a COPD patient too much oxygen could actually depress his or her respiratory drive and inadvertently make a bad situation worse." I shrug slightly. "However, others theorize that a COPD patient's respiratory drive is driven more by what's called the Haldane Effect, and there are others who think it's mostly dictated by what's referred to as the V-Q mismatch. So we may not understand or know for sure." I adjust my headset, acutely aware that Jonathan is hearing every word I'm saying. "Personally, unless someone is in severe respiratory distress, when I'm treating a COPD patient, I aim initially to get his or her oxygen level back to whatever that person's baseline sat is, since that's presumably what the patient's body is accustomed to."

Steve breaks into a smile, and I can almost see the wheels turning in his brain. "That's fascinating stuff, Doc. Thank you."

There's a conspicuous break in the conversation when Jonathan fails to add a reply. Steve seems to notice, too, because he glances toward his partner before cycling another set of vitals on the patient. As the quiet drags on, I sit back on my bench and silently huff out a breath—probably with enough force to cause my own carbon dioxide levels to temporarily shift. I don't care that Jonathan didn't reply to my teaching moment. I do care, however, that everything suggests Jonathan is legitimately bothered by what happened during this patient encounter. While I can understand Jonathan's reaction to some degree, it doesn't sit completely well with me.

I emerge from my thoughts when Jonathan pulls into the ambulance bay at Lakewood. I pull of my headset, open the back doors of the rig, hop out, and move aside. Jonathan gets out of the driver's seat, shuts his door, and jogs past me to help Steve get the patient's stretcher out of the ambulance. Jonathan then pushes the patient's stretcher inside. Steve follows. I trail behind them.

"Good morning," Kathy calls to us from the charge nurse's station, letting us know she's running the show for the shift. "I assume this is the gentleman with COPD?"

"That's correct," Jonathan replies.

Kathy glances at the patient tracking board that she has open on her computer monitor. "Looks like you can take him to Room Eighteen."

I give Kathy a smile before following the paramedics down the busy corridor. As we go, the curtain leading into Room Eighteen is drawn back from the inside, revealing that one of the ED techs, Penny Cavanagh, is waiting to help us. Penny is only in her mid-twenties, but she's excellent at her job. She has a friendly-yet-determined gleam in her brown eyes, the curls in her brown hair appear perpetually spring-loaded, and she's so short that she has to roll up the legs of her scrubs so they won't drag on the floor when she walks.

"Respiratory therapy is on the way," Penny announces as Jonathan wheels the patient into the room.

I enter the room behind the others, slide out of the way, and assess the situation. Dr. Jesse Santiago, another of the ED's super attending physicians, is standing near the cardiac monitor. Beside him is a guy I've never seen before; the guy is dressed in black scrubs and a long white doctor's coat. He's really lean in a fit-appearing way. He has sandy blond hair, which is slightly messy, and a goatee. His brown eyes are big with energy and interest as they shift fast around the room. I almost grin at the sight of him. Though I've never met this guy, I think I already have pretty good sense for what makes him tick: he's got the recognizable look of someone who obsessively rides mountain bikes, loves extreme sports, and considers energy drinks a basic food group . . . in other words, he's one of those high-intensity people who, if they decide to go into the medical profession, inevitably decide on emergency medicine. I steal a peek at his badge:

Lee Molloy, MD
Emergency Medicine Attending Physician

Yep, as I suspected, he's one of our new ED attendings, and it looks like he's being trained by Dr. Santiago today.

Jonathan begins providing the ED team with report. While he speaks, the nurse gets the patient connected to the cardiac monitor and then begins drawing blood from the patient's IV. Someone from respiratory therapy arrives, exchanges a fast look with the physicians, and starts the patient on another nebulizer treatment. Penny sets up to obtain an ECG. A tech from radiology appears outside the room and waits with the portable x-ray machine, which he'll use to get an image of the patient's chest.

Jonathan finishes report, and he and Steve drive their now-empty stretcher out of the room. I give Dr. Santiago and the others on the ED team a quick smile before I exit to chase after the ALS crew. As I step out of the room, letting the curtain swing shut behind me, I glance around the overcrowded corridor. Steve is heading over to a corner, clearly trying to find a place where he can hear while he talks on his work phone. Jonathan is pushing the stretcher out the door that leads to the ambulance bay. If Jonathan is aware that I'm not anywhere nearby, he doesn't seem to care. I feel a pang of something I can't quite identify. Hurt? Disappointment? Frustration? It's hard to say.

Still distractedly observing Jonathan, I make a move toward the ambulance bay to join him, but I wind up nearly crashing into a man who suddenly emerges from around a curtain of another exam room.

"Oh, hey, Elly," I hear the man say in a deep, familiar voice.

I grin and look up at tall, naturally commanding Dylan Gillespie, one of the third-year residents. Dylan is observing me with his classic impossible-to-read expression. When I first started residency, Dylan's trademark look intimidated me. I've since learned, however, that Dylan is one of the coolest and nicest guys out there. Also, at this current moment, Dylan is displaying the remnants of what was undoubtedly a very enviable tan, much like Savannah and Dr. Kent. Not that Dylan's tan is surprising. After all, it was his younger sister, Danielle, who was the bride at the recent beach wedding.

"Hi, Dylan," I greet him in return. "How are you?"

"I'm well, thanks. I take it you're on your EMS rotation?"

I nod.

"Grant is on the rotation, too, isn't he?" Dylan's expression still gives away nothing.

I nod again, more slowly this time. Something painful stabs at my heart as I'm reminded of the last interaction I had with Grant. What happened the other day at the fire station has been weighing heavily upon me every moment since. I know Grant would never mean to hurt me, but his words cut deeply. That whole discussion with Grant felt terribly strained and wrong. I—

I suddenly remember that Dylan is standing beside me. Clearing my throat, I decide to change the subject of our conversation.

"Hey, I heard your sister's wedding was incredible." I smile. "Congratulations to you and your family."

"Thanks." Dylan shows a smile in return. "It was great. I'm really happy for her."

My inner romantic is now awake, and so I can't resist asking, "And of course, I have to inquire if—"

"Doctor Gillespie, please come to Room Four," Carrie's voice blares out from the ED's ancient PA system. "Doctor Gillespie, please come to Room Four."

Dylan glances up at the overhead speakers and then puts his concentration back on me. "I guess I should go check on that." He begins backing up. "It was nice seeing you, Elly. Hope the rotation is going well for you."

Dylan turns away and starts walking through the fray, headed for Room Four. Looking past him, I can see Carrie standing in the entryway of the room. She has a concerned furrow to her brow as she waits for Dylan to reach her. Carrie has good clinical judgment, so if she's worried enough to call the doctor into the room, there's something bad going on in there. Whatever the issue may be, I hope the patient will be okay.

Admittedly, as I observe Carrie, I also can't help thinking about something that has been on my mind for a week now: did Grant notice the way Carrie was flirting with him last Saturday night? More importantly, did Grant *like* the fact that Carrie was flirting with him? What happened after I saw them that night? Did—

No, I can't do this. I can't worry about to whom Grant may or may not be attracted. I'm moving on. I'm leaving behind all the years of silently loving Grant without being loved in return. And if I need any further validation that I'm making the right choice, all I need to do is think back to the humiliating remark Grant made while he and I were working on our project at the station the other day. Grant thinks I'm pathetically rushing out into the dating world. He doesn't think of me in a romantic sense beyond that. He doesn't think of me romantically at all.

So yes, I have to move on from Grant. I also can't give up on the idea of pursuing a relationship with someone else, and right now, I'm exploring the idea of pursuing a relationship with Jonathan.

Jonathan.

I sigh, and I turn again toward the ambulance bay. How do I really feel about the potential of a relationship with Jonathan Blackrock? I still don't know. The more time that goes by, the more confused I become. Is that normal? I don't know the answer to that, either. I shouldn't get discouraged, though. After all, matters of the heart aren't easy or straight-forward. Love doesn't hit you in the face the moment you meet someone.

At least, it usually doesn't. Right?

Lost in thought, I make my way to the ambulance bay. As I step outside, I look over at Jonathan, who's standing near the driver's side of the ambulance and scrolling through something on his phone. Jonathan raises his head, and his eyes meet mine. I slow my step. There's a pause, and then Jonathan gives me a smile before he turns away, pulls open the driver's side door, and gets into the rig.

I blink a couple of times. How am I supposed to interpret that? What was Jonathan trying to communicate? Was he trying to apologize? If so, what, exactly, was he apologizing for? More importantly, why was he upset in the first place? Or was he never actually upset at all?

This romance stuff is a mess.

I climb into the back of the ambulance and take a seat on the bench opposite Steve. It's a quiet ride to the fire station. Steve and I get out, and Jonathan and Steve prep the ambulance for the next call. As the two paramedics finish their work, Steve's personal phone begins ringing. Steve answers the call and casually strolls into the fire station, leaving Jonathan and me alone together.

I'm not sure what to do next. I assume that if anyone should address what happened during our last call, it should be Jonathan. However, Jonathan remains busy doing something on the laptop in the front of the ambulance. I'm not even sure Jonathan is aware that I'm still standing here. So I turn away, pull open the door that leads into the station, and head inside.

As I make my way down the hall, I glance through the big window of one of the office doors to my left. I see Steve seated at a workstation inside, his feet propped up on the desk while he continues his call. Looking straight ahead once more, I resume moving down the corridor, passing more offices, which are all unoccupied. I then reach the kitchen. No one is around here either. Everything feels particularly empty, quiet, and stifled, kind of like I do. I peer up at the clock. Since I have nothing to do with my time until there's another call, I might as well do some chart reviews. So I retreat back down the hall, enter one of the vacant offices, and plunk myself down in front of a workstation.

I'm soon immersed in my work. I have no idea how much time passes before I hear the office door being opened. I pause with my eyes still on the monitor. I suppose I should have prepared something to say to Jonathan, who's undoubtedly coming in to finally talk over what happened during our last call, but I have nothing cued up in my mind. I'm going to have to wing it. Sitting up taller, I look toward the doorway. My heart slams into my chest.

It's not Jonathan who's stepping into the room. It's Grant.

What is he doing here?

In an instant, I take in the unexpected sight of Grant, who's standing in the doorway. He's dressed in a long-sleeved shirt and jeans. His hair is tousled. He hasn't shaved today. His brow is furrowed, and his gaze is intense. As I stare up at him, the embarrassment and pain caused by Grant's remark the other day hit me with renewed force. Even worse, though, is the gut-wrenching realization that this is the first time in my life that I've felt genuinely uncomfortable in Grant's presence. There's a wall between us now—a wall that has never existed before—and it's the most devastating feeling of all.

The strained, uncertain silence drags on. Finally, I can't take it any longer, and I blurt out:

"What are you doing here?"

Grant blinks fast. Keeping his eyes fixed on mine, he takes another step into the room.

"I'm sorry for catching you off-guard like this, El, but I—

"Elly?"

I jump, and my insides lurch when I hear Jonathan out in the hall. I see Grant's brows snap together as he turns toward the door. I'm hardly breathing as I follow Grant's stern gaze. Before I'm ready, Jonathan appears in the doorway. When Jonathan spots Grant, he halts, and his smile vanishes.

"Doctor Reed," Jonathan says in succinct tones. His steely-eyed stare remains on Grant while he motions toward me. "Are you here to . . . ?"

Grant's left eyebrow arches, but flattens an instant later. The transient change to his otherwise-unreadable expression was so quick that I'm sure I was the only one who noticed. I'm also likely the only person who detects the extra beat Grant takes before he replies:

"Good morning, Paramedic Blackrock." Grant surprisingly adopts a relaxed, friendly expression. He moves to one of the unoccupied workstations on the other side of the room. "I stopped by to review some charts this morning. Do you happen to know if it's all right if I use this office today?"

"Huh?" Jonathan's own eyebrows go up. Gradually, his posture relaxes. "I mean, yes. I mean, as far as I'm aware, there isn't anyone planning to use this office today." He actually shows something like a smile. "So I think you're welcome to use the room."

"Great. Thanks." Grant sits down at the desk and casts a casual glance over his shoulder at me. "I take it you're reviewing charts, too?"

I'm so baffled by whatever it is that I'm witnessing between the two men that for a long second I can't formulate a reply.

"Yes," I finally answer Grant, drawing out the word.

"Cool." Grant faces his computer, says no more, and gets to work.

The only sound in the room is that of Grant typing on his keyboard, until I hear Jonathan clear his throat and ask:

"Hey, Elly, do you have a moment?"

Grant stops typing.

I shift in my seat again to look Jonathan's way. His smile is broader now; it's like nothing weird just transpired, and nothing unusual happened during our last call. I, however, remain perplexed and uneasy. Nonetheless, I maintain my composure as I push back from my desk and get to my feet.

"Sure," I reply to Jonathan.

I walk past Grant, who doesn't stop his work to even give me a look as I go by him. I step into the hallway to join Jonathan, who continues appearing self-composed and unbothered. Jonathan shuts the office door behind me and tips his head toward the kitchen. He and I begin walking down the hall.

"Elly, I guess I probably owe you an apology for how I reacted during our last call," Jonathan unexpectedly says.

I snap my head his way. Jonathan's expression has suddenly become serious, and his gaze is fixed straight ahead.

Jonathan meets my puzzled gaze. "I guess what I—"

A shrill sound from Jonathan's pager and the simultaneous blaring of the automated alert from dispatch cut off the rest of what he's saying. Jonathan's jaw clenches as he halts and pulls the pager from the holder on his belt.

"Hypotensive patient with abdominal pain," Jonathan tells me as he turns around and starts charging for the garage.

I spin on my heels and catch up with Jonathan as he speeds down the corridor. Steve pops out of the other office, his phone still in his hand, and he joins us. We burst into the garage, and the next thing I know, I'm in the back of the ambulance, and Jonathan is driving the rig out onto the road.

I peek out the back window at Grant's car, which is parked in front of the station. An aching sense of longing and sadness fills me as I watch the station and Grant's car disappear from view.

Thirteen

There's a chill in the evening air, and a harsh breeze is rustling the trees, causing the last of the leaves to fall to the rain-soaked pavement below. Cinching my coat tightly around me, I duck my head against the rain and wind as I lock my car and scurry across the parking lot, guided by the glow of the streetlamps and the glare of the fire station's own exterior lights. I'm soaking wet by the time I reach the covered area in front of the station's main door. With raindrops rolling down my nose, I ring the doorbell to alert the crew members inside that I've arrived for tonight's shift.

The sound of the doorbell echoing through the station fades away. In the stillness that follows, it suddenly hits me: it's yet another Saturday night, which means I now have less than a week before this EMS rotation is over. After spending over a year eagerly awaiting this experience and excitedly wondering how it might impact my future career, the month itself has flown by in a strange, emotion-saturated blur. I've barely had a chance to pause to catch my breath, let alone analyze how I think the rotation is going or what I'm going to take away from it. Of course, much of the whirlwind hasn't been due to the actual EMS work. Rather, this rotation blindsided me with profound challenges to my heart, and along with those challenges came questions and decisions I never could have anticipated. And now, though the dust isn't even close to settling yet, this month is practically over. After this overnight shift, I'll have one more overnight shift in a couple of days, and then my shifts will be done. A few days after that, on October thirtieth, Grant and I will present our project to Dr. Priest and a committee of other attending physicians, and that will mark the official end to our EMS rotation.

Even then, however, my EMS experience won't really be over. Not quite. On the night of October thirtieth, Jonathan and I will be attending Lakewood Fire and Rescue's gala together. After that, my time in this EMS world will conclude.

Or will it?

Not only do I need to decide about whether or not to pursue an EMS fellowship, I need to decide how I feel about Jonathan. As I've done countless times since Jonathan asked me to attend the gala, I can't help wondering: once my shifts are done, and the glitz and glamour of the gala are over, what will be next for Jonathan and me? We obviously won't be working together anymore, and that alone will significantly alter the dynamic of our relationship. So when I return to working in the ED while Jonathan continues his work at the station, how will interactions change between the two of us? Jonathan previously made it clear that he's interested in moving our relationship forward. Is that what he still wants? Is that what I want?

I don't know.

It has been one week since Jonathan seemed irritated because I provided advice on managing that COPD patient. For the rest of that shift, however, and during the two shifts we worked later in the week, Jonathan behaved as charmingly charismatic and interested in me as ever—more so, actually—and I found myself enjoying Jonathan's company as much as always. Yet I couldn't convince myself that I was falling head-over-heels for him, either. The end result was that the fierce battle between my heart and mind continued raging.

The logical side of me recognizes that Jonathan and I have the potential to be a great match. The romantic side of me points out that I've never experienced the exhilarating, undeniable thrill of love when I've been in Jonathan's presence. My inner romantic also stubbornly continues referring back to Grant for comparison, highlighting how I knew without question that I was falling in love with Grant on the day I met him, and how I've been in love with Grant ever since. In rebuttal, my logical side kicks back in, sternly pointing out that my romantic feelings for Grant have never been reciprocated, whereas Jonathan is actually showing interest in me. To further hammer home the point, my logical side also reminds me of Grant's excruciatingly hurtful comment about how I was just rushing off to date the first person who asked me out, and the ambivalent way Grant treated me when he came to the fire station to work on charts a week ago.

A roll of thunder yanks me from my thoughts. I shake the rain from my hands and rub them together to fight off the damp chill while I continue waiting by the station's front door. Amidst all of my confusion, one thing is clear: when this rotation is over, not only do I need to take some serious time to review how this EMS experience went for me, I also need to sort out my feelings about Jonathan. It's not because Jonathan has made me question his interest. It's because I'm still trying to understand my interest in him.

A motion inside the station catches my attention. I squint as I peer through the glass door to see who's coming to let me in. My body jolts when I spot Grant jogging across the foyer with his naturally athletic strides. Grant's brows are pinched together, and his eyes are locked on mine. My heart rate skyrockets, and my stomach plummets. With my internal war of thoughts and emotions resuming at full force, I'm becoming both sick to my stomach and unable to catch my breath. I'm not sure whether I should feel thrilled or humiliated to be in Grant's presence right now. Speaking of Grant, what is he doing here, anyway? Why . . .

I feel the color drain from my face when into my head pops the calendar for the rotation, which I last checked a few days ago. I now remember that this is one of the days during the month when Grant's shift overlaps with mine. Lakewood Fire and Rescue typically increases its staffing during its busiest hours, so on Saturday afternoons and evenings, the agency often assigns two BLS and two ALS crews to Station Fourteen. And if I remember the rotation's calendar correctly—and I'm almost certain that I do—Grant and his crew have been on a mid-day shift, which ends at midnight. This means that for the next five hours, whenever our crews aren't out responding to different calls, Grant and I will have to hang out together in the station.

I grimace. I can't believe that I forgot about this. Few things get me more rattled than running into Grant unexpectedly, and that's when everything is going well between us. Right now, because things aren't going well with Grant and me, the shock of running into him is a hundred times more distressing. My last few encounters with Grant—running into him while I was on a date with Jonathan, Grant's hurtful remark while we were working on our project, and the aloof way Grant treated me at the station a week ago when he came to review charts—have all been awkward and strained. So it's going to take everything I have to maintain my composure in his presence tonight.

Before I've managed to fully collect myself, Grant has already reached the door. He quickly pushes it open and steps back so I can enter.

"Geez, El, it's raining hard out there. Please get inside." Grant's jaw muscles are tensed as he looks past me to get a view the growing storm. "You haven't been waiting out here long, have you?"

"What?" I blink. "I mean, um, no."

Ungluing my feet from the ground, I step past Grant to enter the foyer. Not only am I still recovering from the shock of running into him tonight, I'm also surprised he's answering the station's front door. As it was explained to me on my first day of the rotation, it's standard practice that one crew member is always assigned to monitor the front door and answer it whenever the bell is rung. This is in case someone arrives who's in need of immediate help. The expectation that a designated crew member will remain vigilant about monitoring the front door is the reason why the doorbell rings so loudly inside the station, and also why there are monitors mounted throughout the building that give those inside a view of what's happening at the entrance.

So the only reason I can think of to explain why Grant has answered the door is that all four crews must currently be out on calls . . . but that doesn't make sense either. If Grant's ALS crew is out on a call, why isn't he with them?

I have no idea what's going on.

So what else is new.

After entering the foyer, I halt and coach myself to draw in a stabilizing breath. Okay, I can get myself under control. No, I wasn't expecting to see Grant tonight. Yes, the last few times when he and I have interacted, it has been a disaster. However, Grant and I do need to work together for the next several hours, so we have to be kind and professional, despite the strain that's hovering between us.

After cycling another breath in and out of my lungs, I turn to face Grant. Despite the badness of our recent interactions, I find that Grant's familiar, steady presence is as immensely comforting and welcoming as always. Cautiously, I show him a smile.

"Thanks for letting me in."

Grant lets the door swing shut, and he makes sure it locks. He appears to take an extra moment before shifting my direction. His blue eyes again fix on mine. There's a pause, which causes me to hold my breath, and then Grant shows me a genuine smile in return.

"You're welcome, El."

All at once, the cutting chill of the rain on my skin is replaced by the warmth of relief and happiness. Grant's tone is sincere. His smile is real. In just the few seconds we've been interacting, it's already starting to feel like old times again. A flicker of hope ignites inside me. Maybe Grant and I can discuss what has happened lately. Maybe we can fix whatever went wrong. Maybe we can restore our friendship . . . the friendship I cherish . . . the friendship I don't know what I would ever do without.

Emotion rapidly rises up from my core. Of course Grant and I can fix our relationship.

We've been friends since high school. Our bond is made of heartier stuff than anything a misunderstanding or words spoken in the heat of the moment could destroy. In fact, I should say something to Grant right now, before any more time goes by. After all, Grant and I have always been able to talk about (almost) everything, and at this moment, what's most important is making things right, even if neither he nor I totally understand why things went wrong in the first place.

I open my mouth to say something, but I hear someone approaching from behind me, and I quickly close my mouth again. Grant's gaze shifts over my shoulder. His smile disappears. A blink later, however, Grant's expression shifts again, becoming empty and conveying nothing. With the footsteps getting louder, I turn around to see who's coming our way. It's Jonathan. As he saunters into the foyer, Jonathan focuses on me and breaks into a grin.

"Well, good evening, Elly." Jonathan reaches my side and brushes my arm with his hand.

My eyebrows rise fleetingly. Not that I think Jonathan's gesture was inappropriate, and it certainly didn't make me uncomfortable. His touch wasn't necessarily unwanted, either. However, as always, the situation simply confuses me. Jonathan's touch, though brief, was enough to convey that he believes there's more than a strictly professional relationship between us. I suppose this is true. Frustratingly, though, I can't understand why I remain so . . . ambivalent. I also can't understand why, at this very moment, even though I'm looking at Jonathan, I'm more aware of Grant. I can almost feel Grant's gaze upon me, and that alone is enough to make my face flush and my breathing hitch. I silently exhale with frustration. Why am I so discombobulated?

Because you're still in love with Grant.

I flare my nostrils, doing my best to ignore the voice in my head. I need to shake off thoughts of what can't and won't be. I make myself focus harder on Jonathan as I show him a smile.

"Good evening to you, too," I tell him.

Jonathan's grin widens in response before he looks over to Grant. "Thanks for answering the door. It took me an extra few seconds to realize someone had pushed the bell." He chuckles and puts his dark eyes back on me. "Didn't mean to leave you out in the rain. We were in the lounge and—"

"Blackrock, get back in here!" a guy's booming voice carries into the foyer. "They're on the ten-yard line!"

Jonathan whips his head over his shoulder, looking in the direction from where the shout came. Quickly putting his attention back on me, Jonathan shows yet another grin and starts backing down the hall.

"I'm gonna go see if they score this touchdown, okay?" Jonathan tells me, jerking his thumb over his shoulder in the direction of the lounge. "I'll be right back."

Spinning away from me, Jonathan jogs the rest of the way down the corridor, rounds the corner, and disappears from view. Moments later, I hear people break into cheers and applause. Ah. So the ALS and BLS crews who are working here tonight aren't out on calls after all. That explains why Grant is here, too.

Grant.

I clear my throat and turn Grant's way once more. Grant doesn't notice me watching him, however. While the cheers from the lounge carry through the air, Grant is keeping his eyes locked on the now-empty corridor. His stare is stone-like, and a muscle in his cheek is tensed. Finally, after the sounds of the celebration die away, Grant exhales hard and runs a hand through his hair. He then shifts his eyes my direction.

A questioning pause hovers in the air.

"Are you all right?" Grant asks in a low voice, breaking the stillness.

I don't hide my look of confusion at his question. "Yes. Why wouldn't I be—"

"El." Grant takes a step closer to me. His chest rises and falls with another breath. "I have to be honest here. I—"

The strobe light in the foyer starts flashing, and the automated, robotic, monotone dispatch alert begins blasting out from the PA system. Grant and I both freeze, and then a split-second later, we spin around in unison and run down the hall. Upon reaching the kitchen, we're swept up by a tornado of activity. The four crews who are working tonight—ten EMS personnel in all—are racing from the lounge area toward the garage. Everyone's pagers are going off, the piercing sounds adding to the chaos. A few crew members are shouting to each other over the noise. The lights in the building are still flashing, and the deafening dispatch announcement is playing on loop.

"Doctor Vincent!" someone calls out.

I peer through the fray. Steve is waving his arm to get my attention, and when I spot him, he begins motioning for me to follow him to the garage. I nod, yank off my jacket and toss it onto the kitchen island, and dart through the crowd to reach Steve's side.

"Two-car MVC. Multiple patients," Steve tells me as we rush for the garage. He puts his pager into the holder on his belt and continues speaking loudly enough that I can hear him above the clamor. "They're dispatching all the crews from here, and some crews from other stations, while we're waiting to be updated on how many patients are involved."

My body finishes making the jarring transition from emotion-laden small talk in the foyer to adrenaline-pounding, heart-pumping, critical-care mode. As Steve and I continue racing down the hall with the others, I spot Grant up ahead. He's running next to a member of his ALS crew, and his expression is one of total concentration as he appears to be getting briefed on the preliminary details of the call, much the same way Steve just briefed me.

One of the BLS providers sprints ahead of the pack to reach the door that leads into the garage. She throws open the door and darts through; the rest of us rush into the garage after her. The hurricane of activity grows as everyone splits up into their respective crews and bolts toward their designated vehicles. Like always, the ambulance that Steve and Jonathan are using is parked closest to the door. Steve pulls himself up into the driver's seat, dons his headset, and begins speaking to someone from dispatch. Without breaking stride, I go the opposite direction and sprint to the back of the ambulance. Jonathan is there, pulling open the doors. Jonathan helps me inside, climbs into the back of the rig with me, and slams shut the doors. I hear the doors of the other ambulances closing in rapid succession. All the garage doors begin rolling up. As I take a seat on one of the benches, Steve hits the siren and advances our rig out of the garage first. Rain starts pelting the windshield and hitting the ambulance's roof with staccato sounds. Heart pounding, I throw on my headset and stare out the back windows, watching through the rain as the other three vehicles emerge from the garage, creating a blinding display of flashing lights against the dark sky.

"Confirmed two-car MVC," Steve informs Jonathan and me through the headset as he begins speeding down the road. "Per police, we've got one green patient in Car One, and two red patients in Car Two."

"Copy that," Jonathan replies, watching through the opening that gives a view up front.

"It's gonna be messy out there tonight." Steve glances at Jonathan and me through the rearview mirror. "Let's get the doc in a vest."

Jonathan pulls his attention from the windshield and looks over at me. "Right. Copy that."

Jonathan slides to the edge of his bench and quickly pulls open the bottom drawer of one of the supply carts that are braced against the wall. He digs out a reflective, fluorescent-yellow vest from the drawer and tosses it over to me.

"Keep that on while you're out there." Jonathan closes the drawer. "It'll help make sure you're visible, and it will identify you as part of the crew."

"Got it." I hurriedly slip the oversized vest over my sweater.

Steve begins slowing our rig as he maneuvers through the torrential downpour. He hits our siren so it lets out a longer shriek. My pulse rate spikes at the sound. We must be approaching the accident. I anxiously lean forward on my bench and peer out the windshield. We're on a dark, narrow, remote road now, and the rain is falling harder. As Steve rounds another sharp curve, our headlights suddenly illuminate the crash scene. I suck in a silent gasp of horror.

Two mangled vehicles are jackknifed at strange angles near the center of the winding road. The front ends of the cars are facing, suggesting this was a head-on collision. One of the two vehicles is a black SUV, and based on the trail of metal and other debris that it left in its wake, it appears the SUV was driven across the center line and then smashed, head-on, into a small green hatchback that was going the opposite direction.

My stomach churns as I begin getting a clearer view of how badly the hatchback has been demolished; I can only imagine how fast the SUV must have been going when it collided into the smaller car. Aghast, I keep staring out the windshield, trying to process the nightmare of what I'm seeing. The SUV also has significant damage, but it's not nearly as obliterated as the hatchback, since the massive SUV was far better able to absorb and disperse the potentially lethal amount of energy that was exchanged in the impact.

Steve turns around our rig and backs it in close to the accident scene. As he positions the front of our ambulance so it faces the direction from where we came, I realize he's doing so to ensure we'll have an unobstructed route away from the crash, if and when we must speed off with a patient who needs emergent transport to the hospital.

Jonathan and I throw aside our headsets and spring to our feet, and as soon as our rig is brought to a stop, we throw open the back doors and jump out. The rain stings my skin like tiny daggers as I frantically spin in a circle to take in a full view of the apocalyptic scene. The crash is hauntingly lit up by the headlights of the EMS

vehicles and the eerie glow from the red flares
that police officers have put down on the road.
Pieces of both cars are strewn across the whole
roadway. The hatchback has smoke rising up
from under its hood, despite the rain. Fluid is
spilling out from the underside of the SUV and
oozing across the road. The stenches of gasoline,
rubber, and burning flares are filling my nostrils.
Relentless noise is hitting my eardrums.
Commotion is everywhere.

I shiver, though whether from the rain or
the sight of what I'm witnessing, I can't entirely
say. Not only are there multiple patients who are
potentially critically injured and in need of
immediate care, this scene is extremely
hazardous. There's other traffic that must be
diverted. The hatchback continues to smoke.
Fluid keeps spilling out from the SUV. This is a
dark night and a heavy storm, and we're on a
small, winding road. There's no question that
this is going to be a dangerous, difficult rescue.

One of the BLS crew's captains is standing
in the middle of the fray. He has donned a
reflective orange vest that has "IC" printed on the
back in huge lettering, indicating that he has
assumed the role of Incident Commander. Using
a bullhorn, the IC barks orders to get everyone
organized. Some firefighters in full bunker gear
are assessing the safety of the scene and working
to get it secured. The other BLS providers, and
the ALS crews, are hastily donning PPE and
retrieving their medical equipment from the rigs

The IC keeps the bullhorn to his lips as he
orders Grant's crew to care for the driver of the

hatchback, and then he commands Jonathan and
Steve to care for the passenger in the same little
car. In response, the two ALS crews run toward
the small vehicle. Grant and I share a worried
look through the rain, and then Grant sprints
after his crew while I run the other way and race
around the back of the battered vehicle to reach
the passenger side. I skid to a halt, my eyes
widening. The doors on this side of the car are
crushed so badly that Jonathan and Steve aren't
able to open them to access the people who are
trapped inside.

Steve and Jonathan shout to the IC that
they can't get to their patient. I hear Grant's crew
members yelling that they're not able to open the
doors on the driver's side either. The IC barks
more orders over his bullhorn. A group of
firefighters races over to the car, lugging heavy-
duty equipment along with them. I dart out of
the way. Within seconds, the hatchback is
completely surrounded by the crews. From the
slippery, muddy shoulder of the road, I watch
restlessly as the firefighters ready the tools they'll
use to pry open the car. The seconds that pass
seem to take hours, for I know the two patients
who are trapped inside the car have severe
injuries, and every moment of delay in getting to
them puts their lives at increasing risk.

The harsh sounds of bending metal fill the
air as the crews start prying off the car's doors.
My pulse is racing as I raise myself up on tiptoe,
trying to get a better view of the vehicle's
occupants. Unnervingly, though, all I can see are

two slumped-over figures silhouetted by the glow of the headlights from other vehicles that are on the scene.

The storm continues to rage. Thunder rumbles through the sky, and flashes of lightning illuminate the dark clouds overhead. I wipe the water from my face, and my eyes fly across the rest of the scene once more. Not far from where I stand, two EMS crews are attending to the driver and sole occupant of the SUV, who I can now see is a middle-aged man. The man is sitting up in his seat and conversing with the crews. Shockingly, the man is smiling, and his expression is glazed-over in a pleasantly detached sort of way. It's like this man—the person who caused this horrific accident—is oblivious to the situation or doesn't care.

The crews continue assessing the man, and as they open wider the SUV's doors, several empty alcohol containers fall out of the vehicle, hit the ground, and roll across the road, stopping at my feet. I stare down at cans and bottles as a sickening, infuriating realization hits me: the man in the SUV is drunk. He was driving drunk when he swerved across the road and smashed his mammoth vehicle into the little hatchback that was going the other direction. Because he chose to drive under the influence, he has severely injured—perhaps even killed—the innocent people who are trapped in the other car.

I make myself look away, but I remain shaken to my core by one of the things I've never been able to come to terms with. Why—*why*—in a DUI crash, does it always seem that the person who caused the accident is barely scratched, but the driver's victims sustain catastrophic injuries? And why does it always seem that the perpetrator of the accident is later found to have a long record of prior DUI events? It's one of the cruel injustices that I will never understand.

I'm pulled back to attention by more sounds of twisting metal and shattering glass. I flinch at the noise and whirl around to look again at the little car. The firefighters finish tearing off the doors on the passenger side, at last providing access to the patient who has been held captive within. Immediately, Jonathan, Steve, and several BLS providers lunge in to reach the patient.

Still worriedly trying to see the two occupants of the vehicle, I stumble around the front of the car to get to the driver's side. The demolition crew that has been attacking this part of the car finishes prying off the door, and the glow from the road flares reaches into the destroyed interior of the vehicle, giving me a view of the young man who's behind the wheel. Another wave of horror crashes down upon me.

The young man in the driver's seat can't be more than twenty years old. His face is disfigured from cuts and swelling, and his features are saturated with blood. The car's deflated airbags hang limply around him, having done their job to blunt the impact of the crash before deflating a microsecond later. Shards of glass from the broken windows cover the young man's hair, face, and clothing. To my relief, at least, the young man is awake. However, his breathing is rapid and shallow, and he's wincing like it hurts to breathe.

Grant's ALS crew members, as well as several BLS providers, start assessing the young man. Above the commotion, I hear the driver let out a weak moan and utter:

"My . . . little brother . . . please don't let . . . him die."

I pull in a shaky breath and stagger back from the car. There's a rushing sound in my ears, and my head gets light. This young man isn't worried about himself; he's worried about his little brother, who must be the passenger. My throat constricts as achingly painful emotions— emotions I usually keep locked away—rise to the surface and consume me. I know the agony of losing a little brother. It's a pain that never goes away. It's a loss that haunts forever.

We cannot allow this young man to suffer such misery. He cannot lose his little brother tonight.

I sprint through the rain back around the front of the car so I can get another view of the passenger side. As I draw close, there's a break in the crowd at last, and I finally catch a glimpse of the little brother who's in the passenger seat. I freeze, growing cold.

No. Please no.

The little brother—a wiry teenager—is covered in blood, but through the terrible stains of red I can see that his skin is ominously ashen. His eyes are closed. He's not moving. I can't even discern if his chest is rising and falling.

For one more dreadful moment, I remain frozen on the shoulder of the road as the rain pounds down upon me. It takes everything I have simply to remember to breathe.

"He has a pulse!" Jonathan shouts to the other crew members. "I'll take his airway. Get his c-spine stabilized and start some IV fluid!"

I break out of my shock. The little brother is still alive. With determination and resolve coursing through me, I charge even closer to the car, joining the EMS providers who surround it. Peering through the chaos, I see Steve placing an IV in the patient's right arm, and the firefighters stabilizing the patient's spine and getting him fitted in a cervical collar. Meanwhile, with intubation equipment in-hand, Jonathan is climbing over the top of the wreckage to fit his massive frame into the car's tiny backseat and position himself behind the patient's head.

The firefighters finish stabilizing the teenager's cervical spine, and then they tip back his seat as far as it will go, trying to give Jonathan access to the patient's airway. Even with the chair tipped back, though, the patient's position is significantly suboptimal for intubation, especially given how constricted Jonathan's movements are in the small, smashed car. My apprehension ratchets up even more.

From the backseat, Jonathan leans forward so he's hovering over the patient's head. He inserts the laryngoscope into the teenager's mouth and begins trying to get a view of the vocal cords. I clasp my hands to my chest, holding my breath as I watch and wait. Injury, blood in the airway, and spine-immobilization precautions all make intubating a trauma patient hard under the most controlled of circumstances. Attempting to intubate a trauma patient when it's dark outside, you're crammed inside the mangled backseat of a car, and the patient can't be positioned properly is almost an impossible ask.

A second passes. And another. And another. My chest tightens even more painfully with each passing moment.

"What's the word, Blackrock?" Steve shouts as he starts infusing normal saline through the patient's IV.

"I can't see the cords!" Jonathan's jaw is clenched as he makes another attempt.

"Pressure's dropping!" a BLS provider calls out.

I flick my eyes to the cardiac monitor. The patient's blood pressure and oxygen level are both falling. This patient is about to go into cardiac arrest.

There's an eruption of jarring noise on driver's side of the vehicle, and I whip my head toward the commotion. The crews that are attending to the young man who was driving now have him in a cervical collar and on a backboard, and they're carefully extricating him from the vehicle. The young man is still awake. He's receiving supplemental oxygen via a nasal cannula, and fluid is running through an IV in his arm. The cardiac monitor that he has been attached to shows his heart rate is elevated, but he's otherwise hemodynamically stable.

"My . . . brother! I don't want . . . to leave my brother!" the young man cries out with desperation in his voice. "Please . . . don't let him die!"

"Pulse is dropping!" shouts the firefighter who's monitoring the little brother's vital signs.

I gasp and look back to the passenger side of the car.

"Blackrock?" Steve springs to his feet. "What do you have to work with?"

"I still can't get a view!" Jonathan calls out. "Airway is not secured!"

"Then get out of there." Steve checks the monitor. "We'll—"

"Sat keeps dropping!" the BLS provider warns.

A shock runs through my body, from my head to my feet. This teen is on the verge of coding. If we don't act now, he may die.

The world around me suddenly seems to come to a standstill. It's as though everything has been put on pause. In the complete and total calm, I can still hear the older brother pleading with us to save his sibling, and images of my own brother again rise up from my memory.

It hits me even harder: the young man cannot lose his little brother; this teenager cannot die.

"I've got airway!" I sprint the rest of the way to the car.

I push through the crowd, ignoring the stares of everyone else on scene. My mind is focused on one thing and one thing only: securing this patient's airway.

"Blackrock, out of the car!" Steve orders, backing up to make room for me to get into the vehicle.

Jonathan looks at me. Sweat lines his brow. He peers into my eyes for one more split-second, and then he puts the intubation equipment down on the backseat and climbs out the driver's side, giving me room to crawl in from the other direction. I dive into the vehicle and turn in the tiny space so I'm at the head of the patient. Even though I'm so much smaller than Jonathan, it's still extremely claustrophobic in here.

I grab the intubation equipment, lean forward over the patient . . . and freeze. Once again, all I can see are images of my brother in my mind's eye. My hands begin to shake as I think about the fact that I've never intubated a patient outside of the ED before. What if I can't save this patient? What if I'm the reason that the young man loses his brother tonight? What if—

Motion draws my attention toward the front of the vehicle. Grant is standing by the hood of the car, and he's watching me closely. Meeting Grant's steady, unwavering gaze, I swiftly feel myself grow focused and calm once more. My hands become still. Grant, the person who knows me better than anyone else does, understands what's going through my mind in this moment. Grant knows the pain I've carried from losing my brother. And still, with his gaze, Grant is telling me that he knows I can do this.

I can do this.

My thoughts sharpen, and everything around me disappears. With motions that are quick and sure, I intubate the patient. A blink later, the world comes back to life around me.

"Tube is in!" I shout.

One of the BLS providers climbs into the car so she can start bagging the patient to administer to him the oxygen he needs. Another BLS provider helps me get safely out of the car via the driver's side. As soon as my feet hit the muddy ground, I spin around to continue anxiously watching the fast-paced resuscitation. It seems only another second passes before the crews have the teen extricated from the car. In a flurry of sound and activity, the patient is put on a stretcher and wheeled over to our ambulance. Steve climbs into the driver's seat and starts the engine. Jonathan and two firefighters get into the back to attend to the patient. I race through the rain and hop into the back of the rig with the others. Someone closes the doors behind me.

With its siren wailing, Steve pulls our ambulance away from the scene. We fly down the dark, winding road while Jonathan attends to the patient and one of the firefighters gives a rapid-fire report over the phone to the Lakewood ED. I glance out the back windows, and I see the ambulance occupied by Grant's crew following closely behind us; undoubtedly, they, too, are headed to Lakewood so the older brother can also get the care he needs.

Before I've even caught my breath, we've pulled into the ambulance bay at Lakewood. In another burst of coordinated activity, one of the firefighters opens the back doors of our rig and climbs out. I go next. Jonathan, the other firefighter, and Steve pull the teenager's stretcher out of the ambulance and practically run as they wheel it into the ED. I scamper after them, and just as I reach the building's entrance, I hear two more rigs pulling into the ambulance bay. Looking over my shoulder, I see Grant's ambulance and one of the BLS rigs. My stomach churns when I realize the BLS rig must be transporting the man whose intoxicated driving caused all this tonight.

Doing my best to refocus, I sprint into the ED. The department is as loud, crowded, and chaotic as ever. Without slowing my pace, I take a right, pass by the charge nurse's station, and head into one of the resuscitation bays. As expected, the resuscitation bay is bursting at the seams with people, overwhelming noise, and storms of activity. Attending physicians, residents, nurses, techs, registration personnel, radiology technicians, respiratory therapists, and social workers are rapidly dividing up themselves into three separate teams, with each team preparing to take on the care of one of the new trauma patients.

As soon as Jonathan and Steve finish wheeling our patient into the room, the first ED team jumps into action, getting the teen transferred onto one of the ED stretchers. While the team begins working to stabilize the patient, Jonathan starts barking report over the commotion. Moments later, Grant's crew wheels in the older brother, and the second ED team, which is gathered around the other empty stretcher in the room, calls for the crew to hurry their direction. The last team of ED providers— the team assigned to care for the driver of the SUV—hurries out the door to take care of their patient in the adjoining resuscitation bay.

The tension in our room explodes as the resuscitation of the two brothers commences at full force. Everyone is talking loudly. People are rushing about. Exams are performed, initial x-rays are taken, and labs are drawn. The little brother is whisked off to CT, and as soon as he's wheeled back into the resuscitation bay, the older brother is taken away to get the further imaging he needs.

Eventually, as is typically the case once the initial stabilization of a patient is accomplished, the resuscitation bay settles into a highly charged quiet as care for the patients continues. From the corner where I've been watching, I exhale a breath and check the clock, astounded by how much time has passed since we arrived with our patient. It seems like only seconds ago.

"Hey, Elly."

I jump when I hear my name. Quinn Meyers, one of the ED's great first-year residents, is walking fast across the resuscitation bay to reach me. I blink a few times, Quinn's friendly face becoming the first one out of the swirling haze of ED providers that I've focused on since I got here. As she continues heading my way, Quinn peels off the blood-covered PPE from her tall, wiry, athletic frame. Her curly hair, which is pulled back in a low ponytail, is bouncing as she walks.

"Hi, Quinn," I greet her, not hiding my tone of concern as my eyes flick back to the patients.

Quinn discards her PPE and gets my side. "I wanted to give you the good news: your patient—the younger brother—is going to be all right. He has a concussion, of course, as well as a small subarachnoid hemorrhage and a really small pulmonary contusion. He'll be admitted to the trauma service for monitoring, but Jay Moen, the on-call resident tonight, is already anticipating that they'll be able to extubate him before the night is over. Even the attending, Doctor Briggs, has said she expects the patient to make a complete recovery." She shows me a reassuring smile. "The only other thing his workup revealed is that he has a non-displaced right wrist fracture, which is nothing that Erik Prescott and the rest of the ortho service can't manage." Her eyes shift to the other side of the room, where the older brother is located. "From what I've heard, the older brother is also doing well. He has a small pneumothorax and a closed head injury, so he'll be admitted for monitoring, too. The second-year resident, Brittany Chen, has everything well under control over there, as you can imagine, and Doctor Briggs says he should also make a full recovery."

Quinn's words soak in, and then the oppressive weight that has been upon my shoulders lifts. For the first time since I saw the crash scene tonight, I feel as though I can breathe.

"Thank you, Quinn." I give her a hug. "Thank you so much for telling me."

"You're welcome," Quinn replies kindly.

As I finish emerging from my critical-care haze, only then do I happen to notice that Quinn has the fading remnants of a tan. My inner romantic lets out a little cheer. Undoubtedly, Quinn attended Danielle's destination wedding as Dylan Gillespie's date. Quinn and Dylan have been dating for about six months now, and they're rock-solid and adorable together.

"Well, now that everyone is stabilized in here and care is transferred to admitting service, I should go check on my other patients," Quinn tells me. She shows another sincere smile. "I'll see you soon, El."

"See you soon, and thanks again," I tell her.

Quinn scurries out of the room, and as I watch her disappear into the madness outside the resuscitation bay's door, my pulse rate finishes returning to normal. I look around the room again, and now I start processing the faces of everyone else who has been caring for the brothers tonight. The charge nurse, Laura, is talking on the phone; she's probably working with the hospital's bed manager to get the inpatient rooms for the brothers arranged. The team that was caring for the younger brother was spearheaded by Dr. Tammy Sanders, another of the ED's great attendings. The others on the team included the nurses, Tom and Hadi, the ED tech, Finn, and another woman whom I'm not familiar with. She appears to be only a few years older than me. She's tall, she has shoulder-length, dark blonde hair, and between her lithe build and strikingly gorgeous features, she basically looks like a supermodel in scrubs. Her aura is one of quiet confidence, strength, patience, and kindness, and there's a wise gleam in her brown eyes. With growing curiosity, I glance at her badge:

Dr. Adrienne Hayes, MD
Emergency Medicine Attending Physician

I nod to myself. Dr. Hayes is another one of the new attendings here at Lakewood, and I already sense I'm going to like working with her.

I turn my eyes to the far side of the room, watching as the care of the two patients continues to be transitioned from the ED teams to the admitting service. The ED team that was caring for the older brother was overseen by Dr. Wilma Fox. The team also included a guy with curly brown hair who, based on the way Dr. Fox is meticulously monitoring everything he does, is probably another new ED attending. The rest of the team was made up of the nurses, Pete and Kathy, and the tech, Penny.

I finish scanning the resuscitation bay, which is littered with discarded PPE, empty IV fluid bags, bloody gauze, syringe packaging, latex-free gloves, unused blood tubes, and a plethora of other items that were used and tossed aside during the duel resuscitations. A quiet, intense hum is permeating the air as everyone goes about their tasks. Two of the radiology techs are putting away the portable x-ray machines. Brenna from respiratory therapy is adjusting the ventilator settings for the teenage patient. The infamously militant attending physician from the trauma service, Dr. Briggs, is striding back and forth between the two patients' stretchers, overseeing their care, which is being provided by the three residents she's supervising this evening: Jay Moen, Erik Prescott, and Brittany Chen. In a back corner of the room, the Lakewood ED social worker, Dwayne, is talking with Cassandra Barlow, the social worker who typically works at University Hospital. I've seen Cassandra pick up an occasional shift around here, and I'm guessing she'll be working here more often once the bigger ED opens.

After I finish looking across the room, I realize the EMS crews have already left the resuscitation bay. I take a step toward the door to go after them, but pause to look back one last time. As I gaze upon the brothers and contemplate what happened tonight, all the emotions I've been fighting to keep suppressed suddenly threaten to burst to the surface. Facing forward again, I hurriedly exit the room.

My emotions are still raw and dangerously close to the surface as I start heading across the department to rejoin my crew. When I pass the adjacent resuscitation bay, I hear the totally unexpected sound of a man's laughter coming from within. I shift my eyes toward the sound, and I stumble as I come to a stop. Inside the room is the intoxicated driver who nearly killed the two brothers tonight. The man is sitting up on his stretcher, laughing loudly while he watches a sitcom on television. A tray filled with hospital food is beside him, and he's contentedly consuming the meal at his leisure. Even from where I'm standing, I can still smell the alcohol radiating out of him.

I look away, sickened and chilled by the man's ambivalence to what happened tonight . . . and to what nearly happened. I can no longer hold back my emotions. My face flushes. My vision blurs with tears. Ducking my head, I race for the door that leads outside so I can leave the emergency department behind.

Fourteen

With my head still down, I rush out to the ambulance bay. For one moment, I'm aware of the cold, wet nighttime air. A moment later, all thoughts of the weather are forgotten when I run into someone who's strolling toward the ED doors.

"Whoa, Elly. I think we've got to stop meeting like this." Jonathan chuckles as he grabs my upper arms so I don't slip from our collision. "Have no fear: we weren't going to leave you behind. I was . . ."

Jonathan trails off when I raise my head to look up at him, and the lights of the ambulance bay illuminate my tear-streaked face. Jonathan's eyebrows rise as he takes in the sight of me. He lowers his arms to his sides.

"What's wrong?"

At first, I contemplate contriving a story about accidentally spraining my wrist in the resuscitation bay, or some other such nonsense, to hastily explain away my tears. It's what I would do, if Jonathan and I had a strictly professional relationship. We have more than a professional relationship, though—at least, I think we do—and if I'm truly intending to embrace that, I need to know I can open up to him. I need to be able to be honest.

I sniff and wipe the tears from my cheeks. "That last call stirred up a lot of emotions for me," I explain, my voice soft and shaky. "For one thing, it was hard to see how unbothered the driver of the SUV was, despite the fact that he nearly killed two people tonight." My throat is becoming so thick I can hardly speak. "And also, you see, when I was younger, my—"

"Hey, I understand, and I'm so sorry." Jonathan pats me on the back. "In this line of work, we see some pretty hard stuff. Folks like you and I are resilient, though, which is why we're able to do what we do." He gives me an encouraging thumbs-up and glances past me at the ED. "I'm sorry to cut this short, but if you'll please excuse me, I have to go grab the laptop that I left in the resuscitation bay. Feel free to ride up front with Falco on the way back to the station."

Jonathan gives me another smile, slides past me, and jogs off to the ED. I stay where I am, staring straight ahead. I hear the squeak of the sliding glass door as it opens for Jonathan and then closes behind him once he's inside. After the sound fades away, I continue staring at nothing.

Does being *resilient* mean never getting bothered by what we see in our lines of work? I don't think so. To me, being *resilient* means that despite seeing the horrors close up, and despite experiencing the brutal emotions first-hand, we somehow still find a way to help those who need us. It doesn't mean the work doesn't take a toll, though, and it doesn't mean we should ignore how we feel.

I glance over my shoulder and look into the ED through the sliding glass door. I don't see Jonathan. Instead, I see the man who was driving the SUV tonight. Hadi is steering the man on his stretcher over to one of the hallway treatment areas. Since the intoxicated man is being placed in the hallway, it means he has been cleared from a medical standpoint, and he's simply going to remain under ED observation until he's sober enough to be discharged. Shivering as I continue watching him, I see that the man is still eating, smiling, and chatting to everyone who passes by him. He's utterly and disturbingly oblivious to the seriousness of what has occurred tonight. The man's situation remains a sickening contrast to the fact that there are two innocent boys being admitted because of injuries that the man inflicted upon them.

Suddenly, flashbacks of the crash scene infiltrate my mind, and then memories of my own brother—some more vivid than others— start filling my thoughts. I look away from the ED, but my breathing still grows strained, and my head gets light. Nausea is rising into my throat. I anxiously peer around the ambulance bay. I can't join Steve at our rig. Not yet. I'm not ready to pretend everything is okay.

Turning the other direction, I walk fast to the far end of the huge ambulance bay, seeking refuge in the shadows. Rainwater from a clogged gutter on the overhang starts splashing down upon me, worsening the chill that already consumes my body, but I don't care. I wrap my arms around myself, close my eyes, and draw in one breath after the next, trying to settle my emotions.

"Elly."

I hear his voice—Grant's voice—and my heart nearly bursts. It's the one healing, reassuring sound that I need in this moment. I open my eyes and turn around. Through the shadows, I see Grant walking my way, paying no heed to the rain that's rolling down his face and soaking his shirt. Grant's eyes never leave mine as he finishes crossing the ambulance bay to reach me. Without hesitation, he wraps me in his embrace.

"Are you doing okay?" Grant asks.

I collapse against his chest, my tears mixing with the rain. I don't reply to Grant's question, but I know I don't need to. Grant understands exactly how I'm feeling in this moment. No one else could possibly understand how this night has affected me—no one else could ever understand *me* the way Grant does. There's no one else I would want right here beside me, comforting and supporting me.

In Grant's embrace, I sense the wall between us disappear. All is forgiven. All is right. I squeeze shut my eyes as my tears fall harder. What would I do without Grant? How could I have ever expected to love anyone the way I love and cherish him?

"El?" Grant says quietly.

I tip back my head so I can see into his blue eyes. "Yes?"

Grant swallows. "El, I—"

"Hey, Elly?" Jonathan's voice carries through the air.

Grant and I jump apart. My body is hot and tingling, and my heart is racing. Grant is soaking wet and breathing fast as he watches me through the rain.

"Elly, are you around?" Jonathan calls again from the other side of the ambulance bay. "We're ready to go."

I still haven't taken my eyes off of Grant. He hasn't taken his eyes off of me. In a rush, it hits me harder than ever before: I love Grant, but there's no point in loving Grant.

Clearing my throat, I make myself pull my eyes away from Grant, and I call over my shoulder to Jonathan, "I'll be right there."

The ambulance engine is turned over. As the rumbling sound fills the air, I look at Grant once more.

"Thank you," I whisper to him.

"You're welcome, El," Grant replies.

Saying no more, I spin around and hurry off to join my crew. As I climb into the back of the rig, I hang my head. My heart is breaking all over again.

Fifteen

"Congratulations, you two. This is one of the best projects ever submitted by any of our residents." Dr. Priest pushes back from his desk, gets to his feet, and shows Grant and me a smile.

The other attendings who've been listening to our presentation—including Wes Kent, Jesse Santiago, Ned Godfrey, and Tammy Sanders—start voicing their agreement with Dr. Priest's remark. Leslie Yamada and Lynn Prentis are also beaming at Grant and me. Even the battalion chiefs from Lakewood Fire and Rescue are nodding their approval. I exhale with relief. I was confident that Grant and I had a solid presentation prepared, but it's still a relief to hear we've made a great impression on everyone. In particular, I'm grateful to know that if I ever need a letter of recommendation to apply for an EMS fellowship, anyone in this room would probably be willing to write one on my behalf.

Dr. Priest comes around his desk to reach Grant and me, and he shakes our hands. "You should both be immensely pleased with what you've done. Not only was this an informative presentation, but the metrics you taught the crews about will make the care they give to patients even better. This was a learning opportunity for all and something that will have a positive impact on patient care going forward." He looks between Grant and me, and his smile becomes amused. "If I recall correctly, the two of you have a long history of doing school projects together, and it certainly seems your chemistry paid off here."

Grant and I exchange another glance.

Dr. Priest checks his watch. "Well, it's almost one in the afternoon, which means we've occupied enough of your Friday already. We'll let the two of you get out of here, and we'll take care of the formal grading process." He leans closer and jokingly lowers his voice. "Don't worry. I'm pretty sure you'll both pass."

There's a round of laughter from the others in the room.

"Thank you for your time, everyone," Grant tells the crowd, as calm and collected as ever.

"Yes, thank you," I echo. "We appreciate everyone being here today."

Grant strides toward the door that divides Dr. Priest's office from Leslie's. I follow after him. As Grant pulls open the door and steps back to allow me to exit first, I hear Dr. Priest call out:

"Elly?"

I stop, shoot a fast, questioning look over to Grant, and then turn back around so I'm facing Dr. Priest and the rest of the crowd.

Dr. Priest is observing me seriously now. "I know this rotation was particularly important to you, wasn't it?"

I have to squelch a sudden prick of nerves. I have no idea where this conversation is leading.

"Yes, it was," I reply evenly.

Dr. Priest nods. "Grant told me this outstanding project was your idea. Not only that, I'm hearing you've been doing an excellent job on your ride-alongs, and that you've even stepped in to help with patients when necessary." He breaks into a new smile. "I think that if you do decide to pursue a fellowship in EMS, you've proven you would do an outstanding job."

My nerves are displaced by another wave of happiness. "Thank you so much, Coach."

Dr. Priest gives me a playful salute. I salute back and then spin toward the door. Grant is watching me with a proud gleam in his eyes, and I have to resist the impulse to throw my arms around him and let out an excited cheer. Instead, face flushing with excitement, I give Grant a smile before leaving the room.

I continue through Leslie's office and out into the hallway. I stop, and in the second or two that passes while I wait for Grant to join me, my mind takes me back to a month ago, when Dr. Priest called Grant and me into his office to inform us that we would be doing our EMS rotation together. At the time, I thought I knew what I would be getting into. However, there was no way I could have anticipated how life-changing this EMS experience would be.

"Earth to Doctor Vincent."

I jump and realize Grant is standing beside me. He chuckles at the startled look on my face. I give him a roll of my eyes before we begin walking down the hallway.

"So what did you think?" Grant inquires once we're far enough away from Dr. Priest's office not to be heard.

I tuck my hair behind my ears. "I think it went all right, and I'm relieved it was so well-received."

Grant doesn't reply. I check his way. He's grinning.

"What in the world is that look for?" I ask, starting to smile myself, though I don't know why.

"I think you're being a tad modest and humble." Grant gives me a nudge. "Come on, you know that presentation went more than just *all right*, and it was more than *well-received*. That was a huge success, and it was all because of you."

My cheeks redden. "It definitely wasn't all me. You were a major part of this, Doctor Reed."

Grant meets my gaze. "And I was more than happy to do it."

We reach the foyer by the elevators. Grant halts in his tracks, causing me to do the same, and faces me directly. He's still grinning, but there's something probing in his eyes now.

"So what are you doing with the rest of your day?" Grant asks.

My stomach sinks. The gala. I haven't told Grant that I'm going to the gala with Jonathan.

I'm not sure why I haven't told him; I guess I've never really had a chance or reason to do so. Grant and I have been busy preparing our presentation, and otherwise we haven't seen each other since our shifts overlapped last Saturday. To be honest, I've been so focused on the presentation this week that I nearly forgot about the gala altogether.

Grant seems to be peering at me more closely. "Do you want to go get something to eat? You know, to celebrate the completion of our rotation and the success of the presentation?"

"I would really like to go," I tell him honestly with a sigh. "But I can't. I'm going out on a date tonight, and I have to go home to get ready."

"Ah." Grant's expression reveals nothing. "You're going out with Jonathan again, I assume?"

"Yes."

Grant scratches his head. "I see. Far be it from me to pretend as though I understand anything a woman goes through during the date-prep process, but you're not going out until tonight, and yet you already have to start getting ready?" His tone is devoid of judgment . . . devoid of anything, really. He checks his watch. "Isn't it kind of early to start getting ready?"

I sigh again and rub my forehead. "Normally, yes. Tonight is different, though."

Grant pauses, still engrossed in studying his watch. "Oh?"

Resigned, I drop my arm back to my side. "You know the gala that Lakewood Fire and

Rescue is putting on this evening? The one we both got an invitation to?"

Slowly—very slowly—Grant finally looks up at me. "Yes."

"Jonathan asked me to go with him," I explain. "As his date."

Grant's eyebrows gradually rise. "That sounds like kind of a big deal."

"It is . . . at least, I think it is, and that's why I need to start getting ready now." I do my best to adopt a humorous smile. "I certainly can't claim to be an expert on these types of things, either, but from what Mackenna told me, between hair, makeup, nails, and everything else that comes with prepping for a black-tie affair, the process is going to be an all-afternoon event."

"I see." Grant keeps looking into my eyes.

I wet my lips and restlessly press the call button for the elevator. "So, anyway, that's why I should probably head out." My smile is becoming increasingly forced. "I'm scheduled to have a video call with Mackenna soon; she's going to help me get ready from a few thousand miles away."

Grant starts backing up toward the door that leads to the stairwell. "Then I'll let you get going."

The elevator pings, and its door slides open. I step inside and turn back Grant's way. He's already on the other side of the foyer.

"You're not taking the elevator?" I ask, though I know the answer.

"Nah, I could use a chance to stretch my legs." Grant pushes open the door that leads into the stairwell. "I hope you have a really great time tonight, El. You deserve it."

I blink hard. "Thank you."

The elevator door begins sliding shut. The last thing I see is Grant stepping into the stairwell and disappearing from view.

Sixteen

"Ladies and gentleman, hasn't this been a fabulous night so far?"

The emcee's smooth voice carries out over the PA system, and in response, a round of enthusiastic applause fills the ballroom. Basking in the glow of the spotlight, the emcee adjusts his bowtie, puffs out his chest, and continues looking out at the hundreds of guests and dignitaries who are attending the gala. The elegantly dressed audience members are seated around circular tables, which are situated throughout the space. I can't help grinning as I watch the emcee work the room. With his sequins-accented tuxedo, polished smile, and well-practiced movements with the microphone, the man is clearly in his element.

The applause continues. I'm still grinning as I put down my pumpkin-spice hot chocolate, which was served in the fanciest mug I've ever beheld, and I begin clapping along with the rest of the crowd. Seated beside me, Jonathan is smiling in his dashing way as he starts applauding, too. I watch Jonathan out of the corner of my eye, studying his profile. There's no denying that Jonathan looks jaw-droppingly hot tonight, dressed in his well-tailored suit. He looks so hot, in fact, that he almost doesn't seem real. It's like I'm sitting next to a model or a movie star, not an actual person.

The venue for tonight's event is as glamorous as my date. The hotel's ritzy ballroom feels like something out of a Bavarian castle. High overhead, huge chandeliers are glistening. Beautiful flower arrangements and delicate twinkle lights further adorn the space. The air is carrying the invigorating sounds of softly clanking glasses, animated conversations, and the music that's being performed by the band on the stage far to my left. In front of the stage, there's a large dance floor that's currently vacant. On the opposite side of the ballroom, elaborately decorated tables display information about the items and events that have been donated to the silent auction.

Jonathan and I perused the auction information when we first arrived, and I nearly syncopized from shock. When I initially heard "silent auction," I assumed it would involve something like what my classmates and I did back in elementary school, when we made brownies and cheap jewelry, or offered to wash people's cars. Tonight, though, there's quite a bit more than a batch of burnt chocolate chip cookies available to bid on. Some of the biggest names and companies in the region have donated things like tropical vacations, spa treatments, motorcycles, and high-end purses.

I was obviously way off regarding the auction, but my guess for what the rest of the gala would be like has proven to be pretty accurate. We're well into the evening's festivities now, and every minute of it has felt as Hollywood-meets-fairytale-ish as I envisioned a gala might be. We've enjoyed musical entertainment, socializing with other elegantly-dressed guests, a delicious dinner, rich desserts, and after-dinner drinks. Everything about tonight has been perfect.

At least, that's what you're telling yourself.

I attempt to ignore the voice in my head, and I make myself busy smoothing down non-existent wrinkles in the skirt of my dress, being careful not to chip my manicured nails in the process. I don't know when I last bothered to give myself a manicure—it's not exactly something I worry about when my daily routine often involves placing a chest tube to manage a patient's hemothorax. Thankfully, though, with Mackenna's invaluable patience and guidance via our video call earlier today, the process of getting ready for my first-ever black-tie event went smoothly. I put my long hair in a loose up-do. I did my makeup more dramatically than usual, especially around my eyes. I happily decided my gown was as gorgeous as I thought it was when I first fell in love with it in the store—it's a blush-colored, v-neck, floor-length gown . . . and it even has pockets. It is the loveliest thing I have ever worn.

You're wishing Grant could see you in this dress.

I cringe when the voice in my mind makes yet another rather rebellious remark. Sitting up taller, I sternly remind myself that I should be concentrating on the man I'm actually here with. Like everything else this evening, Jonathan has been textbook-level perfect. Not only does he look too good to be real, he picked me up right on time, complemented the way I looked in a gentlemanly way, and managed to open every door for me between his truck and the ballroom. He has made sure my every need is met. He's introducing me to his friends and colleagues. His conversations with me have been pleasant and comfortable, and—

But you don't talk to Jonathan in the same type of meaningful way that you talk with Grant.

With a frustrated sigh, I close my eyes, commanding the voice to leave me alone. There's no point in thinking about him. I—

You love him, Elly.

The undeniable truth hits me like a lightning bolt, causing my skin to tingle and my pulse to race. I reopen my eyes, working to catch my breath.

I love Grant Reed. I've always loved him. I always will.

Heat rises up from my core, stealing my breath once again. There's no possible way to deny it any longer: Grant is the man I want to be with here at the gala. Grant is the man I want to be with forever.

It doesn't really matter that Grant is a doctor, does it?

The voice in my head resonates with profound, almost spiritual-like clarity. I work down a swallow. Contrary to what I've been telling myself all these years, it doesn't matter that Grant has also chosen to go into the medical field. That alone doesn't make a relationship impossible. The truth, which I now understand clearly for the first time, is that I've been using the example of my parents' divorce as a reason to justify hiding from something that scared me. I've been using my past as an excuse to play it safe for my future . . . a reason for not confessing to Grant how much I care about him.

All at once, for the first time in a very, very long time, my heart and mind call a truce. The war inside me ends, and all becomes peacefully still. In the calmness that follows, the sensation I experienced long ago—the feeling that hit me while Grant and I were freshmen in college—the desire to tell Grant how I truly feel about him—takes over my body and soul once more. I grip the edge of the table as one thing, and one thing only, drums through my mind in time to the beating of my heart: I need to tell Grant that I love him. He needs to know how much he means to me. He needs to understand.

You want to tell Grant the truth, even though Grant doesn't love you in return?

"Ladies and gentleman, it's time to open up the dance floor!" the emcee declares, interrupting my thoughts. "So get on your feet and dance the night away!"

The band launches into an upbeat tune. There's a renewed wave of excitement throughout the ballroom as people start getting up from their tables and making their way toward the dance floor, laughing and talking as they go.

"Well, what do you say?" Jonathan turns in his chair to face me, and he shows his picture-perfect smile. "Would you care to dance?"

I stare back at Jonathan, my mind racing. I not only need to sort out what to do about Grant, I must also figure out how to handle the Jonathan situation. It's not fair to lead Jonathan on, but I don't want to drop a bomb on him in the middle of his agency's biggest event of the year. So all I can do in this particular moment is smile and give him a nod. Jonathan's own smile widens in response. He stands up, reaches down for my hand, and helps me to my feet. He leads me to the dance floor, and the next thing I know, Jonathan and I are dancing . . . but no matter how I try, my heart remains with someone else.

I don't know how much time goes by before I realize that Jonathan has fallen still, which brings me out of my distracted daze. Lifting my eyes, I do a double take when I discover that Jonathan is watching me with a furrowed brow but a smile upon his lips.

"What is it?" I inquire.

Jonathan is still smiling in a resigned sort of way. "I'm not the man you want to be dancing with tonight, am I?"

My eyes get big. "What?"

Jonathan lets go of me. "Elly Vincent, you're one of the most gorgeous, intelligent women I've ever met, and I really wanted there to be something special between us." He sighs. "However, though I tried hard to convince myself—and to convince you—otherwise, it's time for me to accept that I'm not the man you want, and I don't think I can be the man you deserve."

I don't react until I'm certain I understood what Jonathan just said. I then take both of his hands in mine.

"Jonathan, you're a brave, charismatic person, and I know you'll make some lucky woman very happy one day. She's out there, somewhere, but you're right: she's not me." I release his hands. "Thank you for giving me the opportunity to get to know you better."

"It was a pleasure, Doctor Vincent." Jonathan smiles again. "Thank *you*."

We observe each other for a couple of seconds, and then I motion around the ballroom and say:

"There's still a lot for you to enjoy here tonight, and I don't want to wreck your evening by making you leave early on my account. Please go have fun. I'll slip out and get a ride home. If anyone asks about me, just tell them something came up, and I needed to leave."

Jonathan's forehead creases. "That's incredibly generous of you to offer, but I don't want to leave you—"

"Don't worry about me." I show him a reassuring smile. "Honestly, it will make me happy knowing you got to enjoy the rest of this gala. I don't mind heading home on my own. I promise."

Jonathan looks around the room and then refocuses on me. "You're sure?"

"I'm sure." I nod. "Go enjoy your night. You deserve it."

Jonathan takes a step back and gives me a slight bow. "Doctor Vincent, once again, it has been a pleasure. I'll look forward to seeing you in the ED."

"Likewise, Paramedic Blackrock," I reply sincerely.

Jonathan gives me a final tip of his head, and then he turns on his heels and walks away, soon becoming lost in the crowd. Once he's gone, a sigh escapes my lips. Standing by myself in the middle of the dance floor, I feel both immensely full and profoundly hollow. It's a strange juxtaposition, and there's nothing for me to do about it in this moment except to go home.

Just when I turn and make a move to leave, the music swells, and at the same time, the crowds in my path seem to part, revealing someone else who's standing alone on the dance floor. I stop with a gasp, and for one long moment, I wonder if I'm simply dreaming, but the fervent way my heart is beating tells me that what I'm seeing is real.

Grant is here. And his eyes are locked on mine.

Everything around Grant and me seems to disappear. Even the music fades away. The only thing in the whole Universe is Grant. Just Grant. Only Grant.

Unable to move or breathe, all I can do is continue staring at Grant, absorbing the incredible vision of the man with whom I'm desperately, completely, and devotedly in love. Grant has never looked more handsome than he does tonight. He's wearing a tuxedo—a classic tuxedo that perfectly fits his tall, muscular frame. Grant's thick black hair his combed, and his face is cleanly shaven to reveal the strong angle of his jaw. And Grant's eyes—his vibrant blue eyes—seem to shine with a light of their own as he observes me.

"G-Grant." I put a shaking hand to my chest. "I didn't think you were . . . I mean, what are you . . . ?"

Grant strides closer. "Why are you out here by yourself? Where's your date?"

I actually manage a light laugh. "It's a long story, but the short version is that I don't have a date . . . at least, I don't have a date anymore."

Grant comes to a stop in front of me. He searches my face closely. "So there's . . . no Jonathan?"

"There's no Jonathan," I reply simply. "He and I are better off as friends."

Grant is still for a moment. "Well, then, Elly Vincent, may I have the honor of this dance?"

"Yes, Grant Reed," I answer quietly, "you may."

Grant's gaze never leaves mine as he holds out a hand to me. I stare back at him while love, fear, hesitation, devotion, uncertainty, and desire collide inside me. I look down at the hand he has offered, and at last, I dare to place my hand in Grant's strong, steady grip. The contact shoots sparks up my arm that spread throughout my body and make my heart beat even harder. I gasp softly at the thrilling sensation and raise my eyes back to Grant's face. Grant still doesn't look away as he puts his other hand on the small of my back, draws me in close, and then, with calm and certain movements, begins leading me in a dance.

The room comes back to life around us. Everything is warmth, bliss, and light as Grant and I move across the dance floor to the music. My love for Grant is flowing through me unchecked, filling my soul completely and causing my heart to feel as though it might burst. Held in his embrace in this magical, dreamlike moment, I don't want anything but to gaze up at Grant. My lifeline. My purpose. My everything.

Grant smiles as he continues guiding me around the floor. A magnetic energy seems to envelop us, connecting our souls in a new, wonderful, powerful way. All-too-soon, though, the song ends. Grant brings us to a stop in the middle of the dance floor. Instead of letting me go, Grant keeps his arm upon my waist and his other hand around mine. We continue staring at each other while the couples around us turn toward the stage to applaud the musicians. As I look into Grant's eyes, I can't help wondering: did he feel what I felt? Is it possible . . . ?

Grant lowers his arms back to his sides and steps back from me.

I sigh and release the breath I had been holding. No, Grant didn't feel what I felt.

You still need to tell Grant the truth, regardless of how he feels about you.

I hear the voice in my head again, and I can't argue with it. I don't want to argue with it. Grant deserves to know, and I can't live this half-truth any longer. I—

The band strikes up a fun melody, and the crowds burst into cheers and applause. The levity snaps me out of my haze. I shake my head slightly, like doing so will jiggle my thoughts back into place, and I put a more quizzical look on Grant.

"I didn't realize you were planning to come tonight," I tell him, fumbling for something to say to start the conversation.

"I wasn't planning to come," Grant replies right away. He pauses, brows pulled together, and his eyes leap across the room. He then looks at me again while tipping his head toward a set of French doors that lead outside. "Would you mind taking a walk with me?"

I glance toward the doors. "No, of course I wouldn't."

Grant nods, gently puts his hand on the point of my elbow, and begins guiding me through the throng. His touch ignites another fire inside of me, and my legs get so wobbly that I almost tip over in my heels.

Once we break free of the throng, my mind finishes coming back into focus, and then my stomach knots and my heart begins racing for a different reason: I'm about to confess my true feelings to Grant. After all these years, I'm finally going to tell Grant that I love him. This will be the point of no return. Our relationship will never be the same after this. The only thing that's buoying me up right now is the relentless feeling that I need to tell Grant the truth. I don't know what will happen when I do so, but I do know it's the right thing to do . . . for both of us. And I know I'll forever cherish the years we spent together, and I will never forget the dance we just shared.

Grant leads me through the French doors and out onto a veranda, which is gorgeously adorned with white lights and flowers like the ballroom itself. Grant closes the doors behind us, which dampens the sounds of the party down to a soft hum. In the near-quiet, I look across the stunning scene. Overhead, instead of chandeliers, stars are shining in a cloudless sky. The view from this second-story veranda is of the hotel's twinkle-light-illuminated gardens, which stretch out as far as the eye can see down below. I hear the breeze softly stirring the trees and the trickling of the garden fountains. Though it's late in the evening, the air is being warmed by discreetly placed outdoor heaters. The windows of the ballroom are concealed behind tall shrubs that rise up from huge, ornate planter boxes.

There's no one else out here, and so it feels as though Grant and I are by ourselves in an enchanted forest.

Grant turns from the doors to face me. He pauses, his expression serious, and then he strides to my side and motions to the wide stone staircase that leads down to the gardens.

"Care to join me?" Grant's tone is casual, but there's no mistaking the focus in his gaze.

"Certainly."

I fall into step beside him, pretending to be unfazed, though I'm rapidly becoming a nervous wreck inside. What, exactly, should I say to Grant? How can I accurately articulate what I feel? Can I ever clearly explain to him why I kept my feelings hidden all these years? How is Grant going to react when I confess? Will he ever talk to me again?

My mind churns, and my heart pounds as Grant and I walk down the staircase. I glance his way a time or two, trying to get a read on his mood so I can better strategize about what to say. Not surprisingly, though, Grant's expression reveals nothing. His eyes are fixed straight ahead, and there's a muscle twitching in his cheek. Otherwise, he's impossible to read.

Grant and I reach the bottom of the stairs and begin strolling one of the garden paths, which is gorgeously illuminated by white lights, which look like fireflies against the night sky. When we come upon one of the beautiful fountains, we stop to watch the water as it sprays and falls in its soothing, mesmerizing way. I'm not sure how much time passes while we remain quiet, but the feeling inside of me—the relentless feeling that's compelling me to confess to Grant—finally grows so strong that I can't hold in the truth any longer.

"Grant," I say, my entire body pulsing as I spin toward him.

"Elly," Grant states at the same time, facing me.

We both pause. Grant's eyebrows rise, as do mine. I open my mouth but close it again. Grant does the same.

"You first," we both tell each other, speaking in unison again.

There's another pause. Grant clears his throat. I bite my lip.

Tell him, the voice in my mind commands. *You have to tell him.*

"I love you."

I hear the words pass my lips, the emotion behind them so powerful that it's nearly enough to draw the rest of the air out of my lungs. Heart flying and legs quivering, I have to turn away from Grant and reach to the edge of the fountain to steady myself. Everything feels so surreal. I just told him. I told Grant the truth. After all these years, I confessed. I . . .

I then become completely still as the last few seconds replay in my mind.

I wasn't the only one who just said *I love you*, I realize.

Grant said it, too.

My whole body gets hot, and my heart begins pounding even harder. I grip the edge of the fountain tightly as I attempt to make sense of what just happened. Is it possible? Can it be true?

Does Grant . . . love me?

Slowly—so, so slowly—I turn Grant's way. He's staring at me, his chest rising and falling fast as his eyes search mine.

"Did you just . . . ?" I trail off in a whisper.

"Are you really . . . ?" Grant's eyes are growing wide.

I stare. He stares.

I have no idea what to do. I don't dare believe this is true. I'm afraid it's only a dream, and if I move too suddenly, I'm going to wake myself up.

Grant's eyes flash like fire. He takes a purposeful step closer to me. "I came here tonight because I desperately wanted you to know that I've been in love with you since the day I met you, and up until now, I've been too petrified to tell you the truth."

I stare at Grant a moment longer, processing what he just said, and then my shock and doubt vanish, and incredible joy rises up from my core and fills me completely. My heart soars. This isn't a dream. This is real. Contrary to what I always thought I knew, Grant loves me. He *loves* me.

Grant loves me.

All at once, I understand Grant perfectly and completely. The look in his eyes and the emotion radiating from his countenance unequivocally confirm the truth of his words.

Grant loves me. He loves me in the endlessly devoted way that I love him.

All this time . . . all these years . . .

I let my tears of joy begin to fall. "Grant, I've loved you ever since you introduced yourself to me in English class. You won my heart that day, but I've always been too scared to let you know."

Grant does a double take. "Are you . . . serious?"

I giggle at his shocked expression. "I'm serious."

Grant blinks a couple of times, and then he slowly breaks into the most incredible smile I have ever seen. His blue eyes sparkle, and he tips back his head and lets out a deep, carefree laugh. The glorious sound carries through the gardens before fading away. Putting his eyes back on mine, Grant says:

"Up until this moment, I thought you didn't care about me as anything other than a friend. That's why I never told you how I felt. I didn't want to lose the friendship we shared."

"That's why I never told you how I felt either. I loved you too much to say anything."

There's a charged beat of silence as an unspoken question suddenly hovers in the air. Then our gazes lock completely. A wild, hot energy starts swirling around Grant and me, answering that unspoken question without words. Grant's pupils dilate, and something about his gaze makes my whole body quiver with anticipation. In one swift movement, Grant cups a hand against the back of my head and wraps his other arm around my waist. He pulls me in against him and fearlessly presses his lips against mine.

Heat, joy, fervor, and love unlike anything I could have ever imagined explode within me. I throw my arms around Grant's neck and begin kissing him passionately in return, becoming more awake and alive than I've ever been in my entire life. Grant and I explore one another lips through our untamed kiss, communicating the intense emotions we've been secretly carrying inside us for all these years. Grant pulls me in tighter as he keeps kissing me. I collapse into him, sharing his kisses with equal desire.

At last, Grant slowly pulls his lips from mine and leans back to view my face. He smiles as he slides his arms so they're both around my waist. I keep my arms draped around his neck, my lips still wonderfully on fire from the memory of Grant's touch. I gaze up at him, never wanting to look away. Though I've seen Grant's handsome face thousands of times before, I'm seeing him in a new way for the very first time.

Grant rests his forehead against mine. "You really didn't know how desperately in love with you I've been all this time? You? The master of reading other people's emotions?"

"I really didn't know. I never even suspected," I reply, snuggling against him. "After all, in high school, I was a book nerd, and you were the homecoming king. In college, the dynamic really wasn't that much different. You always moved in a different social circle than I did. So of course I didn't think you loved me; I wasn't like any of the girls you dated."

Grant leans back once more to look right into my eyes. "You most definitely weren't like any of those other girls. You were more intelligent, witty, gorgeous, kind, and ambitious than all of them combined." He shakes his head. "Deep down, I knew that I was wasting my time pursuing anyone else; I knew my heart would never belong to anyone but you. However, I didn't think you cared about me in the way that I desperately wished you did, and so I tried to move on." He leans down and brushes his lips against my forehead. "I attempted to get over you so many times throughout the years, El. I tried to make myself fall in love with someone else, but it was no use. It was you. It was always you." He kisses me again.

I close my eyes and let our lips linger together before I look at him again and reply, "Admittedly, I was extremely vigilant about keeping up the walls around my heart. I was certain you didn't love me, and so I didn't want you to know how I felt about you. I didn't want to lose our friendship."

Grant nods. "I was the same way."

I sigh and rest my head against Grant's chest. "My resolve almost broke down once, though. I almost told you how I felt, but I stopped myself."

Grant softly strokes my cheek with his hand. "What made you decide against it?"

"You told me that you had decided to go to medical school." I tip back my head to see into his eyes. "I was scared to love you, Grant, and so I told myself that a relationship between two physicians couldn't work out. It was easier to tell myself that than it was to confess to you my true feelings and risk the heartbreak."

Grant peers deeply into my eyes. "You were scared to love because of what you saw your parents go through."

I nod. "I had experienced a lot of loss already, and I didn't want to lose anyone else. So I told myself pursuing love wasn't worth it. However, no matter how often I told myself that over the years, my heart never truly believed it. My heart has always believed in romance. My heart has always wanted you."

Grant takes my hands in his. "I know our careers will present challenges, but I promise you that I will never put anything or anyone before our relationship. Nothing means more to me than you."

My breathing hitches. As Grant's words finish soaking in, they free something inside of me. The painful memories from my younger years finally get put to rest, and my fears are gone.

"You mean that, don't you?" I whisper.

Grant doesn't answer. Instead, he releases my hands, reaches into an inside pocket of his jacket, and pulls out a small object, which he holds up between his fingers. As the soft glow of the twinkle lights glints off the object, I realize Grant is holding an old coin. A fifty-cent piece.

Our fifty-cent piece.

"Where did you find that?" I gasp softly.

"I've kept this with me ever since we last exchanged it before we graduated from college." Grant reaches for my hand once more. This time, he turns over my hand, places the coin on my palm, and gently closes my fingers around it. "I've dreamed of the day when I would be able to give it back to you."

In astonishment, I rub my fingers against the coin. The feel of it in my hand is so very familiar. So full of memories. So perfect.

Grant looks off into the distance. "Long ago, I resigned myself to a life of keeping my feelings for you a secret, no matter how miserable it would make me." His brow furrows. "Recently, though, when I saw that I might lose you to a guy who didn't deserve you—to a guy who didn't, and couldn't possibly ever, love you the way I love you—I needed you to know how I really felt." He works down a swallow. "That day when I came to the fire station, I wasn't there to work on charts. I was there to tell you the truth."

My mouth drops. "What stopped you?"

Grant looks at me again. "I realized that I had no right to interfere, no matter how desperately I wanted to do so. If you were falling for someone else, it wasn't my place to intervene, even though it was agonizing to think of you with someone else." He takes my free hand in his. "I didn't come here tonight expecting anything, yet I was compelled to come find you. I wasn't trying to change your mind; I only wanted you to know the truth that you deserved to hear. When I saw Jonathan leave you behind on the dance floor, though, that was when I dared to hope that I still had a chance. I dared to believe I hadn't lost you yet." He raises my hand to his lips and kisses it. "Please forgive me for being such an idiot all these years. I love you, Elly Vincent. I always have, and I always will."

I slip the coin into a pocket of my gown and fall into Grant's embrace. "There's nothing to forgive, Grant. We loved each other, and we wanted nothing but what we thought was best for each other. We were even willing to suffer in silence for one another when we thought that was the right thing to do." I exhale a sigh. "I love you, Grant Reed."

Grant puts his hands on my cheeks and kisses me once more. Just then, the faint sounds of another slow song that's being played in the ballroom begin floating through the air. Grant slides one hand to my low back and takes my other hand in his. We share another kiss, and then, under the starry sky, Grant and I begin to dance. As I rest my head against Grant's chest, swaying with him to the music, I know that no matter where our journey may take us, Grant and I will be dancing together for the rest of our lives.

Epilogue

"Ladies and Gentleman, we warmly welcome you to the celebration marking the completion of Lakewood Medical Center's new, state-of-the-art emergency department!"

Boisterous cheers and applause fill the hospital's auditorium, which has been decorated with balloons, streamers, and posters for tonight's big event. Up on the stage at the front of the room, Mark Prescott, the president of Lakewood Medical Center, is standing behind the podium and smiling at the crowd, looking sharp in his high-end business suit. Beside him is Lakewood's vice president, Tanya Eggertson, who's also beaming proudly as she looks over the audience. While the cheering continues, Mr. Prescott and Ms. Eggertson exchange a nod, and then Mr. Prescott leans closer to the microphone and adds:

"I would like to invite up the man who has been the inspiration and driving force behind this project from the beginning. The man whose tireless devotion to the cause has made all of this possible. The man whose dedication has led to the opening of an ED that will improve the lives of countless patients and ED staff members. Ladies and gentleman, let's hear it for Doctor Wesley Kent!"

Thunderous applause fills the room. As Dr. Kent walks up to the stage, I cup my hands around my mouth and let out a cheer, and then I resume clapping enthusiastically along with the rest of the crowd. Tonight's audience includes nearly all the emergency department staff members, except for those who are working, as well as several hospital big-wigs, dignitaries from the community, members of various EMS agencies, media personnel, and representatives of the companies and individual donors whose funding helped make the ED build happen.

While Dr. Kent takes a place behind the podium, I do another scan of the room. I can't help smiling at being surrounded by so many of my colleagues and friends. Near the back of the room, Austin is boosting Rachel up on his shoulders, piggy-back style, so she can see over the crowd to watch what's happening on the stage. On the other side of the auditorium, Quinn and Dylan are exchanging amorous looks that I'm guessing they think no one else notices. In the middle of the crowd, Lynn Prentis is with her husband and three teenage children. Next to Lynn, Leslie Yamada and her spouse are corralling their two young sons. And scattered across the rest of the audience are most of the ED's attending physicians, including the new hires, as well as residents, nurses, social workers, secretaries, techs, radiology technicians, registration personnel, and individuals from environmental services. My smile widens. They're all part of my Lakewood family, and I consider myself extremely lucky for it.

I'm about to return my attention to the stage, but I pause when I spot Jonathan Blackrock standing on the far side of the crowd. His eyes meet mine, and he gives me a tip of his head. Jonathan and I have crossed paths frequently in the ED in the four months since my EMS rotation, and I'm glad to say we've transitioned to a solid friendship. As I wave to Jonathan, I do a double take when I notice that third-year internal medicine resident, Tara Hess, is standing close at Jonathan's side. I hit Jonathan with a pointedly curious look. His smile widens, and a happy gleam fills his eyes. I shift my attention back to Tara, noting she looks quite happy, too. I give Jonathan a nod of approval, make a mental note to ask Tara about her new romance with Jonathan, and grin as I shift my focus back to the stage.

Dr. Kent accepts a plaque from Mr. Prescott. True to his character, Dr. Kent remains completely humble as he thanks the various individuals and companies who played a role in the construction of the new emergency department. Dr. Kent's humility is both genuine and touching, and it's particularly notable given the fact that, as Mr. Prescott said, he alone was almost the entire reason the ED build ever happened.

Almost.

Dr. Kent's dark eyes find Savannah Drake in the crowd. The audience goes still. As Dr. Kent gazes adoringly down at Savannah from the stage, he appears to swallow with emotion. He thanks Savannah for the bravery and resolve she showed a little over a year ago to save the ED build, as well as for her unwavering support and encouragement she has shown ever since.

There's now a massive round of cheers for Savannah. She blushes as she lovingly gazes up at Dr. Kent in return. My inner romantic dances happily as I watch the two of them; the energy between Dr. Kent and Savannah is so palpable that I can sense it from the other side of the room.

"What has you so amused, Doctor Vincent?"

I look up at Grant, who's standing beside me, and I smile. "Let's just say that my inner romantic is celebrating the good vibes that are currently being exchanged between Wes Kent and Savannah Drake."

Grant softly kisses my forehead. "Mark your inner romantic as yet another reason why I love you so much."

"Aw, thanks." I kiss him back, the feel of his lips on mine making me giddy, like it always does.

My phone, which is set on *vibrate*, lets me know I've received a new text message. Pulling my phone from my purse, I check the message and smile. It's from Mackenna. She's wishing me a happy Valentine's weekend with Grant, and she isn't shy about noting, as she has done approximately one million times over these past few months, that she always knew Grant and I were meant to be together. She finishes her text with a long string of emojis, including hearts, kissy faces, winky faces, and grins. I laugh, shake my head, text her in reply, and put away my phone. I'm keeping my fingers crossed that Mackenna will choose to come to Lakewood as an ED attending when her residency is over, and I also hope she'll be lucky enough to find her own soulmate one day.

Dr. Kent concludes his remarks, and then Mr. Prescott ends the official ceremony. Sappy music starts playing over the PA system. People begin chatting, migrating over to the refreshments table (which is filled with unidentifiable *hors d'oeuvres*), and admiring photos of the construction process that are on display around the room. As I observe the scene, I catch a glimpse of Hadi and Tom sneaking over to the audio-visual table to change the music to something more upbeat. Meanwhile, near the doors, Pete is paying a delivery guy for a huge stack of pizzas. Carrie and several other ED staff members have climbed onto the stage, and I think they're setting up a lip-syncing machine. I smile to myself again. Yes, these are definitely my people, and with a crowd this size made up of mostly emergency-medicine types, it won't be long before this formal event evolves into a real party. As it should. Lakewood is opening its new emergency department at long last.

Grant slings his arm over my shoulders. "So what would you like to do first? Steal pizza from Pete? Change the music when Hadi isn't looking? Help Carrie set up the lip syncing competition?"

I laugh. "I'm game for anything. I'll let you pick."

Grant dips his head closer to mine and says in my ear, "How about a moonlit stroll?"

A shiver of delight ripples down my spine. "Yes. Absolutely yes."

Grant smiles alluringly, takes me by the hand, and begins carving a path for us through the fray as we head for the exit.

"Doctor Vincent," I hear a familiar voice call out.

I halt, causing Grant to do the same. We share a fast look, and then we both turn around. Dr. Priest is approaching.

"Good evening, Coach," I greet him.

"Good evening." Dr. Priest stops in front of Grant and me, and he breaks into a smile. "Elly, I received your request to write a letter of recommendation for your EMS-fellowship application, and I just want to let you know that I'll be honored to write that letter on your behalf."

"Thank you. That means a lot." I break into a smile of my own. "After my EMS rotation was over, and I finally had a chance to catch my breath, I knew for sure that a focus on EMS was what I wanted to do with my post-residency career."

"Well, I'm proud of you, and I know you'll be great at it." Dr. Priest leans in, adopts a humorous expression, and lowers his voice. "And as you know, Lakewood's emergency department doesn't have an EMS medical director . . . at least, not yet. Perhaps, though, with the opening of the bigger ED, adding an EMS director to our staff in a couple of years might be precisely what our department needs."

My smile gets huge. "I'll keep that in mind. Thank you again."

Dr. Priest winks. "You bet." He looks between Grant and me. "Now you two go have a good night. I'll see you around soon."

Dr. Priest walks away, his trajectory taking him past the table of boring refreshments and directly toward the corner of the room where Pete is handing out pizza.

Grant turns to me. "If I'm not mistaken, Doctor Priest just invited you to apply for the role of first-ever EMS medical director at Lakewood, once your fellowship is over."

"That was my impression, too. I can't believe it." I put my hands to my cheeks, which are flushed with happiness.

"I can." Grant draws me in close and kisses me. "There would be no one better for the job."

"Hey, everyone!" Carrie's high-pitched voice echoes out from the speakers, triggering ear-piercing feedback.

Everyone goes silent and turns toward the stage. Carrie is standing by the podium, holding a microphone.

"It's time for lip syncing, so get up here!" Carrie adds, grinning and waving enthusiastically.

Renewed cheers, applause, and laughter fill the auditorium as people rush the stage. Hadi is the first to get to the microphone. He promptly cues up an eighties tune and begins belting out a tone-deaf rendition of the song.

Grant and I exchange another look. I can tell he's struggling to keep a straight face.

"Hmm. It sounds like we now have two options for how we can kick off our Valentine's Day weekend," Grant tells me, his lips twitching upward. "We could endure listening to several hours of excruciatingly painful lip syncing, or we could take that moonlit stroll we talked about." He finally breaks into a grin. "Do you have a preference?"

"I admit it's a hard choice," I reply with a giggle. "However, I think I'll choose the moonlit stroll."

Grant takes my hand again, puts it to his lips, and kisses it. "Say no more."

My heart flutters as Grant resumes leading me through the crowds. We stop by the coat closet to grab our things, and then we head for the exit. As Grant pushes open the door, and a rush of cool February air swirls into the auditorium, I glance over my shoulder one last time to view the celebration honoring Lakewood's emergency department and all who work there. Smiling contentedly, I then look up at Grant and nod that I'm ready. He smiles in return and gives me another kiss. We step outside, letting the door shut behind us.

One era of our lives at Lakewood Medical Center is over, and another era is about to begin. I cannot wait to see what's in store.

Acknowledgements

I've heard it said that writing a novel is a solitary process, yet no one writes a book alone. This certainly has always been my experience, and I'm profoundly grateful to all those who helped make this novel possible:

My wonderful readers, who inspire, support, and motivate me every day.

Maria Spada, the most delightful and talented cover designer in the world.

My invaluable proofreaders, who helped ensure this story was spiffed up for publication.

My cherished ARC readers, whose enthusiasm helps make the dream of storytelling possible.

Madeline, the woman I can always count on for insightful blurbage assistance. Mad, you ARE the blurbage queen!

The HBWG. Of course.

Nick, my unwavering support, my gold standard for swoony heroes, my go-to for "Hey, is this how a guy would really react?" questions, and my best friend.

And Cookie, my sweet, loyal writing buddy and unfailingly devoted companion. Thank you, friend, for all the writing-break walks you took me on over the last twelve years. Thank you for napping contentedly and patiently under my desk while I wrote. Thank you for being the most loving, faithful dog a girl could ever hope for. Thank you for choosing me. I love you forever, little pal.

About the Author

TJ Amberson hails from the Pacific Northwest, where she lives with her husband, the most wonderful guy and the best on-demand story advisor ever. When she's not writing, TJ might be found enjoying a hot chocolate, pretending to know how to garden, riding her bike, video editing, or playing the piano. She loves to travel. She adores all things cozy and holiday-themed. She cheers for happily-ever-afters. And she thinks there's no such thing as too much seasonal décor.

With a love of several genres, TJ Amberson writes clean romance and romantic comedies, and clean fantasy adventures for teens and advanced tween readers.

www.tjamberson.com

Facebook: authortjamberson
Instagram: tjamberson
YouTube: realtjproductions
Pinterest: tjamberson

Thank you!

Dear Reader:

Thank you for reading CHANGE FOR LAKEWOOD MED (Book Four of the Lakewood Series)! I've been excited to tell Elly and Grant's story for a long time, and I'm thrilled you've been part of the experience!

If you loved this novel, please consider helping others enjoy it, too! Here are some easy ways to do so:

*REVIEW IT. If you love a book, post a review! Reviews don't have to be fancy or long. Every great review helps significantly. (Not to mention, a great review makes an author's day!)

*ANNOUNCE IT. Give the book a shout-out on social media!

*RECOMMEND IT. Recommend the book to friends, book groups, librarians, teachers, and reading forums.

Thank you!
-TJA

Made in the USA
Las Vegas, NV
31 May 2022

49592818R00174